THE MUDDY FORK
& OTHER THINGS

THE MUDDY FORK
& OTHER THINGS

SHORT FICTION AND NONFICTION

BY

JAMES CRUMLEY

CLARK CITY PRESS
LIVINGSTON, MONTANA

LIBRARY OF CONGRESS CATALOG CARD NUMBER: 91-61900
ISBN: 0-944439-39-X [TRADE]
ISBN: 0-944439-40-3 [LTD. ED.]

"INTERVIEW" © 1988 BY BRYAN DI SALVATORE AND DEIRDRE MCNAMER.
OTHER PORTIONS OF THIS COLLECTION HAVE APPEARED IN *WHORES* (1988, DENNIS
MCMILLAN PUBLICATIONS), *PLOUGHSHARES*, *TEXAS STORIES AND POEMS*,
CALIFORNIA QUARTERLY, *ASPEN LEAVES*, THE *LOS ANGELES TIMES*, *OUTSIDE* AND
ROCKY MOUNTAIN MAGAZINE.

CLARK CITY PRESS
POST OFFICE BOX 1358
LIVINGSTON, MONTANA 59047

For the teachers—Verlin Cassill, Dick Yates,
Dick Hugo and Shorty Crumley.

CONTENTS

A Short but Interesting Literary History of Orphans

This book should have been titled *The Muddy Fork & Other Orphans*. And this preface could be called "Stories About Stories." But I'm not old enough just yet to admit to too many orphans, literary or otherwise, and I'd rather save the stories for the next time you buy me a drink.

Most of the magazine pieces in this collection were never published in the magazines by which they were assigned. In fact, they often paid me for the honor of not publishing them. A senior editor at *Playboy* hated my first piece, "Driving Around Houston," so much that he went to the trouble to write an ugly memo, thinking perhaps that I wouldn't find out about it, or remember his name almost twenty years later.

(Editors should always remember that if writers don't remember something, they can look it up in their notes.)

I met some fine people fiddling around with journalism—Debbie Bird from Yellowstone Park, Marc Grossberg of Houston, and my "Heavy" pal, Roy Jenson—but I suspect I had a problem with attitude. I wasn't born with either a hatchet in my hand or a brown stain on my nose. And I'm not sure that nonfiction is not fictional. So, given my opportunities, I don't think it's either melodramatic or self-pitying to suggest that I've been less than successful with the magazine article.

My problem with the short story seems to be that I neither understand it nor think in that form. I was accepted into the Writers Workshop at Iowa in 1964 with my second story, "An Ideal Son for the Jenkins Family"—my first short story became my first novel, a clue I should have perhaps discovered sooner—and at Iowa I had the good fortune to work with Verlin Cassill, a great short story writer and teacher. I also have had the pleasure of long friendships with Ray Carver, Andre Dubus, and Bill Kittredge, a sort of trinity of the American short story.

So I have no excuse for not knowing how to write the little devils, but my short stories don't seem to be stories to me; condensed novels, perhaps, or character studies, or ideas I don't quite understand yet. And I must confess that my most anthologized short story, "Whores," started out as an article about border-town whoring I thought I might sell to *Playboy*. I didn't get through the first paragraph before it suddenly became a story about academics I'd known and not loved, people who tried to live their lives at arm's length.

This confusion of purpose and lack of understanding and direction is not my idea of success.

The interview. Bryan Di Salvatore and Dee McNamer did hard and wonderful work on the interview. All I had to do was survive the life and try to remember it. And decide which parts were fiction or nonfiction, which important or trivial, funny or tragic.

Although I've published four novels, I've started and written as much as a hundred pages of another ten or twelve. Only the two which I still think of as living are included here.

The Muddy Fork is the latest working title of a novel I started in 1969, something about growing up in South Texas. Now that I've grown older and don't much care anymore for the idea of growing up, I'm no longer exactly sure what the novel is about. This version was published in a shorter form by Ralph Beer when he was editor of *Cut Bank*, but the sorry truth is that I put it together one weekend to apply for a grant. (My god, I forgot to get a grant. What sort of literary life is it without a grant? Another small failure. Earning your own living. Without the government's help.) I didn't get the grant, haven't finished the novel, but haven't given up.

The Mexican Tree Duck. Well, it no longer opens exactly like this, and in the latest draft, the next to last I hope, it's not about lost ladies anymore. It's about laughter, love, and betrayal. But it's not finished yet, so who knows what sort of orphan awaits.

This preface, however, is finished. Successfully, I hope.

JIM CRUMLEY
Missoula, Montana
May 1991

Journalistic Lies

Driving Around Houston

In Houston there is a story that goes around that the British consular service considers Houston, because it shares a latitude with Agra, India, a hardship tour, and the consular staff is required to serve only three years instead of four. Houstonians tell the story with a straight face, amended with the flickers of a boyish grin that comes with the punch line. "Why, don't they know that Houston is the world's most air-conditioned city?" Of course it is true, and they are damned proud of it. At least those people who live from air-conditioned house to air-conditioned car to air-conditioned office are proud of it. And if you suggest that life in a series of conditioned cages, however cool and comfortable, is not exactly the best life, they know you are a stranger. People who live in Houston do not think such heresy. And heresy it is, because Houston's pride in itself is religious.

In this air-conditioned paradise on the Gulf Coast plain you can do anything—except be very poor and that does not count because in Houston anybody can be rich—indoors and out of the damp, clinging heat: be born and die of a heart transplant; play tennis, jog, drink, watch football; eat, sleep, breed; and carry on the business of living and making money comforted, surrounded by the confident eddies of cold air that always smell faintly like the odor hovering over a clean aquarium. Heaven as a well-tended fish tank. And if you can afford it, you can do so without the roar of compressors, without random drafts, embraced by limpid air as subtle and cool as a fine perfume, and pray daily to an air-conditioned god that Houston never has a blackout.

The dead are buried outside in the heat, but we are working on that.

In spite of the bridges and ramps and elevations of the freeways, the panoramic views from skyscrapers, I never lose the sensation of being underwater, trapped on the bottom of a hot, sweaty sea. From the moment I step out of the Houston *Intercontinental* Airport (they fly to Europe, South America, North America and Atlantis), I'm swimming. Just above the humid haze an endless stream of cumulus islands floats over me, their bottoms as flat as the land below. Always in the distance ranges of tall buildings, shimmering in the heat, rise like sunken mountains, and on the south side of town the mound of the Astrodome looms like a giant moon descending into the sea.

Just north of the Medical Center, where Houston money has built a city of hospitals, where great surgeons and diagnosticians attract patients from all over the world like pilgrims to Lourdes; just north of where you can live forever, in the Herman Park Zoo, the alligators and crocodiles sleep in the sun with a reptilian patience that makes humans seem quite frail and transitory beings. Old men in hospital robes, their wasted arms clasped in daughters' hands, circle the short chain-link fence, their shuffling feet among fat dusty pigeons; their strangled hearts and stricken flesh shy from the reptiles. There is no intelligence behind those alien eyes that shine as empty as glass eyes in mounted heads, no desire, no hope, and nothing the old men recognize as life, just that infernal patience, that inhumane endurance. Occasionally, as if to mock their watchers, they yawn, mouths agape with a forest of jagged random teeth, then they sleep like stones. One giant, with a smattering of blood and pigeon feathers about his scaly mouth, seems to be smiling.

The old men go away, but time and time again I go back. Usually just after lunch for a constitutional stroll (in search of Houston, no doubt) through the free zoo. Always back to the alligator pen, even though I can't tell an alligator from a crocodile, and I'm never sure why. Certainly I don't intend to slip back at night to release them, as friends of mine once tried to do for a condor in a crowded cage, nor do I talk to them, but each time I return I am reassured. Perhaps their enduring patience in confinement convinces me that I too can bear mine.

Because I feel trapped in Houston. I came for the money (ex-wives, children, bad debts), I tell myself, or on a lark (the exile sneaks back), but once in Houston, it isn't so funny. If I don't run, they may make me live there, and even though I've been gone from South Texas for fifteen years, it all comes back. The prickly heat in my nether regions, the sun like a fist on my head, a landscape hopelessly flat, that fiercely aggressive politeness that masquerades as hospitality. Self-righteous and poisonously narrow minds.

At the zoo snack bar a young mother, perhaps twenty-two but already looking older in spite of tight blue shorts and careful makeup, buys her stroller-bound child a Coke. When the Chicano girl behind the counter doesn't acknowledge receipt of the quarter with a polite thank you, the young mother, sarcasm as hot as the nooning sun on the sidewalks filling her voice, says, "Well, you're welcome," with that hard nasal accent like flat stones falling that only unhappy Texas women have. And in front of the leopard cage, a middle-aged woman grabs her child and hurries him away before he sees that the cats are fucking and not fighting. When I laugh behind her, she doesn't think it too funny, not me, nor the slender pink penis, nor the unplacated female cat.

These are my people, the faces of fear I fear, and although I'm certain that the fear masked with self-righteousness is a universal trait among small-town people, it always seems to me to be particularly indigenous to South Texas. Almost half of the people who live in Houston now and did not in 1960 have moved there from small towns within five hundred miles. The rural displaced—a minority surrounded by city folk, blacks and Chicanos—do not look happy. Unlike the alligators and crocodiles supine in the sun; the male leopard once again patiently bellying-up to his mate.

The first city I visited without my parents was Houston, in the spring of 1957 to take a physical for an ROTC scholarship. One misty and romantic night I rode a bus from my downtown hotel (The Milby, a parking lot now) out to the end of the line, just north of the Shamrock Hotel (the height of Texas *nouveau-riche* elegance then, a faded example for Astrodome tours now—"Why, you know, honey, you could put the Shamrock Hotel under the dome and turn it lengthwise three times.") and because I missed the last bus, I had to walk all the way back downtown. At night. So in spite of Houston's reputation for murder and violent assault, I did it again last spring. Nobody killed me. No police cars stopped, no whores propositioned me, no drugstore cowboys wanted to beat up a hippie. I admit my disappointment, and I also admit that I was more frightened strolling quietly up South Main in Houston, Texas, unarmed, than in a black bar with another white Southerner in the East Village, than in the Wahchi District of Hong Kong, than in the Pasay City jail. Take my fear with a grain of salt: Houston does that to me.

Most people in Houston are interested in making money, except those who either can't or who can afford not to, and fast food franchises make money, so Houston has its share, but they also try to franchise elegance. Think of a Jack-in-the-Box that serves oysters on the half-shell, steaks, and drinks.

The decor is meant to be English, I think, something between Shakespeare's house and a pub, but there is a German stein on the bar and the idea of printing the menu on a giant cleaver has to be peculiarly American. (The perfect spot for a Chinese tong war reunion, I say to the waiter, but he misses the joke and I can't bear to repeat it.) As they serve my steak, which nearly has as much taste as cold oatmeal without sugar, the plumbing gurgles behind thin walls and the hostess brings me a place-card with my own personal name sweetly misspelled on it. Fascinated, as I am by automobile accidents and television game shows, I come back the next afternoon for the post-luncheon lull to eavesdrop on small businessmen and salesmen who should be in their offices but who are hiding in bars. I belly-up to the bar, just down from two real Houston high-rollers, one pure Texas, and one Italian. They scheme big money in loud voices, and they don't even whisper when I start taking notes.

It seems that there are these giant cattle that reside in northern Italy and southern Yugoslavia and the Italian's father has a farm and a small but fine herd of these magical cattle. (The calves wean at six hundred pounds; they eat almost nothing and grow as furiously as a tumor; the cows give milk of such quality and in such quantities that it would shame the teats off a Holstein; the bulls are docile and virile.) If they can get the first herd of them into the States, they can make a fortune, but they have to beat the six-month quarantine. Together, in still louder voices, they work out a plan of bribery and intrigue, of devious routes through South America worthy of heroin smugglers. But of course neither of them needs the money.

All the conversations I overhear in bars, restaurants, and on street corners seem to concern money. "Getting and spending . . . . " Plumbers and welders, still in gray work suits, suckling on overpriced Lone Star beers as they watch a chubby young girl shake her sad nubile breasts, talk wages, prices and the stock market. Salesmen, lost in bragging about contracts won and lost, pause long enough to exchange current dirty jokes and barter telephone numbers—"Trade you a belly dancer in Miami for the number in San Antone"—then it's back to stock options and cost-plus and those mythical salesmen who have become Houston gods, the developers. When they talk about women, their voices are quite businesslike; they reserve the sensual hush for money-talk. At a party in a singles complex, a young man in a modish suit offers to sell me 10,000 hits of speed at a dime apiece, then quotes me the current Denver market price. Jokingly I ask what the price is in Seattle. He tells me, adds San Francisco, L.A. and Kansas City. The Dow-Jones of dope. I believe him. Every white person over the age of thirty that I meet eventually speaks of my banker in that same confident tone of possession that criminals reserve for their lawyers and Baptist preachers for their God.

A young lawyer, whose intelligence and judgment and integrity are beyond question, chides me for thinking that I can learn anything about a city by eavesdropping on conversations, particularly in bars, but then he goes on to explain Houston's low unemployment rate as due to a broad base of commerce and industry, its sensible growth to a lack of zoning laws, and preens over its rising land values right in the heart of the downtown where most American cities are dying. Nothing I hear in bars contradicts that. As long as Houston grows, a man can still get rich, by God, starting with nothing but a good mind, a willingness to work, and a little luck. And to hell with pessimism. If there are too many office buildings being built, then it's just a soft market for office space and the hard market is coming back. Who am I to disagree? Houston is a success.

And always has been, except for one small setback when the capital of the Republic was removed to Austin to avoid the heat, mosquitoes, muddy streets, and riff-raff. Houston was founded as a commercial venture, platted before even the basest core of a town existed, and Buffalo Bayou was deep enough for shallow-draft ships to dock fifty-five miles inland above a sandbar-blocked Galveston Bay. Houston hasn't faltered since. Its unemployment rate is traditionally half that of the nation's. Recessions have little or no effect on Houston. Not even the cutbacks at NASA can rock the economy.

The facts and figures of optimism bombard me constantly, even from those people who want me to see behind the Chamber of Commerce spiel. If I ask politely, "What happens when the growth stops?" I don't get any answers. They understand the question and the consequences, but they look into the distance, their eyes glowing like the buildings on the west side that seem to have gold leaf embedded in their windows. Do they envision, I wonder, a time when, no matter how far one drives in any direction, there is always Houston? Like ripples on a pond, countless circles of concrete loops and node cities, separated by green suburban belts. Houston forever.

Looking north from the twenty-first floor of the Post Oak Tower, it seems that a virgin broadleaf forest stretches as far as the eye can see across the plain. Dark and green and cool, sullied here and there by slashes of asphalt, splatters of concrete, hiding pleasant suburbs. From here it looks peaceful, and perhaps it is.

The woman across the desk wants to know why strangers (she means strange writers) want to know the bad things about Houston, the gloried excesses of the vulgar rich, the barbarian level of culture, the ill-fated minorities.

The rich are always vulgar, culture relative, and minorities ill-fated, I answer, evading her question, and all good copy. Houston seems pleasant, for a city, I tell her. At least most Houstonians make it sound that way, and perhaps it is. But I cannot shake the sense that I'm back in Guadalajara, where a small city of upper- and upper-middle-class Mexicans, perhaps one hundred thousand, lives on the verge of nine hundred thousand peons. No blacks, who are one-third of Houston, tell me how great the city is. Most say it's okay, not quite foot-shuffling and Uncle-Tomming me. No Chicanos tell me how rich they'll be next year. These distinctions are not institutionalized but they obviously exist. Just drive around Houston. If you have a car. Black maids going from the northeast side to the southwest to clean white houses sometimes spend two hours on a bus just to get to work. That's no more an accident than the fact that the I-610 Loop was first finished on the southwest quadrant and is only now being wound up in the northeast. Freeways go where the cars are, cars where the money is, and the money is in white pockets.

Houston is a pleasant city to live in if you are, like me, white, middle class, and fairly straight. But I wouldn't. Not even with your life.

O n another afternoon the Italian engineer-cum-cattle-dealer, sans high-rolling Texan friend (who has gone to Washington to meet with the Secretary of Agriculture), buys me a drink as he has his second, or third, double brandy after a long lunch. He does not know how to spell the name of the giant cattle his father owns. In spite of the air-conditioning, a sheen of sweat slickers his pale face. I would guess he needs the money from the cattle deal, that even if it works out, he will need more. His sadness and frail optimism depresses both of us. He should abandon Houston, go back to his father's farmhouse in northern Italy, repair the three-hundred-year-old plumbing, and live there, occasionally stroking one of the doomed docile bulls. And I agree with his Texan friend: he should lose some weight. Even in Houston, fat people die.

From the new bridge over the ship channel, where even now marine life returns cautiously into the poisonous waters, I watch the sun set grandly behind Houston. A vaulted hazy cloud squats on the city, the air burnished by the sinking sun, and out of it skyscrapers, huddled in their private nodes, loom like medieval towers abandoned to mists. Atop, a few silent cranes are stark against the western sky, hanging their girdered heads in some forgotten shame. The burning haze, which according to Houston is not smog but humid heavy air, might be smoke from the racial explosion Houston is never going to permit, but whatever it is, it suits that part of Houston that thinks itself a city, important, divine. And it suits me: the apocalypse begins.

But just off the bridge, the freeway ends unfinished for the moment, and I am detoured through a quiet lower-middle-class neighborhood, detoured into a southern spring afternoon. Old tires split and whitewashed gather bright flowers, and shotgun shacks stand clean and upright, as dignified and stony as the faces of old hill women. The streets are cratered as if by small explosions, rife with patches where dirt has leaked through the asphalt, and where the pavement fails and the shade trees are frosted with dust, small children stand hip-shot and grandly idle, slaking the dust with garden hoses, while their parents rest peacefully on sagging porches. These are the homes of the men who shovel shit in the name of commerce and industry, and they've been abandoned by the modern world springing up like ragweeds across town. Perhaps it is only my romanticism, my homesickness for rural, small-town America before it was infected by television that makes me think that they do not really mind.

And perhaps Houston only thinks itself a city.

From the seats of money and power, all things come to me second-hand.

Everybody tells me that if I really want to see a Houston success story, talk to Gerald D. Hines, as if he were the essence of Houston, or the king. Gerald D. Hines, the legend: He arrived in Houston in the early fifties with an engineering degree from Purdue and an old car upon which he still owed money, and today he controls over one quarter of a billion dollars of real estate. And the legend is close enough to fact to be called truth. Even the footnotes are nice. When he was selling refrigeration equipment during his first years in Houston, somebody said, "That's one young man who'll be a millionaire," and there is a failed Lincoln-Mercury dealership, made vague by success, where he lost his savings once, and a fine story about a tennis game and the idle conversation afterward, a comment about the high cost of leasing office space, a Gerald Hines retort that he could beat the price, and thus an empire was born. One and Two

Shell Plaza, Post Oak City, and the as yet unbuilt but coming Pennz-oil Place in Houston. One Shell Square in New Orleans. The Domestic Headquarters of TWA in Kansas City. In the back of the Hines Interests brochure, 128 income-producing properties are listed, three industrial parks, and nine projects in progress. The company is called Gerald D. Hines Interests, and empire is the right word.

But I never get to see the man, not because he won't see me, not because he doesn't have the time, but simply because we are never in town at the same time. If you can't see the king, talk to the princes, the ladies in waiting, look at his throne, smell the seats of power.

The Post Oak Tower and the Houston Oaks Hotel sit atop the Galleria Shopping Mall. Admittedly I'm a country boy, but that is no real excuse for the time I spend wandering about the three levels of the Galleria. I return there as I do to my alligators, but my reasons are more complex, and I never leave with any sense of peace.

A lovely vaulted skylight, worthy of a Paris train station, tops the mall, and at the bottom lies an ice rink. In July in Texas, without the usual closeness of ice rinks, children ice skate. And of course the best skater is a tiny black girl still in tight pickaninny curls. I don't know whether to laugh or cry. Beside me stand paunchy rednecks in their best sport shirts and slacks, and young men and women so mod that they can't be natives but their accents say they are. As I watch, open-mouthed, a couple passes behind me, speaking in soft fluted Italian. The smells of fine cheeses and sausages filter out from the open-air shop nearby. My God, this isn't Texas, not Houston surely. But it is. When the first shopping center opened in Corpus

Christi in the fifties, the people from my small hometown flocked there as if to a passing carnival, but this is a three-ring circus, a Babylonian delight. Enter in; innocence is sacrificed here. Enjoy now, for the trumpet must sound. If they had alligators instead of ice skaters, I could live here. At least until we perished of air-conditioned pneumonia. I am so astounded that I hate to remind myself that Fred and Frances Cruz live less than a quarter-mile southeast in an apartment complex that is neither modern nor swinging nor cool—live with a natural grace that makes all this, in spite of the studied tastefulness of the Galleria Shopping Mall, seem as disgusting, discordant, and foul as a neon sign in a tree-dark graveyard. Underneath the seats of power, the nether regions dance. The little black girl whirls like an ever so aptly named dervish, an icy fog clouding the blades of her skates. This is progress.

Upstairs—which is how I think of it, rather than up-elevator—I amble into the reception area of Gerald D. Hines, Interests, sink into a soft couch and wait. Young men, middle-aged men, and even secretaries pass before me with a studied air of confidence, energetic but not frenetic, firm but friendly. Those of us who are but petitioners are obviously waiting; we are welcome but clearly do not belong. The reception area is very tastefully decorated, soft walls, recessed lights, Indian pottery and rugs, a tall potted palm with very slender leaves that do not waver. To the right of the reception desk, behind smoked-glass doors, the hushed tones of big business flicker, shades dressed in expensive suits that do not wrinkle, shoes that do not squeak. In the hall down from the elevators, workmen hammer quietly. The elevator arrives and departs with the regularity of a commuter train, but once the doors open, invisible children laugh within, then the doors slide softly shut. Whatever city I'm in, it isn't Houston; it is a city of its own.

When the company officers speak of Gerald Hines and the company, they speak with affection and pride. They are careful to point out that, while his dress and politics are somewhat conservative, he is very open-minded. (I know the conservatism they speak of—not Edmund Burke's but John D. Rockefeller's—but I'm unsure of which brand of open-mindedness they mean.) They also carefully note that for relaxation Gerald Hines skis the Canadian Bugaboos by helicopter lift or shoots the rapids of the Salmon or Selway River. Admittedly I'm jealous. Last summer I couldn't come up with the $365 to float the Salmon for five days, and if I float it now, I won't be able to rid my nose of the crisp stink of dollar bills floating ahead of me. But that's a silly complaint. In fact, I'm not sure what my complaint is. In the best tradition of American business, Hines Interests provides a good product for a fair price, and they are justly proud of the fine buildings they have erected and will continue to construct. The company is aware of modern urban problems, and I'm certainly too jaded to suggest that there might be more important problems in Houston than a lack of good office space. Perhaps it is that great doses of good old American optimism strike me as criminally foolish in these times. Or perhaps I'm simply saddened by their belief in the old illusion: their empire will rise to immortality instead of dust.

Still uncertain of what bothers me here, I descend in the smoothly swift elevators, for once in my life pleased with my mundane life.

Now that I know I'll never be within the fabled Galleria again, I return to the alligators. But in a Texas July afternoon, they slumber beneath the green stillness of their pond like water-logged tree trunks, cool with emerald moss.

For a city of its size and age and tentative ego, Houston provides the requisite cultural activities so necessary for self-confidence, to convince itself that it is a real city with a real identity. Resident opera, ballet, and symphony. Several good theaters, including the Alley Theater. Art museums in proper quantities. And the wealthy families of Houston collect art, sometimes in unexpected proportions.

When I go to see the Max Ernst show at the Rice Museum, I think that surely I've come to the wrong place. The corrugated tin building is painted gray, a gray as dull as the leaking overcast, as leaden as the puddles spaced across the parking lot to the stadium. Inside, unpainted floors and plasterboard walls, nothing to detract from the show, which is impressive, even if it seems astounding that a single family owns most of the paintings and bronzes. I am told that the largest bronze, Capricorn, when not on display, stands at the end of their private garden, taller than a man, probably heavier than a Volkswagen, one hell of a big garden statue.

Imagine having the neighbors over for afternoon gin and tonics and croquet at the foot of the giant goat-headed god. His mermaid queen reclines at his side, their moon-faced mermaid daughter rests like a gift in his great hand, and his elbow is crushing the jester who is out of jokes.

The museum is free, and I'm glad to have seen the show.

My alligators usually sleep like logs but when they wake, the earth trembles. As I consider two sleepy bull gators, one still, the other crawling slowly from pond to grassy bed, they casually bump. There is nothing of reptilian patience now, but movement as quick as the flickers of a snake's tongue. The incredible bellowing roars boom across the zoo; monkeys scream from newly reached perches, and the big cats are suddenly silent. The fight lasts perhaps five seconds, the relationship between the bulls subtly altered, then they settle back into their still sleep. But the zoo still echoes, tremors of fear fly from cage to cage. Small children still sniffle into their parents' laps. This puny beast's body I wear has leapt back from the fence but I don't remember moving.

(On days when the news from the nation is unbearable, I would gladly give this country back to the Indians; but Buffalo Bayou goes to the alligators—they need the room.)

Whatever its failings, Houston never lacks contrast, the insane juxtapositions.

In the 5800 block of Canal Street there is a beer joint, The Buckhorn, frequented by the displaced rednecks from the declining neighborhood and merchant seamen from the maritime union on the corner. Though I didn't see action there, I assure you it is a tough place. Real anger and a sort of violence that can't be captured on film rumbles beneath the surface. The woman who serves my beer moves behind the bar with the strength and determination of a middle linebacker. Down the bar from me a large raw-boned man in a rumpled post office uniform sports a fresh mouse on his left cheek and new scabs on his knuckles. A sleeping drunk clings to a bottle swaddled in a brown paper bag. Behind me pool balls click, followed by an occasional nasal curse. After three beers I ask the man beside me what's going on across the street, and without looking up from his beer, he says, "Fuckin' Meskins."

He means the mural in progress on the side of the Continental Can Company, a 240 × 18 ft. mural by a proudly revolutionary young Chicano artist, titled *The Re-Birth of Our Nationality*. In the center of the mural, which is a catalog of the Chicano struggle—war, technology, La Raza Unida, César Chavez's UFW—a young couple emerges from a flower that rests on a pile of skulls.

I wonder what it does to the patrons of the Buckhorn Bar to walk out drunk, or sober, and be faced with 4330 square feet of revolutionary mural. Occasionally angry enough to throw mud on it, occasionally shamed enough to come up with ten bucks for paint or a six-pack of beer for the painters.

And so it's done. The 747 lifts me out of the warm sea of Houston. As the city spreads beneath me, I know that no single man can tell you about any city. The best you can hope for is the passionate guess. No heart transplants, no air-conditioned baseball games watched from ornate boxes high in the Astrodome, no astronauts who have mooned their way into business. Like all cities Houston will grow, then someday, some eon away, will die. The alligators won't even rouse from their slumber as they waddle over to breed and sleep and die among the rusted hulks of tankers un-turned in the turning basin. But for now it goes on. Gerald Hines builds buildings, Chicano artists paint them. The meat-market bars in the singles apartment complexes cover the soft slap of flesh with loud music. Houston goes on. And so it's done—my exile has become permanent.

1973

The Way of the Road

Back in the good old days—or at least our most recent version, the late sixties and the early seventies—every man and boy I knew had a hitchhiking hippie-chick story. You couldn't go into a bar anywhere in the West without hearing half a dozen. Everybody had one—white-shoed insurance salesmen, college professors and lightweight marijuana dealers—everybody, that is, but me. For a time there, it seemed as if I were the only man in the West of an acceptable age who'd never been seduced by random sex, roadsides and great drugs.

But it happens, and it happens like this: you're sitting in your favorite afternoon bar, propped on your favorite bar stool—the one at the end so you can watch the long-legged lady bartender for whom you've conceived a long-term, aimless lust—when she suddenly turns to you and says, "You got a car?" You nod a casual agreement, cool and easy, like a man whose 450 SL is tethered just outside the door. "Does it run?" she asks, having seen such casual nodding before. You reckon it does, and she drops her bar towel to the duckboards, dumps her tip glass into her purse and says, "Well, bud, let's see some highway. I'm so bored with this job I could scream."

The next thing you know, you're in the parking lot of the Outlaw Inn in Kalispell, Montana, watching two rich old drunks argue about workmanship, an argument that has been drifting on for several hours, one old man holding out his Cadillac Sedan de Ville as the epitome of the lost art of craftsmanship and the other opting for his Beretta over and under 12-gauge shotgun. As if to prove his point, the old man with the shotgun fires a round of birdshot through the door of the Cadillac. "Goddamn piece of tin," he mutters as the other old boy rubs his thumb around the splintered metal of the hole in his door, wondering if his insurance will cover gunfire. He reaches under the seat for a quart of Wild Turkey, offers it around, then invites all of us down to his lake house for a three A.M. breakfast. Beside you, the long-legged lady whistles softly, impressed, and squeezes your hand as if you've somehow been responsible for this romantic display.

Come daybreak, you're sitting on the end of a dock watching the sunrise over Flathead Lake. On the western shore, the hills turn golden, the brown grass of late summer glowing between the dark blue horizon and the cold black water. Behind you, the lady bartender argues with the old boys, trying to see how far they will raise the ante just to see her naked. One of the old boys keeps repeating, "Looky but no touchy, looky but no touchy," as he hops from foot to foot like a little boy losing an argument with his bladder. You cannot stop grinning. You know damn well you're drunk, the highway miles buzzing like amphetamines in your head, but lordgodalmighty you feel good for reasons you don't even care to examine. It's an illusion, right; but it's your movie.

Then the lady bartender strides down the dock, her clothes in one hand and a wad of bills in the other, and she drops both in your lap, dives into the icy water and stays under for a long minute. When she surfaces at your feet, she smiles and says, "I want to see sundown in some other goddamned place." And you're back on the road again.

Thus does reality become road myth.

Anybody who has ever spent any time on aimless trips through the mountain West knows that the illusion is of freedom, that lovely freedom of the cowboy, the saddle tramp, the gunfighter, any of those lanky heroes of our movie-screen youths. Somewhere out there great horses wait to be tamed but not broken, fast-gun bullies wait to be vanquished and maybe, if the timing is right, Mona Freeman even waits to be kissed tenderly, just once, before we ride off into a Hollywood sunset.

Of course, we know it isn't like that at all. Mostly the road is drunks and strangers, conversations you didn't mean to have and the loneliness of lying, unable to sleep, in a strange bed in a cheap motel while just beyond the drywall a couple shouts and screams their lonesome way into bed.

But when you're locked in your car, nothing but miles and miles of mountains and miles of straight road before you, you can't help but believe you're a free and better man once again. Whatever ex-wives, lost children and bad debts await you at home, you can put them behind you and that ribbon of highway in front, streaming into your face like a concrete wind.

At least it's always been that way for me.

During the years since I first moved west, I've spent a great deal of road time with a pair of brothers whom, for reasons of decency, I'll call the Buffalo Brothers. They're good road companions, good enough drivers, drunk or sober; willing to spend their money, and large enough to keep us out of trouble in most bars. We've managed to spend lots of lost days on the road, drifting down those winding mountain highways, our teenaged illusions fairly intact well into our forties, starry-eyed and slightly discontent.

One time we were dipping our toes into the Inner Circle (a route of bars north of Missoula, Montana) just to see if we wanted to run for a while, sitting in a bar in Seeley Lake, playing pool with a big kid who worked as a sawyer, a really big kid. We could tell because he had neglected to wear either shoes or a shirt, despite a large sign outside warning against such disgusting behavior. What the hell, it was his home bar—even his home pool table, he thought, until the three of us had beaten him several times running. We had drinks backed up from the bets, and it was becoming clear that the kid wouldn't let us leave without an argument. We discussed losing while he was in the john, but when he came out, he stalked down the bar grabbing everybody's beer cans, full and empty, squeezing them as if they were paper flowers. Occasionally, the beer foam shot all the way to the ceiling, and we squirmed uneasily in our seats. It wasn't our home bar, not by a long shot. But the bartender waved at the big kid as if he were a child, then came around the bar, saying, "Okay boys—that's it."

He picked up two dollies, strode over and set them down near the pool table. He lifted first one end of the pool table, then the other, onto the dollies, then pushed the table toward the far wall where he removed a sheet of plywood and shoved the table into a large niche. Then he came back, replaced the destroyed beers, sat the big kid down on a stool, came over and poured our drinks into large paper cups—"to go."

Nobody said a word. It was one o'clock on a Tuesday afternoon. The Buffalo Brothers and I hit the road for home, taking the affair as a bad omen, the illusion of survival without pain, or slow-to-heal black eyes, no longer one we held to at all.

Still, for me, driving around beats everything I know. For instance, it took me four tries to understand that I liked driving to ski slopes far better than I liked falling down them with snow packed into my shorts. Once at Eldora, Colorado, the ski patrol sent up a guy to help this buddy of mine and me off the mountain, trying to teach us something simple, like turning, but then he threw up his poles in despair and led us as we bombed down the slope.

I took that as an omen, too. Nothing at ski slopes appeals to me. You have to climb on or into pieces of machinery, then be carried off the ground, fall down a lot, get so cold that not even a sauna bakes it out of your bones and drink with a bunch of pretentious people wearing funny clothes. Skiing is not my idea of recreation.

And I'm not all that crazy about backpacking. I've done it just three times in the past fifteen years, and every trip was fraught with disasters both major and minor. If you go alone, you get lonesome. If you go with other people, you often discover just who your friends aren't. The fishing is never as good as it's supposed to be; the rain is always wetter inside a tent on a mountain than anyplace else. And I've never been able to pack enough whiskey to make it bearable.

Hunting used to be fun, admittedly; but as I've gotten older it seems too much like work, and I'm a bit ashamed of the thrill I get when I kill a deer or an elk. So I've given up killing them and taken to trading goods or services for my meat. I'd much rather stay in camp all day cooking and washing dishes so that everybody else will feel guilty and give me a share of the meat.

I never cared much for trout fishing, either, since I was raised in southern Texas using trotlines, crank telephones and quarter sticks of dynamite. So I often fail to see the beauty of standing butt-deep in an avalanche of cold water while a barbed hook snaps past my ear. This may go back to one afternoon when I was sitting in the Golden Ram in Fort Collins, Colorado, and a friend of mine came in after a windy day of fly-fishing on the Cache La Poudre. He sat down beside me and ordered a double Scotch straight with a double on the rocks as a chase. His bald head was resplendent: two Renegades and a Royal Coachman were lodged securely in the right side of his scalp. "Don't say a word," he muttered. "Don't say a goddamn word." Quite enough said about the joys of fly-fishing.

I might not use the mountains for the sort of serious recreation that some people engage in, but I like to drive through them. If I'm away from them very long I get as homesick as a bird dog kenneled for six weeks during quail season. I guess I still have a flatlander's awe at the simple size of these mountains. I like to look at them the same way some people like to look at the sea. I like to look at them even from the parking lot of the Eastgate Liquor Store and Lounge in Missoula, where the view includes railroad tracks, an interstate and a battery of gasoline storage tanks.

I leave but always come back to these lovely, perfectly useless mountains, these dingy, polluted western towns where the wages are low and the prices are high and the living is often hard. Judging by the growth rates of western towns, though, I'm not the only person in the country who comes to the West with the illusion of freedom. Not by a long shot.

Ah, no place in the world do the bars strike my fancy quite so well as in the West. They're as much a part of the highway as center stripes and chuckholes, places where you can hitch your pickup to a rail and walk into the illusion of a warm, if temporary, home. You don't even have to have a drink—claim a rotten liver or a rebellious stomach—just belly up to the bar, sip a soda and make yourself quietly at home.

Try the basement bar of the Sacajawea Inn in Three Forks, Montana. The building is in the National Register of Historic Places. Or the bar on the right side of the road in Two Dot, Montana. The beer-can collection is gone now, replaced by Indian artifacts. Or Woods Landing, Wyoming, on a Saturday night. During the summer the gathering of loggers and ranch hands is awesome.

If you're not into history, though, hit the bars in Rawlins, Wyoming. Maybe a guy will come in with three jar lids and a paper pellet. Buy him a couple of drinks and he'll show you how the shell game is played, but don't bet much, because he's unbeatable. Used to be, if you got lucky, you could find a bar on the Colorado-Wyoming border on U.S. 287 where the lady bartender would play pool with you for your hat, but you wouldn't want to play for your favorite hat, not after seeing all the hats hanging on her wall.

Or say you feel the need to clean up your act. Hit the Helsinki in Butte, Montana, have a few drinks, then ask the bartender for the key to the steam bath out back. It'll sweat the road miles right out of your system. Or slip off onto the dirt road between Ovando and Seeley Lake and drop into the Kozy Korner and take a look at the barber chair. Used to be, while you were having a couple of drinks, you could get your hair cut, so you wouldn't look quite so much like a fugitive from justice.

Just pick up any bar alongside the road. Stop and chat. Usually you'll find yourself treated just exactly as you deserve—no better, no worse, than you act. Maybe the thing I like best of all about the mountain West is the people: they don't care who you are, but they do care how you act.

The road can be hard and unforgiving, too. Try hitting Rock Springs, Wyoming, at two A.M. when Interstate 80 is closed by snow at Rawlins. Even if there were any available motel rooms, you wouldn't have the money for one, so you backtrack to Green River, Wyoming, and head south through the Flaming Gorge toward Vernal, Utah, with six inches of snow on the road and no tire tracks. That'll get your attention and hold it for a long time.

Or blow a tire going seventy-five in the middle of Utah's Bonneville Salt Flats. Hit a patch of black ice outside Lincoln, Montana, at any speed. Even do something easy, like drive from Fort Collins, Colorado, to Missoula in seventeen hours in a Volkswagen bus, or in thirteen hours in a Porsche, accompanied by a psychotic passenger.

These things aren't illusions at all: if you make a mistake—one little mistake—you're hamburger meat in a twisted metal bun.

Most people are afraid of cars, and a great many of those who aren't afraid should be. I've driven more miles than anybody except long-haul truckers and traveling salesmen during the twenty-six years I've had a driver's license, and I haven't had a bad wreck since I was sixteen and turned over my father's company car, and have only gotten two speeding tickets in the last twenty years. I'm good at this madness, but even at that, I'm always surprised when I get where I'm going alive. You should be, too. The highway is just a silly dream some of us chase, an illusion of freedom, but dying is unfortunately real.

Last time I took to the road, I set out to recreate the Inner Circle. None of us had done it for years. At first I thought about renting a motor home and gathering up all the old road-time folks for one last tour, but I quickly discovered that I didn't want to do it that way. I took a new woman with me, one who likes the highway as much as

I do, who wanted her hands on the steering wheel and the wind in her face, too.

But too much time had passed, and there were great chuckholes in the Inner Circle. What's the point of stopping at Joe Hall's Awfulburger Bar in Potomic, Montana, when Joe's dead? He'd be proud of the burgers, but most of the goofy signs are gone, the bottle collection, too. It's not the same. Some old woman who is visiting her family troubles the lady bartender for local gossip, and the lady bartender isn't a bit interested. She wants to take off on the Inner Circle with us. And what's Trixi's in Ovando after Trixi sold the bar and retired? Just a nice, quiet roadside stop. The new owners are talking about tearing down the old cabins.

It's mostly memories now. Joe Hall chasing drunks out of his place with a broom, Trixi telling old rodeo tales, all of the travelers young and full of listening. Up at the Roundup, Tom doesn't even remember me, but he buys us two road drinks so he can close the place for Mother's Day. Over at the Kozy Korner, one of the ranchers thinks my new lady is the finest thing since sliced bread, which doesn't make me too happy and makes his wife downright unhappy, so we move on quickly to Seeley Lake for pickled ham hocks and boredom; and almost before it began, the Inner Circle is abandoned.

Only the scenery seems the same. On the hillsides, a scruff of yellow tops the grass, and as the winds shift, the grass leans steadily, patiently before the breeze, and the black, timbered sides of the mountains and the snowcapped peaks still tilt into an amazingly blue sky.

Later we stop at the Outlaw Inn for martinis and shrimp salads, hoping to see a movie star (they're filming a movie, *Heaven's Gate*, around Kalispell), but I don't see any stars until much later, south of Polson, when my new lady has been rocked to sleep by the easy drift of the road. I smoke a dollar cigar and think about being forty, about having survived so many miles since I first climbed onto my father's lap as a child while he let me steer his pickup.

I don't know. I suspect the road is a young man's chore and that time is the most relentless highway of all, but I know that old ribbon of asphalt ain't quite through with me yet.

1979

The Heavy

Okay, tell me one more time—who's Roy Jenson and what's he done? That's the question, and it's asked of me at least twenty times on the way to Los Angeles, asked by writers, editors, movie buffs, and even a Hollywood director.

Well, you would think that a good old boy who has been in the movies for thirty years working his way up from extra to stunt man to double to featured player would get more respect than that. Roy Jenson has been done in by every star worth his salt in Hollywood—out-fixed by Paul Newman in *Harper*; insulted to the quick by Jack Nicholson in *Chinatown*; had his chopper ripped off and his ass whipped by Clint Eastwood in *The Gauntlet*; found himself up-staged by a charming orangutan and asphalted by Eastwood in *Any Which Way You Can*; had his head blown off by Steve McQueen in *Tom Horn*; and, insult of insults, been gunned down by Goldie Hawn at the end of *The Duchess and the Dirtwater Fox*. And that is only a slight list of his achievements in violence. Even in a low-rent rip-off of the *Walking Tall* sequence, Roy Jenson and Joe Don Baker staged the best, most convincing, most horrifying in its realism, the greatest fight I have ever seen on the screen. Although it seems that not very many people outside the movie business know his name, when he is on camera, Roy Jenson makes looking mean, downright rock-hard bad, look easy, and he does it without falling back on the stylized mannerisms of, say, Jack Palance, or the studied inarticulate threat of the early Charles Bronson. On the screen, Roy Jenson makes looking bad look as easy as James Garner makes looking good.

Without villains worthy of their stature, there are no heroes worthy of our respect. To make the favorite Hollywood myth—that good will prevail over evil—convincing, the threat of terrible and bloody violence and death must be convincing. Without the bad guys, the good guys have nothing to do except look good on horseback and strum their aimless guitars. Without Iago, the Moor is simply another neurotic lost in his own insecurities, but poised against Iago's malicious connivance, Othello achieves that tragic stature meant to break our hearts. Hollywood did not invent the heavy, but without the heavy, movies could only do comedy—which is sometimes fired with the intelligence of a Chaplin or a Buster Keaton, but is too often Chevy Chase playing all three Stooges—or middle-class soap operas like *Kramer vs. Kramer* and *Ordinary People*, or imitation plays like *Tribute*, or one-note biographies like *Coal Miner's Daughter*, or movies about movies—which can sometimes be fine, as in *The Stunt Man*, or boring inside jokes like *Alex in Wonderland*—or bad versions of bad French films, and last, and least, the ubiquitous and cowardly sequel (*Jaws 12 Eats 10*).

Surely it is no accident that *The Great Train Robbery* was the first popular feature film in America. We love violence, we love gunfire, the wonderful explosive crunch of dynamite. We love heroes; we need bad guys for definition.

Roy Jenson does not look like a bad guy as I park in front of his modest house up in the Hollywood Hills. I am half an hour late, and he is waiting in the driveway with a can of Bud in his hand. Although his last experience with a writer doing a magazine piece turned out badly—the writer bought Roy's screen persona, portrayed him in the piece as fat, ugly, gross, drunk, and mean—he ushers me through the kitchen door of his home with the sort of shy, charming hospitality that only born and bred rednecks can master. I am pleased to see that he is as nervous about all this as I am, but we are both large beefy athletic types running swiftly toward beer guts in our middle years. We recognize each other, somehow, working-class kids who have done far better in life than we had any right to expect, a couple of big kids grown now and often mistaken for truck drivers or construction laborers or bartenders, both of us uncomfortable in professions our fathers never dreamed possible.

Roy's dog Baja barks madly at me as I come in the door. I try to make friends, but Roy does not discourage Baja barking. All the houses on his street have been knocked over except his, he explains, and he credits the dog. I understand, agree. When he finally gets Baja to go out the back door, I see the small pool in the back, the patio nestled against a steep and brushy California hill. Everybody in Hollywood seems to have a pool, I say, making dumb conversation. But Roy wants to talk about the hill, the flood a few years back when the slope dropped into his pool so furiously that it splashed his youngest son's tennis shoe all the way to the garage roof, wants to talk about the forty-thousand-dollar retaining wall that gave way under the onslaught of the rain and mud. Roy dug the pool and the patio out by hand, shovel and wheelbarrow, moved five dump truck loads of mud by hand. I am impressed. An old roughneck I worked with down in South Texas, I say, told me once that there ain't no such thing as good shoveling or bad pussy. Roy seems embarrassed, wants to know where we should do this thing, this interview, and after a bunch of hem-and-haw and foot shuffling, we end up in the kitchen like two good rednecks with beer cans in our hands, sitting on stools or propped on the breakfast bar or leaning against the counters. Although I do not know yet where he grew up, I know he grew up in a house where the kitchen was the center of the house, the living room reserved for strangers, preachers, and insurance salesmen.

Although he was born in Canada, after his father died when he was six, Roy's mother—who, as he said, had people there—moved him and his brother to East L.A. during the heart of the depression. He grew up hard, watching his mother work two and three jobs, working jobs himself as far back as he can remember, one of the few white kids in his grade school, getting the shit kicked out of him every afternoon as the Mexican kids dribbled him home from school like an under-inflated basketball. After high school, which was interrupted by a stint of running away and working on the Shasta Dam, he went into the Navy at the end of World War II. Something happened in the service. Whatever it was, he came out and went to college in Santa Barbara to get his grades up so he could play football at a real college. Whatever happened in the Navy, Roy came out, as we used to say in the sixties, radicalized, intending to write a novel about what a piece of shit Navy life could be. Whatever he did at Santa Barbara, he did enough of it so that a few years later when a coach at UCLA, where Roy finally played ball, recommended him to the newly formed CIA, the CIA would not have him. As I understand it, though, Frank Gifford was more than pleased to have him opening holes in the line. Roy made All-Coast three years in a row, then went to Calgary to play professional ball.

Ah, but this is supposed to be about Hollywood, about movies. Damn right. After his first year at UCLA, Roy went back up to Oregon to work in a lumber camp where he had worked the summer before. When he came back to L.A., he ran into a hustler buddy of his at UCLA driving a Buick convertible with those three holes in the front fender. He had a blonde in the seat next to him and a check for a week's work, more money than Roy had made all summer felling trees up in Oregon.

I wanted some of that, he said. And he got some of it. Quickly. He did his first job as an extra working on *Samson and Delilah*.

Then there came acting classes and a contract at Warners, classes with Gifford, then doubling, then stunts and whatnot during the seven years of Canadian ball, back in the old days when a lineman with Calgary made six thousand bucks a season, when he made more in six weeks up at Banff doubling Robert Mitchum in *River of No Return* than he made in four months cracking heads in the Canadian league.

Even if his name did not show on the credits, Roy knew he could walk into a movie, see himself on the silver screen doing stunts and doubling, and that Tinseltown bug of fame and fortune lodged in his chest like a heartworm.

As we sit across the breakfast bar, after we have moved from Bud to Scotch, after three hours of stories, and after Roy looks up and asks, are we doing the interview now? I assume it is all right to look at him in person to see if I can see what I saw on the screen. So often when you see them in real life, actors seem so small. Once, a producer introduced me to John Cassavetes at Ma Maison, and Cassavetes, who looks like such an absolute force on the screen, talent and intelligence sparkling around him, seemed like just another guy, a bright, witty guy you might have known in graduate school, but, hell, I wanted to see that wonderful psychotic grin from *The Dirty Dozen*. Another time, I had a beer down in Sun Valley sitting next to Clint Eastwood. He was not the Man With No Name or Dirty Harry or, hell's-fire, even Rowdy Yates, just a nice, polite guy, whose reputation as an intelligent gentleman among all the Hollywood sharks seemed well-deserved. And still another time, I chased my favorite actor in the whole world, Warren Oates, down a hallway just to shake his hand and give him the love and blessings of all the literate rednecks in America. He had Warren Oates' face, his pleasant smile, but he was a slip of a man, slight leaning toward skinny. I know, I know—we ask too much of them, those silvered icons of our movie dreams, and perhaps it would be better never to see them outside of the movie houses, but sometimes we do.

And Roy Jenson, like all of them, looks somewhat different across the breakfast bar than he looks in the movies. For one thing, the camera flattens his Nordic face, makes him look mean and, forgive me, dumb. In real life, his face is mobile, intelligent, and when he tells a story or laughs or talks about his children, his face lights up and softens, like the face of your favorite uncle who has had the sort of wonderful and adventurous life you long for in all your adolescent love and hope. When he smiles, you feel at home, and although he looks like the sort of man you would not want to hassle in a bar, he does not look like a heavy at all.

All those physical years, though, show, those years of football and stunts. His large hands are twisted, flattened knuckles and fingers angling off in directions designed neither by God nor evolution. The left shoulder droops with the question mark of too many separations, and when he crosses the kitchen for ice and more whiskey, he limps, and you can hear the left knee snap, crackle, and pop with calcium deposits, bone chips, and degenerative arthritis.

Kill the head, they say, and the body dies. But we know that is not how it happens. Last year, easing into his fifties, Roy ran in the fifteen kilometer Fireman's Benefit Run along Mullholland. Finished dead last, he said, but finished. Nearly twenty years ago when he went to meet his wife's family in Yugoslavia, he roared off the plane drunk, picked up Marina, a European actress he had met while doing stunts on *The Great Escape*, and carried her all the way through the airport in his arms, then went to her parents' home and drank all the slivovitz they had in the house. Those days, these days, the physical life—but somewhere along the way, it changed, and

Roy Jenson decided to become an actor. Not a double, not a stunt man, but an actor. And now, not a heavy, but an actor.

Remember *River of No Return*? Remember those frightening scenes with Robert Mitchum, Marilyn Monroe, and the kid charging down the white water in that pissant log raft? Well, it was not them, it was a stuntwoman doing Monroe, a stunt midget doing the kid, and Roy Jenson doubling Mitchum. Looked like a lot of fun, right? Looked like them folks was so scared they were probably sucking cloth washers off their underwear, right? True enough. Try to remember, too, that for every minute of film, those people were surviving three hours of damp terror for two-hundred-fifty bucks a day, and that the worst part, the accidents, the flip over the falls, the simple failure of equipment, never showed up on film.

But if you are the baddest ass in the Canadian Football League, if you have to kick ass because you are a bit too small to play pro ball up there, blocking on dudes with forty pounds on you and tackling running backs who have twenty-pounds and four-yards momentum on you, you sure as hell cannot be intimidated by some sort of movie crap. Right?

I was cool, Roy says, never backed off for a second, but sometimes I would have these nightmares, I would be so scared that I would jump directly out of my bunk in the cabin, wrapped in all my blankets, so scared that I would leap all the way across the cabin and land on the midget in his bunk. Shit, Roy says, he was scared too. I told him the reason big fish could swim, he says, was because they ate little fish, and the midget ate fish for two months before he found out I was shitting him. But we were all scared.

A couple of years later, Roy was doubling Victor Mature in a dog called *The Shark fighters*, working down in Cuba off the Isla del Piñas. It was hard work, eight hours in the water every day, but not dangerous because they used dead sharks equipped with motors. Not dangerous until the day the Roy noticed all the Piñearos working as extras and technical help had disappeared up into the boats. One, two, three, Roy said as he counted the motorized sharks, counted all the way up to eleven, ah, then twelve. One too many sharks. Out of the water, he said, running on the water like Jesus in a 220-yard dash. To hell with that shit, he said.

A few days later, the special effects man had a heart attack, and the first assistant director fell off the wagon. Roy tried to hide the cases of rum in the jungle, but the first assistant director found a .22 rifle and opened fire, shot at Roy until he brought the rum back to the hotel. Scared me worse than the extra shark, Roy said.

Over the years he had done so much of that sort of thing that he cannot remember the names of the movies, cannot remember the falls, the fistfights. I mention a George Montgomery/Yvonne De-Carlo/Tab Hunter oater called *Hostile Guns*—the first time I remember seeing Roy Jenson—but I have to do the whole plot of the movie before Roy remembers it. Seems like I did a thousand of those, he says.

But there are moments. Doubling for Leo Gordon in *Kings of the Sun* Roy Jenson had a moment down in Mazatlan back in 1963. Maybe because he is a striking figure of a man, or maybe because he can carry as much tequila as he can drink, but more likely because he understands in his bones the nature of machismo—which is not some smartass kid trying to face you down as you drive down a street in Durango, and not some drunk Mexican banker showing you his .45 automatic, and not some crazy attitude toward women that sets good, hard-working, independent American women's teeth on edge; machismo means we will be gentlemen no matter how twisted by drink and drugs and life we find ourselves, and, as Ezra Pound so gracefully said, there is some shit we will not eat; no more, no less—whatever, a small band of extras attached themselves to Roy with that sort of devotion that usually only family requires.

In the scene, Roy had to convince his half-dozen followers to run through fire, without fire suits, on the beach, then fight their way through another two thousand Indian extras—and fight they did, wooden swords and shields clattering like gunfire, some atavistic memory working—and they fought all the way to the top, where George Chakaris felled Roy Jenson with a killing blow.

Of course, just like in the movies, everything came to a stop while they set up the next scene. Roy put on a rubber suit, knee pads, elbow pads, which the makeup people sprayed with their version of that wonderful golden dirt-brown we recognize as Indian. And then Roy looked around from the top of the pyramid, watched an ambulance scream through the crowd of Indian extras, thought perhaps somebody had been hurt by accident during the filming of the fight from the beach, then they set the shot, and he did the fall, the longest stairway fall anybody had ever done, down the long steps of the pyramid.

I thought I was gone, he said, but I have always had fast hands, and somewhere down there when I was bouncing way up in the air, I managed to catch a step for a second and slow it down, and I made it all the way to the bottom with only a scraped shin and a little crack on the back of my head, but I was dizzy as hell, could not see shit, but when I stood up, there was this funny silence, these two thousand Indian extras spinning around in my eyes, and I thought maybe I was hurt worse that I thought, then all these Indians started banging their wooden swords against their fucking prop shields, all two thousand of them, and shit man I felt like I was in heaven.

As it is supposed to be, anything you work at for a long time, anything you take pride in doing—eventually, you will be captured by your craft, by the necessary pride of professionalism.

We are down in Studio City now, bellied up at Stevie G's, Roy

Jenson's home bar. I can tell it is home because when we wander in out of the smog-misted sunlight, Roy's friends give him a raft of shit. He has made the mistake of one martini too many and told them that some dude is coming down from Montana to do a piece about him for *Rolling Stone*. "You don't look like no guitar player," somebody says to him as we arrive. And another points out loudly that his oldest son still considers Roy just about the meanest man alive, the ugliest man he has ever seen. These are not Hollywood people, but working people, and they clearly love and respect this big, battered old fart who chews the end off his cigar, bunches his shaggy eyebrows beneath his Copenhagen gimme cap, and threatens to rip their heads off and shit down their throats. I have to admit that I am pleased and easy among these people, pleased to see that Roy is more than a touch embarrassed about all this.

But I am supposed to be working, right, so I ask what it feels like to have a squib explode against your flesh. Roy should know; he has been killed enough to know; but he gives me a lecture about professionalism, about the craft.

Steve McQueen, Roy says, we were friends. Oh, shit, not buddies or anything like that, but friends, you know. He had been to dinner at my house, we knew each other a long time, that sort of thing. He called me here, Roy says, pointing toward the telephone back by the johns, he called me here to do that bit in *Tom Horn*. You know, I must have been a rustler or something, I don't know, but Steve comes in and gives me a piece of paper, a writ or summons or something, and I'm supposed to do this bit, right, supposed to be eating porridge with my left hand, and I've got my gun, see, in my right hand, and I say something like "fuck it," but at the same time I've got to put down the fucking spoon and pick up the squib button off camera—shit, they've spent three hours down in makeup putting this sucker on my forehead and another hour on the back of my head so it'll blow off right—and here I am, I have to do a couple of lines of dialogue, get rid of the spoon, pick up the squib, drop the hammer on my pistol, pop the squib when Steve is supposed to shoot me, make sure that I don't tip over too soon before the special effects people blow the back of my head off, and somehow after all this shit, I'm supposed to end with my boots on the table so Steve can blow me away with his carbine because I missed him and killed his horse.

Shit, Roy says, I'm making a thousand dollars a day for this bit, and if I fuck it up, I get another day, but goddamn I did it right. First take, he says, I'm a professional.

Although I do not know enough about the details of the movie business, when Roy tells me that the transition from stunt man to actor is almost impossible to make, I believe him. When he caught the part of Puddler in *Harper* in the mid-sixties, he made the move. Although he has starred in a couple of Mexican films—and it is wonderful being a star, he says, penthouses and limousines, but they want you to play it broad, mugging toward the camera—and managed to run up against some co-star roles in American movies, some of which are still in the can, it is tough making a living, hard to get respect.

Too often it works out like this: when he came back down from Idaho off *Breakheart Pass*, Roy felt like he needed something physical to do, so he went to work with one of the co-stars off the film, Bill McKinney, doing landscape and tree-trimming work for five bucks an hour, tough work for an old man, and no respect; Roy and Bill were doing one of the other co-stars of *Breakheart Pass*, doing his yard, making things right for a cast party, a party to which they were not invited. The line, Roy said, was drawn just above their names.

Like all of us at the mercy of other people, Roy Jenson waits for the telephone to ring. Tomorrow, he says, I might be on my way to Africa. It's been a good life, he says—then he tells me this story.

When he was working on *The Getaway* down in El Paso, Roy, one of his sons, and a friend tried to fly a Bamboo Bomber, a World War II training plane, from Chihuahua across the Sierra Madre to Los Mochis through heavy weather. As it became clear that they could not make it—they were making 130 knots air speed but not moving an inch; the rocky peaks, as they drifted through the clouds, sat there, still, waiting—Roy started thinking about dying. Frightened, he said, but not scared. His only regret, he said, that his son sat in the back of the plane. Fuck it, Roy said to himself, if we crash, we'll be okay, we'll walk out of these mountains. Hero talk.

But after he told the story, he told me what it meant. All these years, he said, I've always been afraid in front of the camera, in front of an audience. A few years ago, he said, when I decided to be an actor, I was doing Shakespeare, a reading, you know, in an actor's workshop, and some asshole out there beyond the lights was giggling, and I went out there and grabbed the little bastard by the neck. If it's so easy, I said, you do it. But after we nearly bought it, he said, up in the Sierra Madre, and then we didn't, I promised myself I'd never be afraid in front of a camera or an audience again. Never.

What must it be like, I wonder, this big, crazy bastard doing Shakespeare, or, hell, thinking of opening down in Orange County doing *The Gin Game*. Surely it will not be the same as doubling for Mitchum down that furious river, and never close to that magic moment when two thousand Indian extras pounded their fake shields in tribute.

And when I ask, behind far too many martinis now, what it does to a man to make his nut by doing nothing but bad guys, Roy has no answer. He is standing at the top of his driveway now, and I am down on the street. He looks up the hill and says, there's coyotes up there, you know, and hawks, hell, I saw a hawk bust a raven a couple of days ago. Shit, he says, maybe I'm becoming some sort of Zen asshole. I found some pissants, he says, eating the soap in the shower the other day, and I said to myself "fuck it—they ain't hurting nothing"—so I let 'em alone. I don't know.

Nice talk for a heavy, I say up the dark and drunken driveway.

Roy Jenson ignores that, then says, hey, this ain't some sort of number is it? We're friends now, right? And you'll love me till I die, right?

All the philosophical, psychological bullshit trappings run through my head in one quick moment—the dumb pain of the original Frankenstein's monster, the creature from the Black Lagoon rising and roaring with hurt, all of that, all that evil and pain—and I know, now, the best of the bad guys break our hearts, and I shout back up that dark driveway toward that large, limping figure who has calls to wait for, family to love, and bad guys to play to the hilt, and I shout: You bet your fucking life—I'll love you till I die.

1981

Book 'Em, Debbie

The photographer is trying to coax Debbie Bird, Sub-District Ranger at Old Faithful, into one of those staged shots that looks as phony as your Uncle Egbert's toupee. It's the end of summer on the Yellowstone Plateau, and Bird is as cool as the snow spitting from the clotted sky. She's stoic, like a beat cop whose feet hurt, and patiently polite. The photographer tries to jolly her with the suggestion that, should a carful of rowdy drunks happen by, she jerk them out of their vehicle and, say, rough them up. He giggles as if the idea appeals to him.

Bird smiles slightly, squares her compact frame, and straightens her Smokey the Bear hat—her law-enforcement stance. "No," she says calmly. "I'd just point out that they are behaving badly. Then I'd tell them how to behave. They do it. Every time."

Picture the photographer getting the point and smiling sickly, like a man who just swallowed a film can. Print. Somebody laughs into the steamy air and thinks, This is one tough cop dressed up in that ranger suit.

Yellowstone National Park has about as many visitors each year as it does acres of land. Even the most timid tourists want to let it all hang out in the wild, wild West, and somebody has to protect them from themselves and from the animals. And somebody has to protect the animals and the environment from the tourists, and everybody and everything from the occasional lunatic or criminal on vacation. That's why a handful of Yellowstone rangers, including Debbie Bird, are law-enforcement qualified.

Bird makes it clear, though, that rangers wear lots of hats. They are responsible for fire control, emergency medical services, and environmental violations, as well as law enforcement. (Picture a Los Angeles police officer having to engage in a gunfight with a crack dealer, revive him with CPR, and then hose down the bloody mess.)

On a typical afternoon like this one, Bird responds to a call from a Montana Power Company crew that wants her approval for a cleanup job along a power line that they had to replace after the 1988 fires. (Because of the drop in tourism during the fires, there was no crime to speak of that summer; Bird spent most of her time closing off roads and shuttling park employees away from the blaze.) Then she has to take a brisk two-mile hike to the other side of Midway Geyser Basin to check on some volunteer bridge-and-trail work up by Fairy Falls. The drainage burned in 1988, and the blackened snags along the trail stand starkly against the mountain-blue sky. A carpet of new grass, shot with late flowers, rises through the burned stubble of the forest floor. The falls plunge off a rocky ridge, clearly visible beyond the burned lodgepole pines.

Bird pauses, shifts the weight of her gunbelt. "I never wanted to do anything but this," she says. "From the first time I went to Yosemite, I knew what I wanted to do with my life." The summer she finished high school, in 1970, she took a bus to Yosemite and lucked into a job for one of the park concessionaires, a pattern she continued for several years. Then she was a seasonal ranger for a few summers, watching, as she says, "less-qualified men get the permanent jobs." So Bird took an office job for the Park Service in San Francisco and sent herself back to school to become law-enforcement qualified, which for the most part meant that she learned how to operate firearms. "Somehow," she says, "being an interpretive ranger didn't seem, you know, real enough. Not exciting enough." Then she smiles. "The Park Service is more than a job; it's a way of life."

She even married into the Park Service: her husband, Paul Slinde, is Yellowstone's Trail Maintenance Foreman. "A good way of life," she adds, gazing over the landscape. Then she walks back up the trail toward her unit, a permanent spring in her step.

It's no surprise that most law-enforcement incidents in the park, 52 percent, involve resource violations. People with cameras can't seem to stop trying to get closer to the animals than good sense and the law allow. They also have trouble keeping their vehicles on the pavement, their feet on the walkways in the geothermal areas, and their food safely stored according to posted regulations.

Then there are the usual summertime accidents: twisted ankles, misplaced children, broken bones, French photographers gored by bison, and the most common Yellowstone injury of all—"Goddamnit, Edna, that water's hot!"—the burned hand.

For petty violations, no one outdoes the employees of concessionaire TW Recreational Services. Mostly they're college kids, pretty responsible ones, who have to pass a background check. (Back in the days when the Yellowstone Park Company ran the concessions, virtually anybody who showed up for work was hired—transient hippies, criminals on the lam.) But they are kids and occasionally like to get a little ripped and bathe in the thermal features or piss into the spout of Old Faithful, both clear violations.

Traffic can be a problem, too. Oversize RVs, station wagons filled with bored children, and busloads of Asian tourists create enormous tangles on Yellowstone's narrow, twisting mountain roads. Most of the drivers seem willing to stay sober, but in her career as a ranger, Bird has arrested inebriated tourists behind the wheels of trailers, boats and snowmobiles. Several winters ago a smashed snowmobiler nearly ran her over. The driver protested his arrest at some length and volume, but Bird strapped him onto a sled and hauled him twenty-eight miles from Old Faithful to the jail in West Yellowstone, Montana. "When we started out," she says, "he was threatening to sue everybody in sight. By the time we got there, he was begging to go to jail."

Poachers occasionally hit the park, hunting trophies or meat, but mostly they are locals who know their way around and are awfully difficult to catch. So are thieves, who take vacations like everybody else. Sometimes a professional will hit one of the large parking lots just as Old Faithful blows its top, and the odd amateur will rifle a car parked at a trailhead. Still, most of your possessions are safer in Yellowstone than in your own home.

Crime in the park usually isn't very dramatic, but every now and then things do get exciting. Take, for example, last summer's hostage crisis.

A disturbed college student drove all the way from Louisiana to commit suicide in Yellowstone, but once he got there, he couldn't drop the hammer on himself. Thus he had a bright idea: He'd let the rangers do it for him. He walked into the Old Faithful visitors center, pulled a pistol, and took hostage five tourists, two unarmed rangers, and a Yellowstone Association employee. The other rangers inside the building handled the situation perfectly. They remained calm while armed rangers surrounded the center; one even managed to steer a theater full of tourists out the back door. The law-enforcement rangers, with Bird in charge, kept a quiet lid on things until the gunman released his hostages two hours later. After a couple more hours, he exited without his weapon and surrendered to the rangers. Nobody was hurt. That's the way it's supposed to end.

Sometimes crime turns into comedy. Two days after the hostage crisis, a forty-year-old transient broke into the water-treatment plant at Old Faithful. He sniffed a lot of paint thinner, smashed everything in sight, and then dumped motor oil into the water. The next morning, when the rangers found him, he ran into the woods.

When they didn't chase him, he broke into the building again through a window and came out the front door, quite irritated and abusive about their lack of pursuit.

In her ranger uniform, it's easy to forget that Debbie Bird is also a cop. She carries a nightstick and a .357 magnum (which she's pulled several times but never used) and has a street-cop's impatience with slow days. But for two days nothing happens. Nobody tries to commit suicide in Old Faithful's cone. No poachers or pot-smokers rampage through the meadows. No blood is spilled, animal or human. Even the drivers are behaving themselves, refusing to mar the tranquil afternoons. Crime has taken a real vacation.

Nothing happens but the Yellowstone scenery, one of wildest, loveliest landscapes in the world. So we just enjoy it. That's not a crime, Bird says, grinning. It's one of her favorite official duties.

1989

The Great West

In the mid-sixties when I changed my home place from Texas to Montana, I still assumed that Texas was a western state. Now I have been informed that it is something called a "sunbelt state," a phrase that always makes me check my buckle. Texas still seems to me like an odd nation-state in which I am, in spite of birth and rearing, still denied citizenship. That is all right with me. I live in Montana, in the Real West. Maybe.

One of the things I have noticed out here, though, is that about every five years or so, somebody gathers up enough grant money to sponsor a conference of writers, painters, historians, environmentalists, photographers, Native Americans, politicians and, of course, lawyers to confuse the issue by once again trying to define the Great American West. Important questions are raised for those of us who live here: Who owns it? How do we water it? Can we save it? Does anybody care? And why can't we leave it alone, why must we continue to write about it, film it, paint it, litigate over it, and most of all rape it?

I certainly don't have any answers to most of that string of rambling, gambling, hard-riding rhetorical questions, except I know that we can't leave it alone because we love it beyond reason, beyond myth and reality; we love the light, the landscape, the people. It's a sacred place and we understand that if we stop worshiping it, the West, like a sullen god, will disappear. As far as I'm concerned, defining the West is one of those rough, ranch chores I will no longer participate in, like building fence or bucking bales.

I have to admit that I'm not even sure where the West is any more. Except in my heart. When I'm gone, something is missing. Coming back, running fast and free, it is as Thoreau said: "Eastward I go only by force; but westward I go free." Nobody ever said it much better. And Thoreau had never seen sunrise on the Tetons or spent a summer in Choteau, Montana, or a winter in Walden, Colorado. But he understood that whatever "west" meant—the frontier or the freedom or the place where civilization was tested— it didn't take place in town. And western towns can be ugly, no doubt about it. But you can stand on the edge of Casper, Wyoming, in the springtime and stare until your eyes water at the snow-shot rolling hills, and turn around and face the town. The towns aren't the point; the landscape, the history, and the people are, always have been.

Alex Axelrod's *Art of the Golden West* (Abbeville Press) makes that perfectly lovely and clear. Although it is subtitled "An Illustrated History," don't mistake this volume as history in pabulum form, cream-of-white-eyes for dolts. It's for adults, and those children big enough to saddle their own ponies. It weighs about as much as a kid's saddle, but it's worth making your coffee table groan, stuffed with wonderful reproductions, complete with brief but informative profiles of dozens of western artists, starting with Albert Bierstadt and reaching all the way to Georgia O'Keeffe. Along the way, the usual giants of western art are covered, but this is a generous book, and it is a pleasure to see most of the lesser lights standing there beside them. Although the text seems to have an overwhelming amount of information, the prose is always thoughtful and clear, always connected to the reproductions in a comfortably intelligent manner.

But the art. My God, the art! It is astounding. Not exactly like an afternoon in the Gilcrease Museum in Tulsa, but closer to the house.

Of course, western artists have this thing about light. They don't have a lock on it, but they like to paint it. Russell Chatham, who paints a lot of Montana landscapes, says he's never seen the same light here twice. Or anywhere in the West. Maybe that's half a definition: the West is a place where you go to see the light.

The first time it happened to me, my hunting partner and I were sitting in a duck blind on a slough off the Flathead River just outside Dixon, Montana. In the late afternoon, with the sun and the thermometer rapidly sinking, the sun dropped just below the cloud cover. The snow-swaddled peaks of the Mission Mountains twenty miles to the east flared with a furious light. The dried winter grass on the soft hills along the icy black river began to glow as if fired from within. And the light filled the air, palpable as fog, as sharp as the frozen air. I scrambled out of the duck blind to dance on the hard ground. Luckily, my partner was too bewildered to shoot me. After the light faded, we drifted over to the only bar in Dixon and discussed my behavior.

I've seen a few grand vistas since then, but that lovely moment is still absolutely clear in my memory. Unfortunately for the West, the sun goes down just as prettily over the Berkeley Pit in Butte, Montana. The huge abandoned wound in the earth is slowly filling with water; the water looks to be full of heavy metals, and at sundown the pit glistens with an unearthly light. It's pretty, I suppose, but as toxic as some outer-space virus.

It seems the West always has been a place where the consequences of unbridled greed are particularly visible. Or, as the case may be, insidiously invisible. The West always has been the economic slave of outside interest, a colonial territory. First, they trapped almost all the beaver, then killed all the buffalo. Then they practiced a little genocide on the native population, then lied to the hordes of immigrant farmers. First, they said it wasn't really the Great American

Desert; then when it was, they said there was so much of it it didn't really matter. So the farmers dropped their shiny new plows into 30,000 years of prairie sod, and made damn certain that the Great Plains would never be great again. Now we've got convicted junk-bond dealers out of jail on bond, "harvesting" our trees to provide the Japanese with cheap lumber.

The stories are endless about the rape of the West. They're all sad and somewhat crazy, but none as sadly crazed as the story told in *Bravo 20: The Bombing of the American West* by Richard Misrach with Myriam Weisang Misrach (Johns Hopkins University Press). It isn't enough that we've spent a couple of centuries out here letting scavenger birds foul our nests, now they're bombing us. What next, pray tell?

Here's the story in a nutshell, or make that bombshell: In 1952, in spite of all the other bomb ranges the Navy had at its disposal in Nevada, they began to test high-explosive bombs illegally on public lands just outside the small town of Fallon; the Navy gave it a military label, Bravo 20, but the Northern Paiute, who used to live there and should know, called it the Source of Creation.

Richard Misrach filed a mining claim on Bravo 20, all legal and proper, and before the Pentagon bureaucratic warriors managed to set it aside eighteen months later, Misrach took hundreds of photographs of Bravo 20. Needless to say, they are not pretty, these shots of thousands of bomb craters, filled with liquids that seem to still be explosively dangerous, scattered across fields of shrapnel and unexploded ordnance. These photographs have that sense of horrible fascination you find in photographs of atrocities. You can't stop looking at them, but you wish you could.

The text is just as effective, the facts just as unthinkable. Seventy percent of Nevada's air space is controlled by the military, which makes it tough on the weekend pilot. Fallon Naval Air Station has a few problems itself, environmental ones; the clean-up is called, without irony, "Operation Ugly Baby." A few local citizens, those whose lives aren't based on economics and/or greed, are fighting the good fight out there in the desert. If you can stand a story about how your government doesn't exactly fight fair, how your government passes laws that you have to obey but they don't—if you can stand that tired, old chestnut of a story one more time, this is a great story.

Needless to say, it doesn't end on a happy note, but it does wind up with a great idea, a wonderful idea. Richard Misrach proposed that we make Bravo 20 into a National Park, our first environmental memorial, complete with a visitor center in the shape of an ammunition bunker and sightseeing routes named "Devastation Drive" and "Boardwalk of the Bombs."

If you can get through this book without agreeing with Mr. Misrach's modest proposal, give it away; you don't deserve to own it. "The Bombing of the West" indeed. It's big, it's beautiful, it belongs to us; let's bomb it.

Of course, the West always has been a place that puts a high premium on individual freedom and the almost feudal rights of the landowner. Along with a number of other western writers, I sometimes think we have paid too high a price for those myths, that those myths have done as much harm as all the ravenous corporate lions. Individual freedom is anarchy without an individual sense of responsibility, particularly where the land is concerned, and the responsibility of ownership is not just of the land but also to the land.

I must confess that when I came here from Texas, where almost all the land is privately owned, and found thousands of square miles of public land, I felt as if I had some title to this land. I didn't burn any of it down or take part in any freelance clear-cuts or drive a D-9 Caterpillar to the top of Mount Jumbo just for the view, but like a child I had to be taught how to enjoy that freedom responsibly.

Surely some of that idea of freedom came from the horse culture of western America. The Idea of the Cowboy rather than the cowboy himself. As far as I can tell, cowboys have their own personal brand of genes.

Lots of people work cattle at one time or another in their lives— my great-great grandfather drove longhorn cattle to Kansas in his youth; the oldest picture of my grandfather in my possession shows him working his first job at sixteen, working cattle horseback; even I once sat a saddle for cash money—but they're not cowboys.

Cowboys live and die cowboys. From their mounts, no matter how motley and wind-broke, they look down on the rest of the world. In a very convincing way, I might add. I've talked to old cowboys whittling in the Mexican sunlight around the square in Chihuahua City, stretching out their social security checks, or in old-folks homes at eighty-five, or in wide-spot bars down in Wyoming. They all have several things in common: usually skin cancer, noses pitted like the craters on the moon; crippling arthritis in their hands and legs, hands that struggle with a beer bottle, legs that lend themselves to immobility; and an attitude. To a man, these afflictions were badges of honor, and to a man (not that women aren't cowboys; but the old ones I've talked to seem to have better sense than to fall for their own mythology) they pitied everybody who couldn't live the cowboy life. Worst of all, I believe them.

Nobody has ever successfully explained the cowboy to me, how that devotion to the horse culture trickled down from the Moors to the Spanish to the Mexicans and became one of the dominate myths of the American West. Some people climb on a horse and never figure out how to get off. Maybe that's all the explanation that's needed.

But Richard W. Slatta tries hard in *Cowboys of the Americans* (Yale University Press). He tells you everything you wanted to know about the cowboy but were afraid to ask. He does his best to explain the differences between various types of cowboys that exist, from the Rio Grande do Sul in southern Brazil where the cowboys were often just wild cattle hunters, to the frozen plains of Alberta where he makes the cowboys sound as if they were bad imitations of English gentlemen. The information is interesting, extensive and I'm sure useful. It just didn't answer my questions. As they used to say about the Platte River, it seemed too wet to plow and too dusty to drink, a mile wide and an inch deep.

And at last we confront the *Myth of the West* (Rizzoli International), a book by Chris Bruce published in conjunction with the exhibition by the same title held at the Henry Art Gallery in Seattle. Bruce's approach to defining the West seems to be intuitive rather than intellectual. As a consequence, the book is eclectic and smart, and it does its best to both destroy our preconceptions and redeem them at the same time. On one page, you'll find the stark drama of Georgia O'Keeffe's "Black Cross with Red Sky." Three pages later, Frank and Jesse James stare off the page as if already dead, their pistols cocked across their chests, the barrels not quite parallel. Even the dust jacket, which juxtaposes a detail from one of Albert Bierstadt's dreamlike Yosemite landscapes with a detail from Andy Warhol's double Elvis, slaps the expectations right off your face.

My favorite image: a 1989 Polish Solidarity poster by T. Sarnecki featuring Gary Cooper from the movie poster of *High Noon*. The myth of the West must be about hope, the hope that one good man can save a town that neither desires nor deserves salvation, the hopeful knowledge that the Miller Brothers must be vanquished, no matter if they ride horses or Soviet tanks.

My favorite line: a quote from Jon Szarkowski, "Things aren't what they used to be; and what's worse, they never were." All myths are about nostalgia, in one way or another, but damn few have the decency to make fun of themselves.

This is an interesting and sometimes powerful book, a new way to look at the Old West. You can ride the river with this one.

1990

Anybody Can Write a Sad Song

For reasons best considered over a longneck beer bottle sweating on a rickety table in some worn-out beer joint, a place called, perhaps, "The Green Frog" and located in the desert reaches way beyond frogs (or maybe it's in Arkansas, named "Mamacita's" and run by a former Baptist preacher and his former nun wife), in a place like that, maybe, where everybody lives out their last best chance every day, we can get right down to it, consider life and death, fun and games, love and war, and I can finally admit that for reasons I don't understand, exactly, I have always believed that country music belonged to me and mine.

Me and mine, of course, referring to those unruly and always tiresome clans of Celtic hill people, people who pretty much refuse to believe in civilization, people who have been making trouble for the civilized world ever since they first painted their butts blue and rolled downhill with the velocity, arrogance, and ignorance of stones, breaking the civilized heart of Pax Romana, firm in their belief in the clan, the blood feud, and their odd, wailing music, pipes and bad, bad drums, wild music designed for love and war, cursed to confuse the two, losing all their wars, eventually, and most of their love, the keening cry of the permanently dispossessed, outsiders proudly bemoaning their fates . . .

Okay, enough. I'm a fan of country music, and have been as long as I can remember. Perhaps from those long nights in my childhood when my uncle, home from the Pacific wars, wiled away the baby-sitting hours with XRLF, Villa Acuña, Mexico. A fan certainly from that moment in the early fifties when my first serious girlfriend cranked up her 45 player wired through a ten-dollar radio to play for me Hank Williams singing "The Wild Side of Life," followed by Kitty Wells singing her lonesome answer: "Too many times married men think they're still single . . ." I knew even in the fourth grade that playing this music in the intimacy of her bedroom constituted some vaguely dangerous pledge of undying puppy love.

So I've remained a fan, pledged to melodrama in love, self-pity, and bad whiskey. Often unfaithful, I freely admit, with everybody from X to Bach, from Shostakovitch to Bob Seger, I have loved country music. It may be a bad habit gone worse. New sociological studies contend with much evidence that bar patrons drink nearly twice as quickly when sad country songs plague the jukebox. I've given up cigarettes and other deadly and expensive vices, but nobody has written the prescription for my musical disease. When things go bad in my life, I still turn to Willie and Waylon, Merle and George, Patsy and Kitty and Reba.

Back in the old days when I first became inflamed with the music, it was called, not very politely, hillbilly music, and it belonged to that part of the music business once called, once again not very politely, race music. Then Elvis put it all together, Howling Wolf and Hank, black and white, the dispossessed outsiders together again, becoming something called the market.

Country music makes up about ten percent of the record business, so we're talking big money now, self-consciousness and academic terms flying like beer bottles in a bad cracker joint. Terms like "neo-traditional" and "country-politan" make me want to hide the silverware, but maybe country music is being taken seriously now because in the time of voodoo doo-doo economics and a Gulf War, perhaps it won't be long before everybody is standing on the outside looking in.

So once again, as in the days when fiddles longed to become violins and Eddy Arnold strapped on a tux and stepped on the stage at Carnegie Hall, hillbilly music wants to be something different, to be taken seriously. Success in America always seems to seek acceptance, either intellectual or moral; it's never enough just to be rich and famous. But country music will always be insidiously anarchic, always out of the middle-class mainstream, always surprising. It seems that now we are in a time of—what shall we call it?—a neon renaissance in country music, lots of great new singers and songwriters, lots of energy and fun.

Clint Black is one of the new kids on the bus. His first single, "A Better Man," was released less than two years ago. When I last saw him in Tucson in December of last year, he was still just twenty-nine years old, and his second album, *Put Yourself in My Shoes*, was tearing up the charts. So let us say the dreaded cliche: he's a phenomenon. Or as a former pedal-steel player from the Amazing Rhythm Aces, Duncan Cameron, tells me, "He's like goddamned Elvis. And a hell of a nice guy, too."

Well, maybe not exactly like the King just yet, but his debut certainly matches, and in some ways surpasses, those of George Strait, Randy Travis, Ricky Skaggs, Reba McEntire, Dwight Yoakam, K. T. Oslin, Garth Brooks, and all the others on this endless crusade to seduce the heart of country music, either by returning it to its bloody blue-grass and/or folk roots, or by extending the metaphor into dangerously rabid rockabilly, or by just doing it in their own finely dedicated way. Clint Black, who was born with a country singer's name and a truly heart-breakingly fine country voice right out of George Jones and Merle Haggard, is one of the dedicated.

Words have been written to suggest that Clint belongs to some new sort of suburban vector in country music, committed to belonging to the middle class rather than bemoaning the fate of the ultimate outsider, the working class. Not true. Clint has never belonged to anything but country music and never been anything but a singer-songwriter-player—talk about a way to learn about being outside—since the day he sat, brokenhearted as only a teenager who loses in love can be, and penned his first song.

Of course, he did some time working on his liner bio, some construction work to keep the wolf from the pickup door, some creative construction on his job history, turning a few days cutting bait into a small career as a professional bass fishing guide. But mostly it was just Clint and his guitar, at first in a band with a couple of his brothers, then as a lonesome cowboy, a single, carting his guitar and PA system from bar to bar across the humid Houston plain, playing happy hours and one-night stands.

"I did everything," Clint says, "except play Steak & Ales where folks go to eat chicken wings and drink beer with their buddies and you ain't nothin' but a live jukebox."

Clint's road to fame and fortune sounds rocky and strange rather than easy, but he seems not to have left any hard feelings along the highway. I find a drummer and a keyboard player in a local band all the way up in Missoula, Montana, Randy and Julie Turner of Smoking Gun, who knew Clint in Houston, remember calling Clint when their lead singer split to offer him a steady job in the band. Of course, it just happened to be the week that his first album, "Killin' Time," hit the charts.

Clint returned their telephone call, they tell me, thanked them politely, and declined, saying, "Things are picking up down here."

No kidding. Several months before, Clint had hooked up with Hayden Nicholas, now the lead-guitar player in Clint's band, a local boy just back from the rock 'n' roll wars in L.A. to take care of his ailing father. Hayden had an eight-track in his garage and an ambitious attitude toward the music that matched Clint's. They became friends, wrote songs together, and with the able assistance of drummer Dick Gay started laying down tracks.

Talk about Cinderella stories. The first demo tape they managed to get into the hands of legendary ZZ Top producer, Bill Ham, was a cut of a country ballad sure to be a classic, "Nobody's Home." As they say, "Those of you who aren't legend by now are doomed to be history." Hayden's the musical center of the tightest road band I've ever heard, Dick Gay is still in charge of rhythm and ironic laughter, and Clint's a star, the kind that draws three thousand fans in a line a quarter-mile long in a white-bread city like Spokane, Washington. And aside from all that, the music is solid, down-home, smart, funny, and goddamned good.

As I confessed, I'm a fan.

But this is the backstory, the stuff I know before I climb aboard a tiny aircraft at the airport in Missoula, Montana, to head for Tacoma, Washington, to get the real story, to dig up the dirt. That is theory, though, and at the moment, the real story is winter-flying in the mountain West, ice flinging off the props and slamming into the fuselage like 20mm cannon rounds, a fifty-knot crosswind at our intermediate stop in Spokane, and a very real typhoon blowing horizontal rain at the Seattle-Tacoma Airport.

As every reader knows, magazines don't do combat pay—the experience is supposed to be its own reward—and musicians who have been on the road almost constantly for eighteen months aren't renowned for their sympathy for derelict journalists, white-knuckled or not.

The odd truth, though, is that Clint and his band are so damned nice and sympathetic that I fear I have fallen among dangerous companions, Christians or Mormons, or serial cannibals.

The facts, as always, are dreadfully mundane. They have the character to be tired without becoming cranky. Also, the fiddle player in the band, Jeff Huskins, sometimes known as Lex Lavender, a classically trained violinist and former competitive body-builder, has infected some of the band with the dread narcotic calm known as pumping iron. Other bands, too: the drummer for the opening act confesses to me that he's so sore that it hurts to shine a flashlight on his hide. When I walk through the musicians as we check out the next noon, I can't tell if I'm walking through the football team or the band.

The night before at the Tacoma Dome, which had been sold out for months, I watched Clint do a "meet-and-greet" with the local country radio station and record-store folks. He is neither short nor tall, and seems to have avoided the curse of weight lifting, but he looks trim and able, slim but strong, perhaps like a professional bull-rider. Given the furious quickness of his success, Clint Black seems to be just as polite and gracious as a young man can be, a credit to his folks, I suspect, and his own good nature. When he smiles, which he does naturally and often, his eyes disappear, like Roy Rogers, as if he feels so good he can't stand to see it. Even though he is obviously worn to a frazzle by the concert grind, he remains tirelessly pleasant, always ready with a smile, an autograph, or a pose for a fan's photograph. Country-music fans are notorious for demanding to reach out and touch somebody famous, a responsibility that Clint seems more than willing to bear with grace and good will. My first impression is that he is too good to be true.

Since I already know and like the music, the show contains no surprises. When Clint follows the band onto the stage, he already owns the crowd. They know the words to every song. Particularly the women. Especially the chorus of "A Better Man." Maybe they respond to the notion that a man can love and lose, admit failure, and forgive everybody in sight.

I know I'm leavin' here a better man
For knowing you this way
Things I couldn't do before, now I think I can
And I'm leaving here a better man.

Perhaps it's not Shakespeare or even Warren Zevon, but it seems heartfelt, decent, and even abiding to the women. It also seems to make the callow Coca-Cola cowboys beside them quite nervous. You have to like that.

As I wander during the set, I notice a radiantly slim young woman in a red leather raincoat and red come-fuck-me heels backstage. Waiting for someone, perhaps, swaying to the music.

After the set, a performance as tight as some of the women's stone-washed jeans, these same women, whom I have just credited with a mature understanding of love and loss, rush the stage, flinging notes and flowers in an adolescent frenzy. I hear that they sometimes also fling panties and bras, but can't verify that personally. A member of the crew standing beside me mentions that Clint's trademark black hats can bring as much as two thousand dollars at auction. Someone else wonders what his shorts might be worth. Before I left home, a friend of mine said that he had heard a Montana ranchwoman, an admirable woman in all ways, call Clint Black an I.O. "What's an I.O.?" he inquired. "An instant orgasm," she replied. I don't know what to think about that, frankly, but something in me suggests that if you don't work for it, it can't be that much fun. Whatever that something inside me is, it also suggests that if I don't ask Clint how he feels about being a sex-symbol, he might take me for a decent human being rather than a journalist. Of course, I'm right. I.O. indeed.

After the Tacoma show, Clint and I chat, then go off the record. I have a couple of beers, then wait for the fun to begin. Clint says it's already over.

"On the road," he says, grinning tiredly beneath his dark glasses and ZZ Top cap, "you spend twenty-three hours a day working for one hour of fun. Playing the music. That's about the only fun there is."

I'm not sure I believe the statement completely, but I can tell that Clint does.

A couple of hours later, I get back to the hotel where we are all staying. The rain is no longer falling sideways but it's still falling. The woman in the red raincoat stands in that hard rain, still waiting.

The next day on Clint's bus as it labors up Snoqualmie Pass, on our way to the winter-apple days of Yakima, we do interview, the verb, a chore that must be as tiresome to Clint as bucking hay bales or shoveling horse manure, but he gives it his best shot. It is part of the job. Toward the end, I suggest this must be exciting, this headlong rush to the top from nowhere.

He gives me that naturally open grin that his fans love, his eyes lost among the laugh wrinkles, and says, "Sometimes I'm so excited I can't keep my eyes open I'm so tired of being excited."

Then we laugh and talk about music while Clint bounces around, trying to catch the clear-cuts and the crags with either his camera or his camcorder. But the clouds kill the light, so Clint fires up his CD player still as happy as a kid with a new toy as we listen to what he considers his musical influences, James Taylor and Jimmy Buffett, not bad influences for a writer and singer of country songs. Then Loggins and Messina, and finally, as we drift through the rocks and sagebrush down into the Yakima Valley, Clint stuffs Willis Alan Ramsey into the player, so I can hear "North Texas Women" and "Good-bye to Old Missoula." I don't believe I've ever seen anybody enjoy music like Clint does, and it's a wonderful sight to see him happy.

The next day, coming back out of the Yakima Valley in a rented car, underneath a big blue sky, Mount Adams standing behind me like a broken tooth and Mount Rainier rising in the west like a contrary moon, I listen to my favorite Clint Black song, "Nothing's News."

> *When the whistle blows at five o'clock*
> *There's only one place I'll be found*
> *Down at Ernie's icehouse liftin' longnecks*
> *To that good old country sound*
> *And talkin' 'bout the good old times*
> *Braggin' on how it used to be*
> *But I've worn out the same old lines*
> *And now it seems nothing's news to me*

The heart-bone emptiness, the absolute hardness of life and love, fill the car with that old country wail. It's almost enough, a tonic against all that landscape beauty.

On the bus, Clint had told me that what he really admired about Jimmy Buffett was that he could write about the good times, catch those happy moments in music. "Anybody can write sad songs," he says, "all you have to do is sit down and feel sorry for yourself." Then he laughs. "I'm too busy for that kind of stuff."

But I must admit to sometimes liking the sad songs.

At the end of the tour for me, in the desert outside Tucson, I ask Clint what he would say if he were doing this piece about himself. "I'd want people to know how hard we work on the music," he says, "and how hard I work to handle all this success without becoming a jerk."

So far so good.

1990

Fictional Truths

An Ideal Son for the Jenkins Family

For Buck Jenkins the luxury of sleeping late on Sunday morning was an empty pleasure: he woke at six o'clock as he had almost every day of his life. He lay very still in the soft light, trying not to wake his wife, Lydia, but the longer he stayed there, the more he wanted a cigarette. His Camels were on the nightstand within easy reach, but he didn't dare light one, not in her bed, not in her bedroom. Finally, unable to be still, he slipped from between the starched sheets and dressed quietly, listening to the undisturbed breathing.

He paused, lighting a cigarette, to look in on his son home on leave. The boy slept heavily. Buck had heard him stumbling through the house at three that morning, making drunk noises, and Buck had smiled to himself, glad to have the boy home again. Buck walked out to his battered Dodge pickup and drove away.

He came back about nine o'clock after spending the morning at the local cafe, talking and drinking those familiar cups of coffee with all his oil-field buddies, a ritual performed each morning, even without the excuse of a working day. Lydia was in the kitchen and had breakfast started. She didn't pause as he poured coffee and sat down at the table.

"Nine o'clock," she said, finally. "I'd better get that boy up if he's going to church."

Buck didn't answer.

"John Robert," she said as she walked down the hall, "John Robert, are you awake?"

"Now," the boy grumbled, "now." Buck walked to the edge of the hall, and listened as he slowly drank his coffee.

"You'd best be up if you're going to church," she said.

"I'm not," the boy answered.

"But you went last Sunday," she said, "You'd better come along."

"Nope," the boy answered.

She waited silently for a bit, then said, "Well . . . come on, now. Your father and I are going."

"Nope."

Buck walked back to the kitchen, hoping the boy would have sense enough to keep quiet. Buck didn't want any more fights between mother and son like those screaming battles of the days before the boy ran away to join the Army.

"Go talk to your son," Lydia said, interrupting his worries, "Make him get ready for church."

He left, but went into the other bedroom, and changed from his khakis to his blue suit. He was struggling with the unfamiliar tie, when Lydia came to direct him to the boy's room.

Buck entered and saw the boy's inquiring glance. Buck noticed the newly strong shoulders and the uniform folded neatly over a chair and the gleaming jump boots under the edge of the bed. He felt that the boy was a good soldier. He was already a sergeant in his Airborne outfit, and had just reenlisted for three more years.

"Your mother wants you to go to church," he said slowly, measuring each word in his mouth.

"So?"

"Don't you think you oughta go? She's missed you this past three years. Don't you think you oughta give her this much?"

"No. Do you?" The boy sat up in bed. "What the hell did she ever give me, huh?"

Buck glanced at the ceiling, put his hands in his pockets, took them out, and then looked at his feet. He didn't want to find out what she was going to do. Goddamnit, he thought, why can't everything be different this time. The phone rang, and he left the room, thankfully.

He spoke into the phone for a bit, then went back to the bedroom, and started changing out of the suit and back into work khaki.

"What are you doing?" Lydia asked, her voice straight and hard.

"Jake called. Got a salt-water pump out up on the Dupree lease."

"Can't it wait till tomorrow? You took this production job so you wouldn't have to work seven days a week."

"It's my job."

She said nothing more. Buck left in his pickup as she dressed.

When he came back after two cups of coffee at the cafe, John Robert had fried bacon and eggs. Buck was again struck—it seemed the hundredth time in the past week—by how much the boy had grown toward being a man. He poured more coffee and lit another cigarette.

"Feel pretty bad, huh?" Buck chuckled, "Some stomp at the VFW, huh?"

John Robert nodded, chewing slowly.

"Got a pump out. Swab went out yesterday afternoon. Too late to change it. Thought I'd do it today." Buck spoke between sips of coffee.

"Thought Jake just called about the pump," the boy said as he finished.

"Aw, he calls 'bout every Sunday mornin'," Buck said shyly, "round nine-thirty so I'll have an excuse not to go to church. I only went last Sunday 'cause you did." He chuckled, "Changed in and out of that damned blue suit so many times it's damn near wore out, and last Sunday's the first time I wore it longer 'n hour." He laughed aloud.

"Why don't you just tell her to go to hell? Be a lot easier, wouldn't it?"

"I couldn't do that. Your momma's had a hard life and . . ."

"Don't I know," the boy said as he stood to gather his dishes, "And I'm only the final burden." He set the dishes into the sink.

"Well, she has," Buck said to the boy's back.

They both knew—because she reminded them regularly—about Lydia's childhood, how she had to pick cotton and chop tomatoes to support three sisters and an alcoholic father. It was the club she used to keep Buck away from the boy, and tried to use to keep the boy away from doing anything that might be slightly dirty. She had made Buck take the "pledge" before she consented to marry him, and she did everything she and the Lord could to keep their son away from the things her father enjoyed—the hunting, the fishing, the oil field, and most of all the booze. She didn't want the boy to touch anything dirtier than a dusty pulpit—nothing so dirty as Buck, who had to work with his hands.

"Hey," Buck said, "You wanna go with me?"

"Where?"

"Up to the Dupree. Could probably use an extra hand. Head ain't been off that pump in five, maybe six years."

"Oh, hell, I don't think so," the boy answered from the sink as he washed the dishes.

"You going somewheres?"

"No . . . not really. Just don't feel too good."

"It wouldn't take but a couple hours. Might stop at Momma Lopez's for a few beers and some tamales."

He paused, then said, "Makes a good hangover lunch." His voice trailed away, "Yeah. We'll stop for a beer for sure. Hair of the dog will make you feel better." Then his voice quaked. He paused, and slowly asked, "Well . . . are you comin'?"

"Oh hell yes, I'll go."

"Well, now, don't go if you don't want to."

"I'll go."

Buck waited in the kitchen as the boy dressed, then quietly followed him out to the pickup. Buck tossed a twelve-pound sledgehammer into the bed of the truck, saying, "That head might be stubborn." The hammer lay loose in the back as Buck drove the pickup over the rough cache streets, and it bounced, banging against the truck bed, crashing blows into the dusty air.

Buck stopped the pickup at the beginning of the muddy road which led to the well. The boy was asleep, so Buck smiled and honked the horn.

"Goddamnit," the boy said as he woke, grumbling, rubbing his swollen eyes, "What did you do that for?"

"Good alarm clock," Buck chuckled, "Pretty damn good."

"Yeah," the boy snorted. He stretched and scratched himself, then glanced around him. "Where in the hell are we?" he asked, then saw the muddy road ahead.

"Hey, you can't get through that stuff."

"Why not?" Buck asked, "Me an' this old pickup can handle it."

"What if we get stuck? I don't feel much like pushing."

Buck just grinned, slammed the pickup into gear, and started down the road. He slipped the pickup into second, riding easy on the accelerator, and moved the truck steadily through the sticky black-land mud.

It took him twenty minutes to drive to the well, and during the trip, he told the boy of the times when there really had been some mud.

"Well, how 'bout that?" Buck asked at the well as they were getting the tools and the new swab, "Whatcha think of the driving?"

"Huh?"

"That driving—how about that?"

"O.K., I guess," the boy shrugged.

They walked to the pump, their boots plowing through the rainbow-sheen of oil on the black mud. The pump was a slightly workable refugee from an old oil rig, a great hunk of metal—once blue, but now chipped and rusted—squatting heavily on two oil-soaked twelve-by-twelve wooden sills.

As Buck stepped onto the pump, he saw that it was covered by a horde of red ants which had been flooded out of their bed by a puddle. He laid his tools on the sills to keep them out of the mud, then wiped some of the ants away from the eight-and-a-half-inch steel bolts which held the valve head on the pump body. He placed a long-handled wrench on the nearest nut, grasped the horizontal handle and pulled, testing the resistance. He pulled harder, then harder, then so hard that his feet slipped from under him, and he fell into the mud. Dazed, he didn't move until he heard the boy's ringing laughter, then he reached for the wrench handle above him. Resting his hand on it for a moment as he got his breath, he then tried to pull himself up. Almost to his feet, he felt the first ant sting his hand. Instinctively his hand recoiled from the handle, now covered with ants, and he fell back into the mud.

The boy was laughing even harder as he reached down to help

his father out of the puddle. He kept laughing, but Buck only grunted as he searched for a stick to scrape the mud from his pants.

As he sat on his haunches, swearing to himself, cleaning his pants and rubbing mud into the ant stings, Buck said to John Robert, "Use that one," and pointed to a heavier wrench with a shorter, hammer-scarred handle.

John Robert placed the wrench on a nut, picked up a small hand-sized sledge, then struck the wrench handle several one-handed blows using his left hand, then again with both hands, but the nut didn't move. He tried the other nuts, but they were as tight as the first, and not one moved. He swung harder as he went around the nuts again, and on the other side of the pump the hammer slipped from his grasp and flew some thirty feet over Buck's head, glancing off the side of one of the oil tanks. He started after the hammer, but stopped when Buck spoke.

"Ain't no use in gettin' mad at that hard iron, son. It can't hear you cuss it or feel you kick it. And you sure as hell ain't gonna hurt that iron, but it'll damn sure end up hurting you." As he spoke, Buck continued to scrape the mud from his pants, and his head was down, watching the stick peel the mud from the khaki, as if he were talking to himself.

"Bullshit," John Robert said, then walked away.

When he returned with the hammer, Buck and he worked steadily, trying to loosen the nuts, trying to break the rusted hold between nuts and bolts. The clang of steel against steel echoed from the metal hides of the three great tanks, filling the noon day as it sounded across the muddy, flat fields. When he rested, Buck watched thundershowers form in the northwest, their rolling grey heads riding on stout columns of rain as they moved in stately, winding paths toward the Gulf. Finally, as he knew would happen, one of the showers moved toward them, and he called the boy, and they walked to the pickup as the first light drops began to fall.

They sat silent, smoking, peering through the damp blue air of the cab at the heavy drops exploding on the hood.

"That's the damned oil patch," Buck said. "Always rains when it ain't supposed to."

John Robert merely nodded as Buck looked at him.

"Guess I ain't got no right to bitch, tho', it's been good to me. Sure beats chopping cedar. My daddy had me choppin' cedar for fence posts from daylight to dark 'fore I's twelve. That's why I run off when I was thirteen," he chuckled. He paused, stared into the rain, then continued. "He'd a skinned my ass if he'd caught me. But your momma's daddy took me in, broke me in roughnecking—God, there was a man could put out the work. He'd work you to death, drink you under the table, then give you the shirt off his back. I never seen anybody run a rig, drunk or sober, as good as him. . . ." He paused again, wondering why he was telling the boy these things he never spoke of—why now after all these silent years should he talk about the hard days—but they hadn't really been so bad.

"Fourteen years old and could work the ass off anybody, then drink 'em to the ground, then work twelve more hours, then start over again. Boy, those boom towns were something—wild, fightin' and drinkin' twenty-four hours a day, and good hootin' days they was, damnit."

"Sounds like it," the boy said, "Mother always made it sound different."

"Aw, she's still mad at her daddy," Buck snorted, "She ain't never forgive him for never keepin' no money. He drunk a lot of it up, but he gave most of it away—didn't ever let his family go hungry, tho', no matter what your momma says. Then when he got killed on that rig up by Goliad, they got the insurance money even tho' he's drunk as a lord."

"I guess he was all right," the boy chuckled.

"Yep . . . damn good days. Things changed now, tho'. Rough-necks get all their work done with machines, plus gettin' two, maybe two an' a quarter an hour. Hell, oil field's a good place to make a livin', now. Say," Buck said, slapping the boy on the leg, "Whaddya gonna do when you get outta the army?"

"Who said I was getting out?"

"Oh," Buck said, "Oh." He would have given anything he could to have the boy working in the oil field with him—but it never seemed to come out right. He couldn't give his wife and his son both what they wanted. Just like when the boy told his mother he was going in the Army, just like that time.

It was another Sunday during the spring before John Robert was to graduate from high school. Lydia had been after the boy to make up his mind as to which of the small Baptist colleges he was going to attend. The boy finally told her that he intended to go in the Army as soon as he finished high school. They had fought over the cluttered table and a silent Buck. One side didn't need his help, and the other didn't ask for it. Lydia ended the argument with tears and screams that she would never—never so long as the good Lord gave her strength—sign his release because he wouldn't be eighteen until six months after graduation, and he just might as well get ready to go to college because he was going. The boy stormed out the back door, slamming it behind him.

Buck sat at the table, still silent, listening to the shine of Lydia's voice as she cleared the table.

"Samuel, you'd best talk to your son," she said, "He's just getting too sassy."

Buck was ready to be angry, but she had confused him by using his Christian name, so he too went out the back door.

It had been a beautiful spring day, and the sky seemed to reflect the deeper blue of the nearby Gulf. The fish wouldn't be biting, but Buck wished that he was sitting on one of the town piers with a rod and reel in hand—but he had something to tend to first. He walked over to the hackberry tree where the boy was sitting. They talked a bit, and after the boy assured him that he could handle the Army even if he never had played football or shot a gun, Buck promised to sign the release. He knew the boy with his dislike of books and buildings had no business at college, no matter what Lydia said about working with your hands. He felt close to his son that day, and tried to tell him about the good feel of hard work, but the boy cut him off.

"Boy, that's all right," he said, "I'll get the papers tomorrow, so I can leave next week. No sense in finishing school if I'm going to the Army. Damn, I hope I get to Germany. They say Germany is all right!"

In the pickup, Buck shook his head wondering how things always got turned around. That wasn't what he meant for the boy to say or even think—but it worked out fine, he thought, just fine.

"Say, I saw the way you handled that hammer," Buck said, "Looks like you're learnin' good things up there."

"Yeah, it's O.K. Fellow learns a lot of things. How to take care of himself and everything."

"Don't it scare you, jumping outta those planes?" he asked, punching the boy lightly on the shoulder. "Damn sure'd scare me."

"They don't give you a chance to get scared. You stop in the door, the bastards boot you right on out. It don't make any difference whether you're scared or not—just boom in the butt and you're flying," the boy said, grinning, "But that's O.K. Jumping's O.K. I've joined a sky-diving club."

"What's that?"

"Well, it's kinda like a game. You try to land in a circle on the ground."

"How?"

"How?" the boy paused, then said, "You free-fall a long ways so the wind won't carry you, then you've got a special chute with a panel out so you can guide it. It's great!"

"Don't sound like it to me," Buck said, shaking his head and laughing.

The boy kept talking, hardly noticing his father's remarks.

"Sometimes we free-fall just for the hell of it. Just like flying if you do it right. You can turn flips and spin while you're falling— looks like the ground is about a million miles away, and you're never going to come down, but you get closer and then you get worried— but you wait. Wait till you get so scared it feels great. Then it gets worse and better and you wait till you know that if you don't open that chute right now, you're gonna ride it right to the ground. Then you wait just one more second longer, and that's the best one, then bang! Pull that cord."

He paused to quickly light a cigarette, then continued.

"Then you just know you waited too long, and that son of a bitch ain't never, never gonna open. But it always does," he said, laughing, "At least it always has," he laughed again, "or I'd be a greasy brown spot somewheres, instead of here.

"Sometimes I almost go to sleep coming down after the chute opens. You been going so fast, then it's like going real slow, and you sorta swing real easy, like rocking yourself to sleep. Then you're so loose, it's like landing on a great big soft bed."

"Hey," Buck asked quickly, seeing that the rain had stopped, "Whatcha doin' next weekend?"

"Huh?"

"You wanna go fishin' with me an' Jake next weekend?"

"I don't think so," the boy answered.

"Why?"

"I'm leaving tomorrow."

"Oh . . . maybe next time, huh?"

"Sure," the boy said, looking away. "Maybe next time."

Buck threw his cigarette out the window, and said, "Let's get them nuts off and fix that damned pump so we can get the hell out of here and get a beer."

He climbed from the cab, stopped to reach into the back for the twelve-pound sledgehammer. "This'll fix those son's-a-bitches," he said, showing the hammer to the boy.

The heavy wrench was still on the first nut, and Buck practiced swinging at it with the sledge as if chopping down a tree. The hammer swung around him easily, lightly like a good double-edged axe, but when it struck there was no crisp flight of cedar chips, only the dull, dead crash of steel. It was easy and smooth at first, but quickly became hard. His swings began to land off-center, almost missing the wrench handle, so he turned the head to use the broad side.

"Getting tired?" the boy asked.

"No," Buck answered, turning the hammer-head straight again, but he slipped his hands further up the handle, choking up.

After several minutes, he paused to wipe the sweat off his forehead with his sleeve. The boy took the sledge from him and started to swing.

"Not too hard, son. Don't want to shear those bolts," he said.

"Be pretty hard to shear an inch-and-a-half of cold-rolled steel, wouldn't it?"

"They're sorta old and rusty," Buck said, "Take it easy. Don't want you gettin' hurt out here."

"Me neither."

They took turns again, hammering calmly, methodically as the sun roared from behind the thunderhead. Its heat dried the ground, then dampened their clothes with sweat. Neither spoke as they hammered into the afternoon.

When Buck rested, he watched the boy, calm and sure, swinging the hammer in clean, lateral arcs about his body. He saw himself thirty years before: the tanned face, the strong jaw, the good hands. At least he looks like me, Buck thought, too bad he's the son of that bitch. . . . He grabbed his thoughts quickly. He hadn't thought like that in a long time; he must be getting tired.

After a long while, after they had spent too much time trying to get the nuts off, and there wasn't enough afternoon left to fix the pump even if they could get the nuts off, Buck knew they should quit, but he refused to be beaten by a dumb mass of metal. He seemed to lose all caution, and hammered wildly, furiously, as if he were under attack. The boy, too, was grunting with effort as he handled the heavy hammer. The pace began to tell, and their strength waned and great cramps stiffened their forearms and the muscles across the backs of their shoulders. Their nerves dimmed, and they no longer felt the ants, and soon their hands and wrists were covered with red welts the size of dimes. Tiny, clicking pulses tickled the backs of their shaking knees, matching the regular pounding which seemed to smash their heads. Then they could do no more, for now, and stopped without a word.

John Robert stepped back, and Buck stepped up, but he just couldn't raise the hammer, yet. He stood there, his shoulders slumped forward, his chest rising and falling under a shirt clapped damply to his skin, his eyes bloodshot, and his arms hanging out at a slight angle because of his raw armpits—too tired to sit, too stiff to fall, he stood with his hand resting limply on the upright hammer handle.

"Let's quit," the boy said from where he squatted too near the pump, "Let's stop this crap."

Buck said nothing, but his head seemed to slump closer to his chest.

You're right, Buck thought, staring not at the boy, but at the wrench handle jutting between them. That's right, no use, just like your momma, and the hunting and fishing we never got to do, all the things we never got to do. Just ain't no use. But out here where work is a man's way of talking, surely out here a man gets a second chance . . .

"Son-of-a-bitch," he moaned under his breath, grabbing the hammer handle with both hands and jerking it behind him.

"Son-of-a-bitch," he grunted, whipping the hammer around him, swinging as if forever.

The head of the sledge crashed past the wrench handle without touching it, driving itself toward the boy, and as the sad face of steel crunched into the boy's forehead toward the middle and slightly above the right eye, Buck felt the soft jar in the handle.

It was almost a year before John Robert returned from the Veteran's Hospital in Houston. The doctors had done the best they could with his face, but his nose was still sharply bent toward his left cheek and there was a depression around his right eye socket where all the crushed bone had been removed, and a glass eye sat idly in the hollow. His brain had been too damaged for mental therapy or surgery to help, and although they couldn't make him control his speech enough to talk, he could go with Buck as he made the rounds of the wells. The boy could fetch tools for his father and keep him grunting company during the long afternoons they spent in Momma Lopez's. Buck drank steadily from four to six each afternoon—now that Lydia was indifferent to Buck and too busy with her Societies to notice—and he watched the boy play with the mongrel dogs which wandered freely in and out of the beer joint.

Lydia asked little of them, just that Buck care for the boy during the day, and that the boy go to church with her three times a week. The boy seemed to like the singing, but became bored during the sermons, and he had a disturbing tendency to remove his glass eye to play with it which upset the other members of the congregation. Lydia slapped his hands sharply until he did it no more. She never asked Buck to go to church, but he went anyway, every time the boy did.

Buck went about his work as always, puttering around the countryside in his battered pickup or fished or drank beer with his son for a constant companion. They couldn't talk, but Buck didn't think about it.

During the next summer, Lydia made him leave the boy home every morning. She wouldn't tell him why, and when he asked, she merely smiled as if she had a lovely secret. The boy couldn't tell Buck, but he seemed to withdraw even more, and sometimes in the afternoons when Buck sent him to the truck for a tool, he wouldn't come back. Buck walked after him, and every time found the boy staring into the distance, his lips moving silently, painfully.

Then one Sunday, Lydia invited the preacher, his wife, and her Prayer Society to dinner. She made Buck stay in his suit after church and eat with them.

With everyone gathered at the table, Buck bowed his head, expecting the preacher to say the grace, but Lydia rose from the other end of the table, walked behind the boy's chair, and placed her hard, white hands on his shoulders.

"All right, son," she said.

The boy fumbled as he clasped his hands, grunted for a few seconds, then closed his eyes very tightly.

"Whhh . . . we thank you . . . you oh Lord . . . for th-th-th . . . for these and all . . . and all our many bl-bl-blessings."

When the boy finished, everyone at the table was crying, except Buck. The ladies and the preacher gave great thanks to Jesus for the moving prayer, and almost miracle. The preacher prayed until the chicken was cold, and all the while Lydia stood leaning over the boy's back.

"Aren't you proud of our son," she sobbed happily to Buck, her face almost soft and young again, "Aren't you proud."

Later that afternoon, Buck drove the boy to a nearby pier where they fished silently until dark.

1963

Three Cheers for
Thomas J. Rabb

After the game, Tom Rabb ran quickly across the crowded football field, dodging the fans who tried to congratulate him. Once in the locker room, he rested on a bench, breathing deeply to keep from vomiting again, his sobs loud in the silence of the room. His team had beaten their old Midwestern rivals that day, had even won a trip to the Cotton Bowl, but there were no happy shouts, no victory celebrations, for the game had been marred by the death of the opposing quarterback. He had been dead when the ambulance took him away, but the two teams didn't learn of his death until the last seconds of the game. Tom Rabb had vomited twice when they told him, and now he tried to keep from throwing up again.

The coach, Tom's father's old college teammate, told him, "It was only an accident. It wasn't your fault. Don't worry, kid." Rabb stared at him with such anger the coach walked hurriedly away.

Rabb sat, his eyes closed, his body shaking, till the others left the room. Then he stood by his locker, and ripped his uniform from his body. He tore the jersey from collar to waist, burst the strings of his shoulder pads and threw them the length of the room where they smashed against the wire caging of the equipment area. His shoes followed, then his pants and hip pads. He jerked off the locker's tape with his name and number printed on it, then opened the door, slamming it back against the next locker with a crash that rattled the whole line. On the inside of the door were the clippings his father had pasted there after each home game when he came to visit his son. He didn't even come, Rabb thought, even he couldn't face me.

The clippings were the concrete evidence of his father's success. He had trained the boy constantly—almost from the moment of his birth—for the single purpose of being a great football player.

TOM RABB SOUTHWESTERN CONFERENCE
LINEMAN OF THE YEAR THIRD TIME

RABB SURE PICK FOR ALL-AMERICAN AGAIN

RABB FIRST ROUND CHOICE OF DALLAS

There was even the article cut from *Sports Illustrated*, and his father had underlined in red, ". . . hardest, most vicious tackler in college ball today."

"Where's the one for 'Killer of the Year,'" Rabb shouted as he ripped them all from the door. He crumpled and tore the paper until it was almost pulp, and flushed it down the toilet on his way to the shower.

The hot water burned in the scrapes and scratches, but it also loosened the muscles and eased the bruises, and his body relaxed—confident as always after a game, finding its perfection magnified by the minor extent of its wounds—but his head throbbed as if split by the blast of water.

Before dressing, he paused before a mirror, wondering what they were thinking. Animal, he thought, beast, like always, dumb brute. He knew. They loved you best of all when they could hear the leather pop way up in the press box. They loved it in the stands, but now you have killed somebody, and they'll hate you for showing them what they really came to see. Could he say he didn't mean to? Of course not. He had learned that long ago, a thousand times.

Once in grade school, as he stole third base in a softball game, he knocked the third baseman out. He was truly sorry, for he hadn't meant to hurt the other boy, and he turned to the crowd that gathered, trying to tell them he hadn't meant to harm or hurt, but they only wanted to congratulate him. He had knocked out the class bully, accidentally, the kid no one liked. He had made them happy, and they weren't about to allow him to say, "I didn't mean to." Of course he meant to—he had dealt the enemy a blow, hadn't he? Later when a teacher accused Tom of doing it deliberately, he had no answer for the charge. He had taken the praise from the crowd, and now must take the blame, too, even if he was innocent. He took the guilt, thinking it worth the price—but he learned that the crowd was fickle, and their praise must be rewon each and every day. He did his best, as it was his nature to please, and he lost the right to plead innocence when his body performed the violence the crowd wanted to see.

He looked at that body in the mirror, the two hundred sixty-three pounds of muscle trained to injure without maiming, to hurt without killing. There was something unremorseful about the solid, clean look of his massive shoulders, something cocky that said, "That's what we're for, buddy," and something in the knotted muscles of his arms and legs that said, "Don't blame us, Jack. We only did what they wanted." He broke his image with a metal chair, scattering the silvered glass, but each tiny piece still reflected him, mirrored the power of his body as he dressed and went to find his father.

He didn't find him, not at the private bar for rich alumni below the press box, not at any of the other private clubs, nor at the hotel. Rabb had a beer at each of these places, and was drunk when he went to his dorm.

He backed his Thunderbird convertible across the lawn, put the top down, and parked under his window. He threw his things out into the open car, the two-hundred-dollar suits, the ninety-dollar sport jackets, the handmade boots, the fine pigskin luggage filled with his other things. He left his records and stereo for his roommate. He smashed the trophies and the pictures of himself on his dresser, and hurled the fragments down the hall, then roared away, his tires scratching cruel ruts through the grass.

It was almost two hundred miles to his father's ten-thousand-acre ranch near Houston where he raised prize horses and Santa Gertrudis cattle which lost him money each year. Luckily the ranch covered several pools of oil so there was no worry about the money.

Tom drove wildly, drunkenly, at first, trying to maintain his trail of violence, but as usual it bored him, and didn't help at all. He often wished he could really lose control, really turn pain into a muscular reaction, but it seemed he never could, so he drove the rest of the way safely, quietly, letting the ache settle somewhere deep within his chest.

When he reached the ranch, he saw that his father's plane was already there as his headlights swept over the runway. There were no lights in the house, so he drove past it to a small square building set in the center of a circular cinder track. The building was a small gym where he had worked out three times a week as a child. Weight lifting for strength. Gymnastics, tumbling, and trampoline work for agility. He had run at least a mile on that track every morning and afternoon from the time he was seven. (He still dreamed of that track, endlessly circling it in his sleep, trotting after fame to the insistent cadence of the leather quirt that slapped against his father's leg. Always in the distance a beckoning crowd cheered him on, and there, too, his father waited, a giant dark figure with a riding quirt slapping softly against his left leg, and if only Tom could run hard enough and long enough, he could get there, and his father would put down the quirt and take him in his arms, and the crowd would come down out of the stadium and really love him . . . but he never reached that haven, for he ran and ran forever in a darkening circle.)

His father was drinking in the small gym, the only lighted building in the night.

"Oh . . . hello, son," his father said, offering the bottle to Tom, "Have a victory drink. You've earned it, boy. That was some—"

"Why didn't you come?" Tom interrupted. "Why didn't you wait?"

"I just thought you'd want to be alone. You know, after . . . that's all. I just thought—"

"Don't you understand!" Tom shouted. "My god, is this what I've been getting ready for all these years? To be a damned killer? Well, we can be proud, now. We've done wonderfully well."

"Aw, it was just one of those things, son, that's all. If they try to do anything," his father said, standing up, "kick you off the team or out of school, or anything, I'll get the best lawyer money can buy, and we'll fix them." He paused to drink. "And I'll send a check to his family, and everything will be OK, you'll see."

Tom covered his face with his shaking hands, and screamed, "The best money can buy, huh? The best goddamn money can buy—buy him back to life, you want to buy something." He turned to the rack of barbells and weights, and pushed them over to crash and ring against the concrete floor. "The best money can buy!" he shouted again. He turned over the trampoline and the horses and broke the guy wires for the high bar and smashed the parallel bars and threw the medicine balls through the windows, shouting, "Nothing's too good for my son!"

His father didn't move as Tom demolished the equipment that helped build his success, and he still didn't move when the boy finished and stood crying in the midst of his wreckage. "Buy me a hole, you bastard," he cried, "or a cage!"

"That's OK, son. Take it easy," his father said, walking toward him, "I know you're upset, but you've got to get hold of yourself, now. You can't let a thing like this get the best of you, you know. You've got to get ready for the Cotton Bowl."

"My god," Tom moaned.

"And you don't want to get a reputation for being temperamental. The pros might not like that, you know."

Tom grunted at each word as if he were being kicked in the stomach.

"I've put my whole life in you, boy. Tried to give you something money can't buy. All the money my father left me, and none of it ever made me as happy as when I was playing ball." His father shook his head. "I've always hated it because I wasn't good enough to play pro ball. I want you to have that, son. You can't buy fame with money, by god!"

Tom's groans took shape as muttered "shut-up's."

"You're gonna be a great football player. Might even make the Hall of Fame. How'd you like that?" His father chuckled as he said, "Did you ever think when you were a little dickens and I had to quirt you to make you run sometimes, did you ever think you'd be a Hall of Famer, huh?"

Tom jumped at his father, swinging wildly, knocking him down with the first blow. His father fell heavily to the floor, rolled over, then began to crawl blindly around the room, crying, "My god, son, where are you, son. Help me, my god, please help me." He saw that his father was crying, saw that he was drunk. He had never seen his father cry.

He fell beside the older man, grasped his heavy chest, and pulled him across his lap, held him, rocked him, tried to comfort the only friend he had in the world. "Daddy, I'm sorry. My god, I'm sorry."

"That's all right, son. Everything'll be all right," his father said as he patted the boy's arm, "You'll see."

Tom tried to explain the next day, but his father only talked of the Cotton Bowl, and when Tom refused, his father never spoke to him again. Tom drove to Mexico City and drank and whored and turned away professional football scouts with contracts in their hands until he was drafted in the spring.

Rabb had never seriously considered the Army as a possible solution to his life, but after being in for a few weeks, he found it, if not pleasant, at least not unpleasant. Often he even felt secure in the anonymity of being US 3255384, a stuffing for a khaki void, and he slipped gratefully into this hole after the four months in Mexico.

He kept to himself, trying not to attract attention by either talking too much or too little, but his presence demanded attention. He was, as usual, the largest and strongest, and, also as usual, was uncomfortable in the company of smaller men, perhaps reflecting their discomfort. For fear of being thought a bully or a threat, he never disagreed with anybody. He agreed with Democrat and Republican, with Catholic and Baptist, with everyone who spoke to him, and everyone thought him slow and stupid for his efforts, a giant throwback.

There was a new problem, though, as he was forced into the company of young men with loud ignorant voices as irritating as they were intolerant. Before, he could walk away from these voices, but now he was surrounded by them, locked in constant company with them. He wondered why it would not be just to destroy these jabbering fools. Often he daydreamed of entering a room and shouting,

"Silence! Think well of what you might say in my presence, and speak only truth and other kind words." Power for good—but the crowd, both the good and the evil, feared power they did not control. They would unite and arm to strike him down if he used his physical strength for any other purpose than as an exhibition. He must follow the rules they made for the games they controlled. So he followed the rules and played the game as he had all his life, and they left him alone to lie on his bunk each night, shining brass and boots, keeping his equipment clean and in good repair, only bothered when they wanted him to play the freak for them, to show his strength or his supposed stupidity. He endured their jokes in silence, and they tolerated him. No one mentioned the death the fall before, and those who connected this Rabb with that incident never spoke to him of it. The public seemed to have forgotten, but Rabb hadn't, nor had he any hope of losing the memory until the morning of the grenade lecture.

Rabb's company sat in a semicircle against a hillside around an arrogant Lt. Kilp who gave a technical lecture on the grenade, its components and their functions. He spoke as if to assembled idiots, repeating each key phrase several times and even less important remarks more often. The talk bored the trainees, and they soon began whispering among themselves. Lt. Kilp reached into a packing case and pulled out a gray grenade, dramatically jerking the pin out. He carefully handed the grenade to the recruit without releasing the handle which activated the fuse.

Orans tried to be nonchalant about the grenade, but it only lasted about one minute, and he was soon sweating and shaking, grasping the grenade with both hands, one wrapped tightly around the other.

The murmuring stopped as soon as it was obvious that the officer was going to let the shaking boy hold the grenade. The whole group watched the grenade very closely. Lt. Kilp was even more arrogant and pompous than before, and continued to strut for another twenty minutes.

Rabb was angry. He wondered why someone didn't jump up and knock the hell out of Kilp, but no one did. They just sweated out the rest of the lecture as Rabb's anger rose.

"Well, Orans," Kilp said as he finished the lecture, "I suppose you are one smart guy that will be careful with his mouth?" He casually took the grenade from the boy.

"Yes, sir!" the boy said, sighing as if he might never speak again.

Lt. Kilp strutted for a few more minutes, holding the grenade, then he shouted, "Dismissed," and tossed the grenade into the company. The handle flipped away with a quiet ping.

Most hesitated for half a second, watching the clumsy bounces of the grenade and the trail of smoke drifting from it, then they stampeded.

Rabb didn't hesitate an instant, but moved as soon as he saw the grenade leave Kilp's hand. He bulled his way through the mass of struggling bodies, of arms and legs tangled in fear, and reached the small clearing around the grenade where the efforts were even more frantic. The grenade seemed both innocent and menacing, but to Rabb it was like a beam of salvation, a meaning, a purpose, and he dove across the last barrier of demonic bodies and covered the grenade with his body, lost finally in the numb waiting for that moment when he, the tool of the crowd, would be their shield, and they would have to love him.

He waited, but it seemed so long, and there was too much red fear streaking across his tightly closed eyes and so much noise pounding in his ears. Then the red became endless black and the noise thunder, and it was so loud and so black and so deep, and he was lost in it.

When he came back, it was from a long way, and all he knew was laughter in the distance, then closer, then above him. Was it that simple? Was that all there was to it? No pain? Who was laughing? He slowly opened his eyes and focused them, and saw the ground, the pine needles green against the red earth, and he couldn't understand, and couldn't think for the booming laughter above him. Reeling to his feet, he saw the grenade on the ground, intact, a small cork laying a few inches away. He still didn't understand, and looked into the laughing face of Lt. Kilp.

His head jerked back and forth with uncontrolled laughter. Rabb understood: a practice grenade.

There were a few nervous titters from the rest of the company, many well within the kill range of the grenade, but most had been too frightened to laugh.

"Stop that!" Rabb shouted into Kilp's face, "You goddamn stop that!"

Kilp stared at him. He noted the name. "Humph, can't you take a joke, Rabb?" looking at his clenched fists.

Rabb wanted now—as much as he had been happy to die a minute before—to feel his fist crash into the face, again and again, until it smashed through the blood and pulp and out the back side. He held himself, and walked away, feeling "stupid" written in ten-inch letters across his back.

There was a slight change in the others' attitudes toward him. As a matter of fact, several guys who had never spoken a word to him nodded and said "Hi" during the rest of the day.

That evening, as he worked on his boots and brass, Rabb was interrupted by S/Sgt. Miller, his platoon sergeant, who wanted Rabb to come to his room down the hall from the squad bay.

Sgt. Miller, a tall, lanky cowboy from Montana, was a thirtyish Korean War veteran who liked the role of the tough sergeant with the heart of gold, and he played it to perfection. He harassed his troops constantly, making them answer him at the top of their lungs, and then he coyly turned his head and cupped his ear and shouted incredibly loud, "I can't hear you, Trooper!" Or he made them do push-ups or run with rolled mattresses on their backs; but he carried out his harassment with such a jovial, fatherly gleam in his eyes and such a boyish grin hiding behind the wide British Guardsman's mustache he affected that no one but a few soreheads disliked him. Most of his troops, Rabb particularly, understood that Sgt. Miller was good-natured and a fine example of the professional soldier.

"Pvt. Rabb, reporting as ordered, Sergeant."

"Stand easy, trooper," Sgt. Miller said, grinning, "Aw, hell, sit down, Rabb."

Rabb sat on a foot locker and Miller straddled the only chair. Miller pulled out a cigar, and said, "Smoke if you like."

"Have I done anything wrong?" Rabb asked, squirming. "If I have, I didn't know it."

Sgt. Miller didn't speak, but elaborately lit his cigar.

"If it's about this morning, Sgt. Miller, I'm sorry, but I—"

Miller interrupted with a wave of his hand. "You didn't know that was a practice grenade? I know that. Lt. Kilp pulls that crap every cycle, and scares the hell out of all the recruits. He thinks it's funny—maybe it is, I don't know, but it scares the hell out of me, too." Miller paused to concentrate on his cigar for what seemed to be several minutes, then said, "I want you to take Olinger's squad."

"How come?" Rabb asked.

"Aw, he's a natural fuck-up. He knows it and don't care," Miller said to his cigar.

"No, I mean, how come me?"

"You soldier pretty good, and you're big enough so none of the guys'll give you much trouble. I think it'll work out OK. OK?"

"Sure, I guess so," Rabb said. "If you think I can handle it."

"Shoot yeah," Miller said. "Move your gear tonight, OK?"

So Thomas J. Rabb became, if not a leader of men, at least the leader's direct agent. He deeply felt the responsibility of leadership. He didn't worry about sounding naive when he told his new squad that he was there for them, to help them whenever and however possible, and if they laughed at his mother-hen efforts behind his back, they couldn't doubt his sincerity.

The gray stripes on the black brassard he slipped on his left arm each morning seemed to make everything all right. If he felt apart from the others, that was fine, that was part of the loneliness of leadership. Now he was captain of his own team, and it was one of the few periods of his life when his relations with his fellow men seemed right. If he still felt lonely just before he went to sleep each night, at least now there was a responsible reason.

The Army, in the person of Sgt. Miller, had given him squad-leader's stripes and a certain measure of happiness, and he, in turn, gave the Army back the same effort he had given his father and football all those years. And his efforts bore the same success they always had. He fired Expert on the range, set a company record on the physical-training test, and a post record on the obstacle course. He was selected to compete for Company Soldier of the Month, and won the honor at the company and battle group level, and was only edged out of the post honor by a young S/Sgt. who was an airborne instructor. The company commander, a tall muscular Negro captain from Texas, spoke to Rabb about considering an application for OCS, promising that it would be approved, but it was Sgt. Miller, again, who gave Rabb the final direction to turn his life—the Special Forces.

Miller had a friend in the Special Forces group stationed on another part of Fort Benning, and he and Rabb drove over to visit him one Sunday. The sergeant was almost as big as Rabb, but had such an air of calm capability that he seemed twice as large to Rabb. The beret, the bloused jump boots, the quiet self-confident voice around the hard core of just plain toughness, sold Rabb at once. He was reminded—in that fateful way that the Army reminded him of football, and both of life itself—of a professional lineman he had dinner with in Dallas the summer before. Both men, the football player and the soldier, seemed neither ashamed nor overly conscious of their size and strength. They had found their place in a physical world, a place Rabb could never find.

But he tried: he took a short discharge, reenlisted for four years as Regular Army, assigned to Special Forces training. Even the other cadre began to treat Rabb as an accepted, if minor, member of their company, and then when Miller met Rabb in Columbus—cadre and trainees couldn't leave the post together—for a trip to a Phoenix City whorehouse, Rabb knew that everything was going to be all right forever.

At night he lay in his bunk after taps, his hands clasped behind his head, his body feeling more able than it ever had, and he thought about the wonderful life ahead as soon as he finished basic. Everything seemed so perfect, he even thought about writing his father—he had neither seen nor heard from him since November—then his dreams exploded in his face like a faulty grenade.

It was the Sunday before the last week of basic training, a week he eagerly awaited for the double pleasure of finishing basic—he wasn't even taking a leave, but was going straight to Advanced In-

fantry School—and his squad was to be on detached duty as ag-
gressors while the whole Battle Group trained on *Squad Tactics:
Defensive*.

He took a nap that Sunday afternoon. He had been on pass with
Sgt. Miller again, and had a hangover. Someone woke him, saying
that Sgt. Miller wanted him outside. Rabb put on his fatigue jacket
and boots, and went downstairs.

There was a flag football game in the wide grassy area between
the large concrete barracks. Rabb's company was playing Charlie
Company, and most of the NCO's and recruits from both were
watching. Rabb ran over to Miller to ask him what he wanted.

"Where you been, boy? Get in there," Miller said, chomping on
his cigar. "We're getting beat."

"Oh . . . I don't know if I ought to . . . " Rabb said, stammering
as if he were still waking up. "I uh . . . I don't think . . ."

"Come on, boy. You're not gonna get hurt," Miller said, grabbing
him by the shoulder. "Get in there. I got twenty on you boys with
Charlie Company's first shirt. Now get!"

He trotted reluctantly onto the field, replacing one of the smaller
linemen at middle guard. He merely stood in the way, and if a run-
ner came near, he grabbed at the handkerchief in the back pocket
rather than tackling the ball carrier to get the flag as all the others
were doing. He played for about ten minutes, seldom if ever bump-
ing into anyone, and not listening to Miller's insistent shouts to "Get
in there, Rabb, boy." Not this time, he thought.

The first physical contact came as he reached around the tailback
for the flag, and the boy lowered his shoulder and ran over Rabb.
On his way back to the huddle, he shouted to Rabb, "Keep out of
my way, dumb ass!" Anger tightened Rabb's stomach, but he controlled it, and said nothing. He heard snickers from the sidelines,

and turned to look. They thought he was afraid: he could tell by their faces, but he didn't care until he looked at Miller, and Miller looked away as if he didn't know Rabb. He didn't have to prove his courage: he was already an All-American twice and almost a third time. But he had been playing the game too long, had too much the habit of proving things to crowds.

He felt it rising in him when he got down on the line. He felt it, and started to run away—but everyone else was playing rough, tackling, why must he always be an exception? Why? he thought, but then the other team came to the line, and his mind went on automatic pilot, and thought no more.

He saw the center's forearm muscles flicker an instant before he snapped the ball, and he charged. He hit the split between the two men who were supposed to double-team him, his forearms swinging like clubs. He hit as if wearing full pads, shoulders and arms blasting the two smaller men apart. He was on the tailback almost as soon as the ball was, his arms blocking any pass. The tailback tried to dance away with a stiff-arm in Rabb's face, then he made a futile attempt to run away from Rabb, but Rabb was faster. Rabb hit him high, his shoulder into the other's windpipe, his arms smashing at the football. Rabb followed him to the ground, lowering his shoulder so that it broke three ribs when they landed. The tailback was unconscious, bleeding from the mouth where two teeth were broken off at the gum line. Rabb rolled up, running back to the defensive huddle. Always run back. Always.

As he ran back, he smiled at the sidelines, expecting to see people smiling back, but the stunned faces hit him like a solid shoulder in the guts. Rabb turned and ran off the field toward his barracks.

Goddamn! Goddamn! Goddamn! Over the line again. How do you keep from stepping over the line when the bastards keep moving it? They got what they wanted, and that wise bastard got his mouth shut good—what more do they want? A football player or a flower girl? Goddamn it all to hell!

At five o'clock the CQ came to Rabb's bunk to tell him the Captain wanted to see him in his office. Rabb didn't even wonder why the CO had come all the way back to base on Sunday. He changed into clean, starched fatigues before he went down to the orderly room.

"Pvt. Rabb reporting as ordered, sir."

Capt. Flowers returned the salute, but didn't say to "Stand easy," so Rabb kept his brace. The Capt. took off his glasses, and rubbed his eyes with the back of his hand. "Well, at least you didn't kill him, Rabb. I suppose that's something." Flowers replaced his glasses, stood up, clasped his hands behind him, and paced around his desk. "Stand easy, soldier," he said without glancing at Rabb who remained at attention. "Stand easy, I said," his voice rising as he spoke.

Rabb changed positions, but was no more easy than before.

"Rabb, I'm from Texas, too," Flowers said. "Went to college and played football in Indiana, though, but I still like to follow Texas football. I saw that game on TV where you killed that boy." Flowers paused and turned his back on Rabb. "I didn't say anything to anyone because I supposed it was an accident, particularly after you turned down the pro offers, but after your performance this afternoon . . . I don't know, now. Was it an accident?"

"Was what an accident, sir?"

"Haven't you been listening?" Flowers asked.

"No, sir."

"Just why not? You tell me that, soldier."

"No excuse, sir," Rabb mumbled.

"What was that?"

"No excuse, sir."

"You damned right there's no excuse for what you did today! None at all! And you can thank Sgt. Miller for not being in the stockade waiting for a court martial right now," Flowers said right into Rabb's face. "If I had my way, you'd be there right now. I could do it myself, you know," Flowers said. "But I've got enough troubles as it is."

"Yes, sir," Rabb said, always ready to sympathize with a good man's problems. "It must be bad for you?"

"What do you mean by that, Rabb?" he asked, stopping the pacing, and turning sharply toward Rabb.

"Nothing, sir," Rabb answered quickly.

"Come on, soldier, spit it out!"

"Well, sir . . . I was just thinking how bad it must be being a Negro officer at a southern post, and . . ."

"That'll be enough!"

"I'm sorry, sir . . . I thought that's what you meant, sir," Rabb stammered.

"I said that's enough! Don't you hear well, soldier?"

"Yes, sir."

"Rabb," Flowers said, beginning to pace again, "I don't know what your game is, or what's the matter with you, but let me tell you right now that I'm withdrawing your orders for Special Forces tomorrow morning. They don't want your kind in a crack outfit like that, and you're not going, and that's final."

"Yes, sir," Rabb said, choking on the pain in his throat.

"Now you listen to me," Flowers said, advancing on Rabb, "You've got one more week in my company, and if you so much as touch the hair on another man's head, I'll have you behind bars in ten seconds. Do you understand?"

"Yes, sir."

"Now get the hell out of my sight, soldier, and watch your step. Not one inch out of line, or I'll have your ass."

"Yes, sir," Rabb said as he snapped to attention and saluted.

Rabb wandered slowly out into the twilight toward the beer hall where he drank until it closed, and then wandered back to his bunk where he lay without sleeping until reveille. He had no hate or anger, even at Capt. Flowers—he just couldn't understand where he had gone wrong, and he searched through the jumbled darkness of his memory for the answer. Finally just before dawn, he relived that game, that death which had seemed so long ago yesterday and so near tonight.

The morning of the game, the coach came to Rabb's room to ask him for the hundredth time that week if he understood just how much the game meant.

"National champions, maybe," the coach said. "Think of that, Tom. Think how much that will mean to your father."

"Yes, sir."

The coach shook his head, and sighed. "National champs. Never thought I'd have one." He looked up. "We can beat them, by god. But you've got to keep on Sedlack," he said, referring to the other team's All-American quarterback.

"Yes, sir," Rabb agreed. "I will."

"You've got to get him. Hit him so hard he can't even think about passing."

"Yes, sir," Rabb said. "I'll try."

And it was a perfect day for him to try. A high blue sky and crisp fall air made the colors and sounds of the pre-game warm-ups twice as real as life. The home stadium was packed—Rabb liked that—and there was even national television to cover the clash between the Texas team ranked number three and the Midwestern team ranked number one. Rabb was ready, and even before the warm-ups he got the good butterflies that told him he was going to be tough. He felt clean and powerful in his pads as if they were to protect the other players from him. The blue sky, the green grass, the thousand colors of the fans, and the cheers—so great to be alive, he thought.

He played a brilliant game, beautiful, hard-hitting ball, clean ball—he thought only weaker men had to play dirty—and he hit with blood in his eye. But Mike Sedlack was tough, too, and he shook off Rabb's hardest tackles, got up smiling and trotted back to the huddle to pass again. The whole Texas team was almost as fired up as Rabb, and they were able to hold the Midwesterners scoreless in spite of Sedlack, but they hadn't scored either as the game moved into the fourth quarter.

The Texans quick-kicked, driving the other team to their eleven. Two plays gained nothing. On third down, Sedlack went back as if to pass, but ran the fullback draw, the off-side tackle and the half-back trapping the middle guard, Rabb. As soon as he stepped through the line without making contact, Rabb knew the trap was on. He lowered his body almost parallel to the ground, driving with all his strength, hoping to blast through the block. The block was perfect, the halfback at Rabb's knees, the tackle higher. His body shuddered in the block, asking the final effort, forcing himself to stay erect. He still had his head down when he hit the fullback, and didn't get his arms around to grasp his body. The violence of the meeting knocked the fullback three or four yards backwards, and kept Rabb from falling down. The fullback tried to circle Rabb, running across the field. When he realized that he had run into his own end zone, he tried to bull his way back out, but was smothered under Rabb's roaring tackle.

The noise was unhuman, unbelievable as the home crowd smelled victory. Their roar was only slightly less than that of Rabb's heart as his team pounded his back, hugged him, and shouted glorious things.

The safety seemed to break up the game, and both teams scored a touchdown within five minutes. The Texans still led by the margin of Rabb's safety with only three minutes to play. It seemed too small, though, as Sedlack started another drive, and moved his team downfield on short passes as the Texans loosened their secondary to stop the long pass. Sedlack rolled out of the pocket to hit the short pass for eight or ten, or ran for four. Even if they couldn't score a touchdown, they were sure to get into field goal range, if Sedlack wasn't stopped.

Rabb was desperate, shifting about in the defensive line, slanting, stunting, anything to get Sedlack. His eyes, all the nerves of his body, were constantly seeking that small signal which would tell him the direction Sedlack was rolling before the play started. *The right guard. Out of line. Not as much weight on that hand. He's pulling! Knee turned out. Pulling right. Sweep? Trap? No. Sedlack rolling! Yes! On the option!*

Sedlack rolled to the right on the pass or run option. His interference waited behind the line of scrimmage to form the pocket until Sedlack decided to run. Rabb broke the rule, and didn't cover his territory, but slid down the line as soon as the play started. Sedlack saw that his receivers were covered as he rolled out, but he slowed to look twice, then shouted the order to run. Rabb shook off two blockers, but the fullback caught him from the blind side, and knocked him to the grass. Sedlack lost the rest of his interference as the end took both guards with a side-body. Rabb rolled over, then up after Sedlack again. Sedlack slowed again to hip fake the outside linebacker so he could get to the sidelines, but after he got by, he was trapped by the defensive halfback coming up fast and Rabb in pursuit. Sedlack moved straight for the sidelines as he realized he wasn't going to make good yardage, and he hoped to at least stop the clock and save a time out, but he had to stiff-arm the halfback to get there, and this slowed him enough for Rabb to catch him.

Rabb caught Sedlack five yards in bounds, but instead of tackling him or knocking him out of bounds, he grabbed Sedlack around the waist. He pivoted on his right foot, and drew Sedlack's body around his, spinning and using their momentum to hurl the lighter boy through the air, flinging him across the sideline grass. Sedlack bounced, turned once in the air, then landed with the small of his back against the curbing of the cinder track which encircled the playing field.

Sedlack's scream was lost among the random noise in the stadium, and few except Rabb saw him arch and claw at his back with both hands. The football rolled foolishly across the track, and Sedlack's body convulsed in one long twitch.

Rabb remembered every detail: he had jumped up and ran back on the playing field. Three plays later the coach took him out, and as he trotted off the field, the stadium rose and cheered a long, thundering ovation that seemed to shake the very skies, and poured over him like a wonderful trumpeting calling him to the gods—but no, Rabb thought, sitting up in his bunk, that's not the way it was at all.

Again: he had jumped up, but before he ran back on the playing field, he had turned to the sideline television cameraman and smiled into the collective eye of the crowd—My god! he thought, you grinned at the camera, and you knew he was dead! You knew it! And you still smiled for your fans, played three plays, felt so wonderful at the long cheer, and all that time you knew what that final twitch meant, and you didn't care! You didn't care at all!

Could it be worse? Yes, for now he knew deep in the marrow of his bones, knew as he knew his pounding pulse and the restless sounds of sleep around him, knew that even now, even knowing, he would, this very moment, still trade that boy's life for that magnificent roar from the crowd.

So there was the fester, and all this—the madness afterward, Mexico, the Army—had been a sham, a cover to hide him, not from guilt, but from lack of guilt. He had cared, once, but by the time of Sedlack, he didn't. What had changed him? His father, that drunken, lonely man? The gaping crowd that he knew really hated him? No, it was him, and only him. They sucked him into a honey trap, and he loved every second, every hurt of it.

As he waited for reveille, the truth of himself seeped into every cell of his body, that large, unremorseful body that betrayed his pained mind—mental pain into a muscular reaction.

The area of Fort Benning reserved for *Squad Tactics: Defensive* was a great oval clearing laying lengthwise up the side of a red-clay hill, a small tip lapping over onto level ground at the base of the hillside, and another tip over the ridge of the hill. The surrounding trees were thinned lower on the slope, but were matted into thick brush higher up. The defensive positions were at the edge of the ridge facing down the hill over the approximately one hundred twenty yards of clearing. The clearing had no tall trees, but there was good scrub brush cover to within twenty or thirty yards of the positions. The aggressor squad, Rabb's under the direction of Sgt. Miller, could attack from any direction, but since they were placed at the bottom of the clearing in a gully, it was more convenient to attack straight up the hill, and this was their usual procedure.

Rabb and his squad were tired. They had attacked the positions seven times before lunch and four times already this afternoon. There were half-a-dozen salt rings on the green fabric of their fatigues, marking the sweating and drying. Rabb seemed doubly tired: the sleepless night was part of it, but there was something else, something worse, almost as if he had spent the whole day covering that foolish grenade, waiting that terrible wait while the fuse burned under him. For the first time he could remember, he felt the taste of defeat, fatigue. Life had beaten him, and he didn't like it. Twice he had barked at his squad. Another time he had shoved one of them as they were running through the brush of the clearing because he was running too slow. He was so tired; he had never really been tired before this day.

"Whewww," Rabb sighed as they rested before the last attack. "One more time, then it's all over."

He heard Sgt. Miller's field phone buzz, but didn't listen to the talk. "OK, you troopers saddle up. Don't keep the general waiting," Miller said as he finished the phone call.

There was a murmuring from Rabb's squad.

"That's right. The general has come to watch his little girls, and we're gonna give him something to watch," Miller said. "Come here, Rabb."

"Yes, Sgt. Miller."

"Rabb, boy, you're gonna be a wounded G.I."

"A what?"

"A wounded soldier. Just like the Germans used to do in World War II. You're going to walk right up on those bastards like you've been hit, and if they come out to help you, you grab one, and hold him."

"What for?"

"The rest of us are going to sneaky-foot around them and come in on their flanks while they're watching you. See?"

"OK," Rabb said, smiling for the first time that day. Earlier that morning, when he told Sgt. Miller about the visit with the Capt., Miller told Rabb that he was sorry, but there was nothing he could do.

Rabb took off his t-shirt. His shoulders seemed to rise out of the baggy fatigue pants, layer upon layer of muscle reaching upward and outward until he looked like a caricature of a circus strong man. "Goddamn, boy, you're a big bastard," Miller said as he rubbed dirt and leaves on Rabb's chest and back, and made scratchlike marks with a stick. "Now take your time going up that hill. We have to have time to get on their flanks without them seeing us. OK?"

"Sure, Sarge."

Miller dragged Rabb out of the gully where the defenders could see them, and acted as if he were beating Rabb. Then he pushed Rabb to the ground, and walked away. Miller whispered, "Make it good, boy, and maybe the general'll give you a medal." He chuckled.

When Rabb staggered to his feet, and stumbled up the hill, he didn't have to act: he did feel wounded in the most vital of his organs. The fatigue still gripped his body, but as he moved slowly up the hillside, he became aware of many eyes on him. The silence reminded him of that single second between the end of the Star Spangled Banner and the first long cheer of the ball game. He felt better, and began to play wounded. He fell twice, and crawled a few yards. Once he lay still for several minutes feeling the air cool on his back as clouds hid the sun, and the pine trees around the clearing seemed to stand in closer formation like dark, silent spectators.

As he rose, he thought, I'll show them, by god. There was no one on this field but him, and he'd give them a whole show. This was even better than making an unassisted tackle in the open field: there was no ball carrier to share in the crowd's attention. He crashed madly through the brush, fell to the ground, and crawled under the brush, only to rise again and scream in pain. He fell about twenty yards in front of the first position, and lay there moaning and crying for help. "Help me! Oh, you bastards, help me." Then he was silent for several minutes, still, but suddenly he screamed as if his soul had been ripped from its temple, and then was silent again.

Finally, he dragged himself toward the positions, pulling along by roots and handfuls of dirt, moaning.

He could feel it in his belly and along the ridge of his spine and among the hairs on the back of his neck. He knew when he was good, when he had done his job well—he had them in the palm of his hand. He could crawl right into the foxhole with them now, and they couldn't stop him. He had them beat and captured already. Maybe he would get a medal. Sure, he snorted. But maybe. The general could pin it on him, then all the troops would cheer, chanting his name across the parade field, slapping him cheerfully on the back. They'd love him again, like before, and they'd know he wasn't a dumb animal. Sure. And his name in the paper, maybe even his picture, and his father would see, and put down the quirt, and they would all come down out of the stands for him. Sure. Please, God, please, he cried silently.

He moved forward, dragging himself with one hand, pleading with the other. His face was twisted and white, and his motion intent. He frightened the two recruits in the forward position, but they remained motionless, the taller one sticking up like a gopher, but the other one was only a timid blur between his helmet and the edge of the foxhole. They waited, unable to help or hinder Thomas J. Rabb.

As Rabb came to the edge of the foxhole, he saw his signal, his sign. The taller one had his weapon fixed on Rabb's head, but the other was turning to seek advice from behind. The taller one started at the sound, and glanced beside him. Rabb seized the rifle with his now demanding hand, and jerked it past his head as the blank went off over his shoulder. At the same instant, he pivoted on his other hand, throwing his body around to kick the turned boy in the back, and then landed balanced in the hole. His jerk had torn the M-1 from the grasp of its owner, and Rabb thrust that butt upward and caught him under the chin. His jaw flopped away at an angle, and his heavy steel helmet, swinging down over his face, closed like a gate, smashing his nose. Rabb knocked the other boy unconscious with his right elbow behind the ear as he made a motion to undrape himself from the side of the foxhole. Rabb heard the shots and shouts as his squad charged from the flanks, and he turned to face an aroused enemy.

He slipped back the bolt of the M-1 to eject the fired blank, and shot a charging sergeant full in the face. He then used the heavy rifle to block a kick from one of the observing officers, slamming the stock across the rising shin. Rabb paused in the hole to eject another shell, waiting as his shoulders shuddered in fluttering, convulsive jerks. He ignored the crying private and the unconscious one, and the blinded sergeant and the crippled officer. Thomas J. Rabb, hero in his own right, master of many situations, then charged forever into the gaping maw of an ever-cheering enemy.

1964

Cairn

When the telephone rang Jamie Donalson threw his pencil on the ledger then slammed it. His father-in-law had thought it would be good for Jamie to learn the business, and Jamie might agree, but he thought of the business in terms of an air-conditioned office, afternoon golf at the country club, and the white-columned mansion on North Peachtree; not doing inventory in the stuffy rear of a drive-in grocery. College in the daytime, drive-in grocery and pregnant wife at night. She didn't show yet but her feet would swell each night during the four hours she helped him with inventory. Jamie would try to think babies, cribs and diapers, but he could only remember her legs that spring vacation they had met in Fort Lauderdale.

But the phone still rang and his wife called from the front of the store.

"I'll get the goddamned thing," he shouted, knowing she would chide him for cursing where a customer might hear.

He picked up the phone, spoke into it for several minutes, then hung up and shoved his swivel chair away from the desk. After he cut off the light, he sat, staring out the screen door, watching the cars swing past on the North Expressway, their sharp outlines softened by the pale green vapor lights.

He washed his face after a bit, mumbling "business as usual" in a quiet voice, and as he passed from the office into the storage area, he absently noted which boxes had been inventoried. Surprised at his lack of grief, then ashamed, he went on up front, his face set in practiced solemnity, a trick he had learned during his thirty days in the county jail.

"Who was it?" his wife asked from behind the counter, her voice tired, fatigue etched into her face, pale under the fluorescent light.

He didn't answer her but stepped past on his way to the beer cooler.

"Who called?" she asked again.

"My grandmother," he said into the open cooler. He pulled out a six pack of beer and a ring of pepperoni, remembering the hard smoked sausage his grandfather made from venison and pork, remembering the old sod smokehouse, remembering as he walked back to the checkout counter.

"You didn't shut that cooler, Jamie," his wife said, a thin patient smile settled at her mouth. "Why did your grandmother call?"

He ignored her and set the beer and the sausage on the counter, took out a beer, opened it. A long hard gulp of beer left easy bubbles climbing the neck of the bottle. Then another and he set the empty bottle carefully in the center of the counter.

"Yes, I know," he said to Gloria. "What if Daddy sees me? Or my probation officer? Or, God forbid, a customer?" he said as his hand searched his pocket for his grandfather's knife, the bone-handled old knife.

"I didn't say a word, Jamie," she said quietly as she went and closed the cooler. "You're the one who'll have to go back to jail, not me."

"You know something," he said, looking down at the knife. "I'll bet I've lost a thousand lighters in the past ten years but somehow I never lost this old knife. Funny." The old blade, thin and curved from endless absent strokings on the whetstone, slipped through the sausage cleanly and left a neat line with curled edges across the formica countertop. "Still sharp too." He sliced another piece of sausage, chewed it, then said, "I'm going to Texas."

"What?"

"You heard me."

"Oh, Jamie. Please." She slumped against the cooler. "Not again. Not now with the baby coming."

"My grandfather is dead."

"I thought he was already dead. Three years ago . . ."

"No, this is a different one. My father's father."

"Oh, honey, I'm sorry, I didn't know. You didn't tell me." She stepped to him and grabbed his large bony hand, the flat hard hand hung on a thick wrist which always looked odd hanging from the sleeve of his three-button Ivy League suits. "I'm truly sorry. You stayed with them a lot, didn't you?"

"Some."

"What happened?"

"I don't know," he said after a pause. "Jessie didn't say."

She asked about the burial.

"Next day or so, I guess. But I'm going."

"Do you want me to come?"

"Guess not. I'm leaving now. Right now." He opened another beer.

"Don't do that. Call Mr. Willis in the morning for permission. He'll let you go. We'll both fly out. Please."

"I think I'm leaving now."

"Please."

"No. Now."

He didn't look at her as he took a picnic icebox and filled it with beer and ice and cheese and sausage.

"Oh, Jamie, what will I tell Daddy?" she moaned as she leaned on the counter.

He stopped and turned with a finger pointed at her. "Tell him to call the damned police. Tell him his stupid son-in-law has blown town with the cash-register money again. Tell him what you want."

Quickly he opened the register and jerked out all the bills. "Give me the car keys." When she didn't move, he reached under the counter for her purse, then dumped everything out of it, scattered everything and picked the keys out of the mess.

"Jamie, please, not again . . ."

"That's right, baby," he said over his shoulder as he carried the full icebox to the '55 Chevy which had been their wedding present from her father. He paused to stare down the long curved tail of the expressway, down to where the cars raced and blinked along its coiled length like pulses, cold, quick and electric. "I'm sorry, baby."

"No, no," she sobbed.

He set the icebox in the front seat, slipped behind the wheel, and without looking back drove away. But in the rearview mirror he saw Gloria sit heavily on the curb in front of the grocery, her figure wavering under the flicker of the neon sign, KWIK IN, her head bowed, her swollen feet stretched in front of her.

He raced the dawn out of Atlanta, across Georgia, and was midway between Tuscaloosa and Meridian when the first light glimmered in the rearview mirror. He'd missed the driving and the drinking during the thirty days Gloria's father had let him stay in jail, but he could stand that. And he'd missed them both, speed and beer, almost unbearably during the six months of probation. But he, though wishing he could blame grief, knew in last night's anticipation that they would be good to get back to. Now he was slumped in the seat, one hand fingering the wheel, one hand caressing the bottle set in his crotch, a grin warm on his face.

For grins, as he said to himself, for grins he supposed he would drop by the old place and for grins he listened to a morning farm report on a local station. That's it, he thought, drop by the old place.

By the small Hill Country place where he had spent most of his summers between tours at various boarding schools and military academies, drop by to stand with the stocky old woman stunted on hairy legs, to watch the old man planted in the red rocky clay of the Hill Country. He knew that his parents wouldn't get back from South America in time, but he would go by, drop in for a bit, a quick visit, and after that, maybe Mexico. Who could tell. Maybe Alaska. Who could tell.

Then, with no warning, the memory of his grandfather swept out at him from the gray morning fog along the road, swift, sudden, like a semi over a sleepy rise. The old man, thin, gaunt old man, as old at fifty as he would ever show. The old man, father to Jamie whose father sought oil in the jungle so Jamie would know more than the dirt farm he knew as a child, but there was Jamie in the summers, spoiled brat from military school. He remembered the summers and the old man's hands guiding his down a whittling stick and he stopped, crying.

He wondered if the old man would be buried in the tattered dusty graveyard in Blanco, but then he thought not. Victor Donalson probably wouldn't rest easy in any ground and not at all in any but his own. Perhaps up the hill above the house among the whispering cedars. No. Then he realized where the grave would be, had to be. Down by the creek, on down the hill from the house where the spring bubbled into a cool stone well where crawdads waited for bent-pin hooks and bacon rind, cool and quiet and shaded by live oaks older than the old man, the air tart with the smell of mint and watercress which tangled along the rock-studded creek. The old man could sleep there as crystal water murmured in a shallower bed, could watch the crab apples ripen and fall in late summer and the squirrels as they chattered about his cairn, could feel his land around him.

For a moment Jamie knew that he would like to dig the grave—

he helped the old man dig the foundation for the new house the last summer he had spent there—but then he felt foolish. No one dug their own graves anymore, though he knew that his grandfather had dug another hole in rocky Tennessee hills for his father; this was 1956 and you paid people to dig your graves; but he couldn't shake the feeling.

He picked up a laconic hitchhiker in Jackson and shared his driving, his beer and his silence all the way to San Antone.

North on 281 and there it began, the rolling hills, the cedar-clutched draws, red clay and rocks, and the land cut here and there by spring-cold rivers which gathered in blue lakes among the hills, a land for goats and deer and useless old men spacing out their days on the dusty streets of Blanco, and everywhere it was summer and a thin coat of red dust had fallen across every face. Blanco, white town, but not white now in the heat of summer, but red like dried blood.

The road was still dirt where it left the town and he followed it out of town along the river for eleven and six-tenths miles to the rocky ford and the mailbox with Victor Donalson's name faded from it and the first gate. He stopped to get the mail but there was nothing in the box. A twig, red dust, nothing. Seventeen and three-tenths more miles from the ford, seven gates to the end of the one-lane crooked track. The first gate was aluminum and easy but the rest were oak and warped by the sun and blue northers and heavy with time. Rusted latch chains hooked on rusted nails. Hinges that sagged and frames that dragged the ground.

Seventeen fine miles of sudden shades, of quiet eyes peeking from the shaded cedar, and springs easing in reverse curves down

hillsides, of sullen ponds fringed in soft-shell turtles sunning and
Buzzard Bluff like a pitted skull across the creek, and then the last
gate. Once on Donalson land Jamie found little changed on the
road. Fresh axe marks showed where the brush had been trimmed
back. The trash weed had been cleared from the fence rows and the
wires were singing tight between the posts.

But there was no one at the new house which had been built over
the foundation hole he had helped dig that last summer. He drove
around the new house, over to the log and sod, round-roofed building, half-barn, half-house, he remembered as their home. After sitting for a few moments in the car, after looking once back at the new
rock house, he got out and walked through the split-log door frame
into the living quarters. It was empty, but for the smells, the kero-
sene, and cold, greasy, dusty, smoke smell of the wood cook stove,
the bite of lye soap, the damp musk of the hard-packed dirt floor,
the ache of harness and horse smells from the barn, and over it all,
like distant music, a dusty trace of hay. Where light speared through
fallen chinks of sod, he could see fat feed sacks and salt blocks and
hay bales, the script and punctuation of chickens.

Later he walked outside to roam the place, this place, the family
place. He cut a link of fibrous stiff sausage from the smokehouse
ceiling and ate it with an apple and a handful of water from the
spring-fed cistern up the hill. And later still he scattered a furry knot
of daddy longlegs off the age-whitened outhouse seat, remembering
the utilitarian dream book, the catalog hours, the guns and the ladies underwear. But it was gone now. The twisted door didn't close
right and fat flies bored holes through aimless shafts of sunlight.
Still later he leaned against the high deer-proof fence around the
fifty acres below the house and he could still see his grandfather
plowing. The old man, the mule and the plow had seemed a great—
complicated but useless—entity which turned up the rocks of the

field, white stones to be thrown in the wagon and hauled away to build fences and fords and now even the new house. "I'm the best damned rock farmer in Texas," his grandfather used to say, and Jamie believed him.

He was sitting on the stone steps of the other house, smoking, when he heard the grind of the pickup on the far side of the hill. As it topped the rise and started down he saw that it was as battered as the one he remembered but it was a newer model. His grandmother sat behind the wheel. He hadn't remembered that she could drive. After the truck stopped he stood up but didn't move. The old woman climbed down from the cab slowly, most painfully it seemed, but her face remained as passive as stone.

"Hello, Jessie," he said.

"'Lo."

"I'm Jamie."

"Of course you are," she said.

"Well, it's been a long time."

"Yes. Give Jessie a hug. You're not too old for that yet."

His arms couldn't reach around the squat woman so he clutched her shoulders and pulled her to him, trying not to smell her age.

"Long way from Georgia, son. You didn't have to come. Aren't ya'll due a baby?"

"I just wanted to come. That's all."

"Come with beer on your breath and a red-eyed hangover," she said softly. "Your folks weren't in Houston when I called so I sent them a telegram. Don't reckon they'll make it. Didn't expect you, but I thought I oughta call."

"Did you have to go to town?" he asked, after he couldn't think of anything to say.

"We've had a phone and electric lights for five, maybe six years now. But you wouldn't know about that, would you?"

"When did he finish the house?"

"Well, he might have finished her that next summer, with help, but it was the next." All this time, this talk, he thought she had stared at the ground because she didn't want to see him, but he saw that she had become so stooped that she had to duck her head and turn it sideways to look up at him. He sat down on the steps.

"I wouldn't have been much help anyway," he said, but she didn't answer. "I, ah, went to Bermuda. Had to go with friends."

Jessie snorted as if no one ever had to go to Bermuda. "Seems like I remember your daddy saying that was the summer you found out how to spend money."

"Yeah, I guess I did that," he mused. He had spent more than money on those sun-struck beaches. His first drunk, his first woman. And after the first week, he couldn't imagine that he had almost gone back to Texas to help an old man build a house because "Might as well, son. Got plenty of rocks." The new house looked suddenly good to him. It belonged to the hillside. He could see his grandfather's marks in the mortar.

"Where are they?" Jessie asked in the middle of his thoughts.

"Who?"

"Your folks," she answered.

"I don't know. Argentina, now, I think."

"Don't you know for sure?"

"We don't keep in touch much since . . ."

"Since you went to jail?"

"Yes. How did you know about that?" he asked.

"We kept in touch."

"They shouldn't have told you. It was a mistake anyway."

"People make mistakes. There's no shame in being in jail. Better men than you have looked out of bars for a time. Don't forget that."

"Yeah," he said.

She asked, "Have you seen your grandfather?"

"Where?"

"Inside of course. You haven't been inside?"

"No. I just got here."

"Well, come on, son."

He followed her blocky legs shaded by wiry gray hair and her clumsy lace-up shoes up the steps. At the screen she turned and asked him if he still knew how to carry groceries and he turned and went back to the pickup. The three sacks were sitting in the newly made pine coffin, simple square-cornered coffin, and he shook his head, then felt guilty for being pleased.

As he set a sack of potatoes on the table, he remembered the Sunday morning pleasure of Jessie's potato pancakes, remembered sitting on a deer stand and chewing on a cold baked potato, remembered . . . but he couldn't remember talking to Jessie as a child. He remembered that he minded her quicker than he did a drill sergeant. Once he had come down from the sleeping loft in the early morning and peed on the dirt floor. Jessie had blistered his butt with a piece of kindling wood until he had screamed "It's only dirt" and she had screamed back at him "But it's goddamned clean dirt" and whacked him again.

"Going to bury him out here?" he asked, smiling, so she could say "Of course" in her own final way.

She took him into the front room where her husband lay on a long plank table. Tightly sewn heavy canvas shrouded Victor Donalson to his thin neck. They stood on opposite sides of the table as the old woman stretched her gnarled hand across her husband's brow.

"How does he look? Had to take him to town to be embalmed—that's the law—but I wouldn't have them make him up or bury him."

"He's fine. Just fine," Jamie answered, looking down on the still, thin face somehow cheerful and defiant in death, meshed and laced with wrinkles, not of age but of use. The thin hair exposed his dry liver-spotted scalp but the mouth puckered firm and unsunken.

"I kept his face uncovered for you, just in case you came. Sit down, I'll close it now."

He sat in a cedar-frame chair and leaned against the rough stone of the fireplace, his fingers tugging at the fringe of hair left on the edges of the stiff deer-hide bottom. Jessie took a large, curved sacking needle and waxed twine and began to fasten the two edges of canvas over her husband's face. She worked slowly, patiently, with a strength of movement Jamie was beginning to remember more clearly.

"How did it happen?" he asked.

"Drunk, the old fool was drunk, out ridin' that damned old mule, drunk. Lightnin' threw him down in that draw over toward the Tillman place. Busted up his right leg real bad, splintered the thigh bone so bad the splinters stuck out of his leg. I went out after him soon as that damn mule came home all wild-eyed and crazy. But I don't walk so good anymore.

"I found him 'cause he was drunk as a coot and cussin' everything in God's creation, found him in the dark, a pile of kitchen matches and a pile of splintered bone and an empty pint laying around, and when he heard me coming he started in on me about not bringing another bottle.

"But he died about ten minutes after I got there, died just like he lived, drunk as a coot and cussin' all God's creation, going to Hell for spite and drunkenness and pride . . . old fool," she murmured. She had been stitching steadily as she talked but finished in silence.

She slipped the last stitch, tied a knot, then bit off the twine, remaining for a second stooped protectively over the old man, patting his cheek through the rough canvas. "Old fool. But goddam he was a man. Not big but a man all the same. He laid down my three brothers and my father the day they told him no jailbird was marrying me, laid 'em out with an axe handle, threw me in the wagon like a sack of chicken feed and drove like hell out of Tennessee . . .

"Make a fire, Jamie," she said quickly. "Your grandfather always got a chill at night when he couldn't get a drink."

Jamie stripped the kindling, built the fire, naturally, easily, and it burned well, then he sat quietly by the fire, listening to Jessie's humming as she fixed supper, listening to the fire, occasionally glancing at the shrouded remains of his grandfather, listening.

He got a late start on the grave because it took him so long to milk the two cows. He was out of practice and his hands cramped but the muted gurgle of a thick stream of milk into the pail told him that his fingers hadn't forgotten. When he laid his ear against the second's belly, he could hear the impatient grumble of her guts. She was used to a faster hand, he thought, grinning.

While he dug the grave Jessie watched from the edge of the stone wall. The ground was as hard as he remembered but it moved with pick and shovel. He worked steadily, quietly, a bandana tied around his head to keep the sweat out of his eyes; he had learned all that that last summer. And it all came back, not easily, but it came all the same, and by noon the grave was half done.

Jessie brought venison sandwiches from the house and he drank long and hard from the well, drank the teeth-achingly cold spring water which tasted and smelled of dirt and rocks and clay and living things, ate the venison, tough but full of taste, then he lay on the grass stretching his sore back and smoking and watching the buzzards, black scratches against the whitened blue, watched the patient drift of their survey.

"You still in school?" Jessie asked quietly.

"Huh? Oh, yeah. Part-time. I'm still running one of Gloria's father's stores . . ."

"After what you did?"

"They were kind enough to give me a second chance."

"Don't make light of it. It lets you go to school."

"Yeah, but maybe after the baby comes I'll go back full-time."

"Still going to be an engineer like your daddy?"

"Well, ah, no. I'm in Industrial Management."

"What's that?"

"Like a business major except that . . ."

"You mean you want to work in an office?" she interrupted.

"Ah, yeah, sometimes. You know. I only need another year for my degree, then maybe I'll go to law school. Corporate law, maybe tax," he said.

"How long's that take?"

"Three, four years, maybe," he answered casually.

"Seems like you been in school a long time now."

"Yeah," he said. "A long time."

"Ever think of being a farmer, like you used to talk about?" she asked suddenly.

"No. That was kid stuff . . ."

"Your grandfather didn't think it was kid stuff," she interjected. "You didn't either. He thought you'd make a good hand, someday maybe even run a place like this. You ever going to graduate?" she asked.

"Sure. Why not?"

"When your father graduated," she said, "we drove him all the way to Houston to watch him and brought him home before he went to South America that first time." She chuckled, looking sideways at him. "Damn Donalson men. They both got so drunk on the way home that I had to drive. Then they got me so drunk that I ran through the gate on the Samuels' place." She laughed, her eyes misty. "Didn't even see it. Victor wouldn't talk to me for a week." She laughed harder, laughed as she must have in the happy pride of that night. "We had to walk all the way home."

They laughed together for a few minutes and in the following quiet Jamie stepped back in the grave and said, "Jessie, I didn't even know he drank. I always thought he was taking medicine."

"Maybe he was. He came from a long line of whiskey drinkers and makers—that's how come he went to jail—so maybe he was."

Later they silently approved the finished grave and the neat mounds of red burnt earth on either side. As they walked to the house, he said, "I'll put him in the coffin, Jessie."

He carried the pine box and the lid into the front room. He placed handmade quilts in the bottom, then lifted the still bundle easily and set it in the soft down folds. He covered him with two more quilts and nailed the top down. The first two nails bent and had to be pulled out but the rest sank swiftly into the pine under firm, sure strokes. After supper he and Jessie sat on the stone steps, watching dusk soften the rocky old hills as secret deer crept into the oat patch across from the house.

The preacher came before first light and all the mourners before him. In the morning chill the old man was lowered into the dew-damp earth. The men helped Jamie fill the grave but he built the cairn alone out of stones he had gathered the afternoon before, white rocks washed in the creek below. As the layers rose in a rough pyramid, he smiled, thinking, it would take these rocks to hold the old bastard down and the old man would smile because the rocks had finally got him down and now he lay brother to the rocks, the stone of his courage, the rock of his strength, and, as Jessie might scoff, the rocks in his head. And Jamie worked his grief into the stone.

The cairn pleased him in the same way that the new house pleased him. Its solidity spoke against time, audible now, soon perhaps a whisper but a long whisper in time, and whatever man whenever who stumbled on these stones would know of the man beneath the land. He tried to think it of no importance but he had built it with his hands and could not deny it and would not try even as he walked away.

Back up at the house the old men gathered about the plank table, stony old men in musty suits and tieless denim shirts buttoned to their raw necks as if bundled against that coming cold, that cold whisper. They talked hunting and weather and the years while the women buzzed in the kitchen, fixing breakfast, chatting quietly in their Sunday dresses. Jamie sat peacefully at the head of the table, watching the sparks wing up the chimney from the damp-chasing fire he had built.

After everyone had gone and Jamie spoke of having to go too, Jessie made him drive her about the quarter section. She pointed out the two government-built ponds which she noted should be stocked with bass. They rode a track over the back side of the place, scattering the various clots of sheep and goats still ungainly from the spring shearing. She made him stop at the end of the valley and talked of how easily twenty acres could be cleared with a bulldozer. And there were planned sites for hunters' cabins and deer stands. On the way back she said twice, pointing at the forty cleared acres of truck vegetables below the house, "Your grandfather spent nearly fifty years digging out the rocks, fighting, and now that it is ready he isn't here to work it."

Back at the house she was out of the pickup and away before Jamie could speak of leaving. He had another cup of coffee, another cigarette, then chopped six months kindling from the wood pile behind the house and he sharpened the double-bit axe. He cleaned his grandfather's guns, the single-shot 30:40 Krag which had killed nearly a hundred deer in season, and the poaching gun, the 25:20, which had killed more, and the old octagon barreled 30:30 which the old man had brought from Tennessee, and the ten other guns. He oiled them heavily, then placed them back in the spike buck racks. He scattered hay for the cows and carried salt blocks up for the goats and sheep and filled their self-feeders, then shoveled manure from the barn and curried Lightning. He milked, early, but late enough so that the Jerseys could wait until morning. But then it was time to go.

After bathing, shaving, changing clothes, fixing sandwiches and coffee, and eating, he went to say goodbye to Jessie. He found her sitting in the afternoon sun on an old milk stool at the door of the smokehouse, snapping green beans from her garden out beyond the corrals. She threw the ends and bad beans to the crowd of clucking hens around her and dropped the snapped beans in the bag of her apron.

"Going back?" she asked without looking up when he stopped among the unconcerned hens.

"Yes. I think I'd best be going, Jessie. I've got an inventory to finish and a stat quiz to make up." As he said that he was going back to Georgia, and just then, he knew that he was.

"Comin' back?" She still had not looked at him but she carefully watched her brown hands work like dancers at the beans.

"Why?"

She peered up at him. "Why? Because this is all yours now. This place."

"But you . . ."

"But I'm an old woman and I want to go back to Tennessee to see my people before I die. My father is still alive and I want to see him, to forgive him, to be forgiven. I loved every day I spent with your grandfather, but he took me from my people and now I want to see them before I die. This is a good place and we made it together. And I don't want strangers working it. I'll leave it set fallow first."

They were silent for a bit while her hands continued their work and Jamie stuck his in his hip pockets and kicked small rocks until she spoke again.

"You'll need money to start, for a tractor and a dozer and to stock the ponds. You can build the cabins yourself, if you remember anything. I would've asked your father to come back but all he knows about land is to poke holes in it. So if he isn't going to work the home place, then the least he can do is put in some of that money he has been trying to push off on us for years."

"He wouldn't do that," Jamie said quietly.

"Don't worry," she said, shaking her head and smiling. "He's still my son and this is still his home and he hasn't forgotten who pushed him off of it, who sent him to college because he didn't belong here. I'll remind him when I see him."

"When?"

"He'll be home as soon as he can. He won't let grass grow on his father's grave before he sees it."

"I don't know, Jessie."

"I do, son, I do."

As he drove to Blanco, to the highway home, he felt absolutely nothing. The gates opened mechanically to his absent hands just as the steering wheel answered them. There was the highway, the white line, other cars, and nothing more, until outside of San Antone he noticed a blister on the palm of his hand just where he liked to hang his hand on the wheel. He moved his hand, tried both hands, but the right hand and the blister and the steering wheel kept rubbing, and he stopped in Schulenberg for a beer.

The drunk that followed was strangely quiet so that by the time that he reached Atlanta, except for the blister, he was still numb, slightly hungover, slightly drunk, and numb. He tried the grocery, without thinking, but it was closed for the night. Then he went home through the city night, down the empty black streets to their apartment in the new brick complex.

When he opened the door he found her sleeping in front of a silent television, her swollen feet propped on a chair, her face pale in the light.

"Gloria," he whispered, shaking her, "I'm home."

She woke and they kissed and talked for a bit, she explaining that she had covered for him and he speaking quietly about Jessie and his grandfather and the farm. He rubbed her feet and legs. She felt the blister on his hand and kissed it.

"It doesn't hurt. It'll be all right," he said as she rested his head on her stomach. His hands would get hard in time.

1964

Daddy's Gone a-Hunting

He liked the easy, uncluttered order of his days now, the long hours of quiet solitude broken only by the hammering echoes of the occasional logging trucks winding down the grade behind the cabin, the constant windlike rush of Hay Creek in its narrow rocky course, and the animals: two tiny chipmunks, serene and quick, making a home in the woodpile, a water ouzel that fluted away from the spring box each time he approached it, swiftly lost in the sun-dappled shade, and a doe who usually moved up the creek out of the hayfield across the road while he had his second cup of coffee. For ten years he had lived with a woman and children; now he lived alone. He rose each morning to silence as the sun cleared the granite peaks in the park east of the cabin, then trotted an easy mile up the Hay Creek Road, walking back down slowly, enjoying the mountain sun, the burned flush on his chest, the cool dark of shaded places, where the memory and promise of winter waited to touch his face. For ten years he had done little housework or cooking, but now he did everything, remembering his father and the small ranch on the flat at Tarkio in the crackle of pine pitch in the wood cook stove, but thinking of his wife as he ate thick-sliced bacon, greasy eggs and butter-fried toast sitting on the front steps in the sun that slanted through the lodgepole pine. It had been ten years since he had eaten a greasy fried egg, ten years of soft-scrambled, cold cereal, and a constant excuse that the smell of bacon frying made her sick, and now he wondered why, wondered how it had begun. Ten years. Sixteen years since his father had died of an old bear wound and

Olympia beer, fourteen years Burke had been away from Montana. He had left alone. Now he was back, alone.

In the afternoons he read, in the early evening bottom-fished the North Fork, and at full dark made the long winding trek down and across the river, through the park, down to the West Glacier Bar, a long slow trip pierced by the eyes of snowshoe rabbits red in the headlights as they considered his passage, down to the well-lit cloudiness of the bar, passing kids sprawled on the porch, out west for a summer lark, and on past the red neon circle and blue name of the Oly sign. He drank slowly, careful to avoid a hangover, unlike himself, unlike the self that gulped nine martinis and embarrassed his wife at every academic cocktail party in the small midwestern town where he taught, used to teach. Occasionally he might shake the barmaid for the jukebox or an extra beer to be nursed during the long return to the dark cabin, to be held, warming in his hand—more than drink, something to talk to, to ask where his life had gone, why he felt so damned old at thirty-two, why the rabbit's eyes turned red, remembering, thinking until sleep closed the gap between dream and reality, and he would sleep close in his bed, knit there by the steady voice of the creek, the cold night air, the clouds falling away from the moon, only occasionally at first jolting awake in a furious sweat as a sudden crack from the fireplace embers broke the silence.

So all his days were the same now, as orderly as fence posts, with no thought of the paper on Tennyson he had come to rewrite, the one he should publish to be promoted, and he sat in the sun, or under a hissing Coleman lamp, and read whatever pleased him, whatever caught his eye on the second-hand rack at the Apgar Motel, and as his eyes and fingers followed the tracks of others through a British India, or down a narrow street with the Continental Op, or across the high windy plains of the 1880s, he thought of the huge pile of yellowed paperbacks left behind by his father when he gave up the ranch and moved to Missoula, to the mill and the shining bony arms of a Bannack-Shoshone squaw. At fourteen Burke wouldn't go, wouldn't heed his father's apologetic warning, "Being lonesome is okay when you're young, son, but when you get old sometimes it grinds your guts worse than a sow trying to get back her cub." If anybody should know, Burke thought that the old man should, but he wouldn't follow him to town. It took the old man's death, four years later, and a burst of late adolescent sexuality. But, he remembered, he had finished the paperback stack that summer. An odd coincidence, perhaps, but probably not.

He propped his book open over the empty coffee cup, cocked his finger at the grazing doe, and wondered how long he could resist poaching her. He couldn't count the years since he last tasted venison, soaked in milk overnight, chicken-fried for breakfast. Couldn't count them. Barbara never chicken-fried anything, said it was bad for their stomachs. Once, when he had chicken-fried round steaks for the girls while Barbara was out fighting the good fight for sex education at an early PTA meeting, he had reminisced about his youth and chicken-fried venison, and his youngest girl, Alicia, had asked, in her mother's shy, coy, heartbreaking voice, "You couldn't shoot Bambi, could you, Daddy?" Or had she said "wouldn't"? Whatever, knowing Erica, the oldest, would repeat his answer to her mother, he avoided the question. "Guess not, sweetie, but I could strangle all the stupid, phony Felix Saltons in the world." When they wanted to know what he meant, he replied that it was an adult joke. The girls had both wailed, refused to eat his greasy old dinner, crying at the horror of being children forever and ever. By way of apology he had read twenty pages of Disneyish drivel before he tucked them into their matching gold beds, watching two chubby thumbs sink deeper into rosebud mouths and four dark eyes grow large and round as they sensed his anger, thought it directed at them, so he tucked them beneath white blankets resplendent with pale pink roses, whose stems had no thorns, and read on until they slept, despite his wife's La Leche League membership, thumbs securely lodged in their mouths, warm, sputtering breaths breaking around them. Gently, ever so slowly, he moved their hands away. Alicia's stayed away, but Erica turned over, moaned, managed to get both her thumb and the satin corner of her blanket into her mouth and even managed to smile around all that. Did loneliness grind your gut, old man? Try love.

Later, when Barbara finally came home, the good fight won, he had made her a cup of orange blossom tea, himself a light Scotch, and had meant merely to suggest that perhaps the girls were old enough to appreciate a little Dickens every now and again before bed and he'd be happy to. . . . But she slept curled in her chair before he could speak, her small hands cradled under her cheek, worn thin and vulnerable by all the good fights.

"Sex education in the schools," he whispered to the sleeping woman. "Well, what about death, disease and life, the thorned roses—where do they learn about that?" he said softly; he'd long ago stopped shouting about that, had learned better.

He didn't and hadn't begrudged his father the right to die in the spare arms of a thin, drunken squaw, and he wouldn't begrudge himself the right to live his days alone again. Now. After all. His last night home and the death of old Tom. Alone. And his nights, too, which were as ordinary as his days, orderly and alone, except for an Indian barmaid over in East Glacier, once, and a forty-year-old high school music teacher from St. Paul, who was in the late process of discovering what she was going to miss in her spinsterhood, twice.

At the end of Barbara's thirty days, he knew. He rented the cabin on Hay Creek until the end of the summer, wrote his terse resignation, *for personal reasons*, with no prospects for the fall, faced only with the prospect of a hermitage winter, ten-foot drifts and below-zero snow creaking under his paces. Then he drove down the North Fork road as fast as the old Ford pickup would go, called Barbara, told her to fly to Birmingham and be damned, told her his only sorrow for the wasted years, his only fear for the children, his only remorse that it hadn't happened childless and sooner.

In the West Glacier Bar, he intended to get drunk in celebration, but it went sour on him and at midnight, still sober, celebrating nothing, he called back, not to relent, but to explain his mistakes. She answered only once, thought his mistakes virtues, wanted no explanations, then left the phone off the hook. After wasting time trying to get the operator to understand, he walked back to the bar under a moon round and amazed in a cloudless sky, across the darkened street and graveled parking lots, toward the red neon eye of the Oly sign, which promised love, laughter and a dreamless sleep.

Had their marriage, their early love, simply been defeated by the years? And the cat was simply an excuse for both of them. Certainly he was already tired of seeing Kaboom floating like tattooed corpses in watery milk, had become bored with acting interested in the senseless prattle of his children and the earnest liberalism of his wife, sick of the phony dedications of his colleagues. And tired of himself, surely, tired of Barbara's endless annual excuses not to summer in Montana, excuses that became insistent offers for him to go alone. Surely she was as tired of him as he was of her. But it only seemed that way now, didn't it?

The night before he was to leave for Montana, they had fought bitterly about her refusal to go with him. He had agreed, hadn't he, and she had after all promised her parents—those slim, glossy, tanned, beautiful white-haired replicas of aging parents, whose breath always glistened with cloves—that she and the girls would spend the summer with them on the Cape.

But that wasn't unusual; they always fought before he left on a trip, fought for all sorts of real and necessary reasons: his fears of dying in the senseless mangle of car wreck or airplane crash; her horror of losing him, in his absence, to death or a strange woman. Then, in the morning hours, both struck finally and totally by their fears, they would apologize, huddled together, then make excruciating, gentle love, the best of their married years, and as dawn dusted the room with soft light, softer shapes, they would recount their first meeting over a library table, relive their first touches in a dark, dusty niche in the stacks, where a medical encyclopedia of World War II shared a shelf with the collected death statistics of five midwestern states, their passion proof against cold facts. Then, while daylight hardened the corners of their bedroom, they paid the final homage to their love.

But not this time. The accusations were too bitter, the fight too long, the years too many to overlook unless they both made the effort. Daylight found them sad in gray light on the sun deck behind the house, his last drink iceless, unfinished in his hand, her last cigarette burning out on the ground, sending a slender pale column of smoke up through the scarce leaves of a dying elm.

"I can't leave like this," he had said, "I'll stay another day."

"Suit yourself," she had answered as the old cut tomcat they had kept since the first year of their marriage, whose main functions in his old age, which began shortly after they had him cut, were eating, sleeping and crapping in the bathtub, sauntered out the back door and into Barbara's lap.

"Go hunting, Tom," she said, shooing him off her lap, maintaining a fiction begun years before.

"Tom never kills anything but time," he commented as he always did, but her smiling, usual line, "Be quiet. You'll hurt his feelings," didn't follow.

"He's not supposed to," she answered, lifting the fat brindle cat back into her lap and stroking him. "He doesn't need to."

Knowing where she intended the conversation to go, Burke rose, kissed her cool forehead, then went straight to bed, hoping for a better day.

Shortly after three o'clock Tom committed suicide with a passing Oldsmobile and at seven Burke was explaining to a still sobbing Erica that she had long since ceased to cry for Tom, that she was engaging in a fraudulent, self-pitying and self-glorifying sorrow. During the resultant hysterics, he angrily slapped Erica, then Alicia, then turned on Barbara with a ten-minute lecture about the place of man and animals in the cosmic scheme, which she endured silently as the girls sobbed under their pink-rosed blankets. And he wound it up threatening to burn those creepy, goddamned blankets if he saw them when he got back from Montana.

Though he wasn't sure exactly what he meant, he realized how much and how long he had hated the children's bedroom, the Winnie the Pooh wallpaper, the stuffed animals, the thornless roses, all the things calculated to protect his girls from life when they needed so much to be prepared for it. When he was Erica's age, he had shotgunned a bear off his old man and helped hold his guts in with one hand while he drove to Alberton with the other. But there were no more bears, Barbara always said. Somewhere the bear's always waiting, he always answered. Somewhere. And he must warn them. He was sorry for Tom, but grateful for this chance to purge himself of ten years' anger.

So glad it took him a moment to recognize the face his wife presented to him, the stern, determined motherface, protecting her children from the world, the one she used to terrify city councils, school boards, state senators, even the President if he dared face her. Her terms were, after his criminal outburst, non-negotiable: he had thirty days to decide if he wanted their—she didn't explain the referent—lives to proceed as always, with or without him.

He supposed that someday he would be ashamed of the obscenity he had shouted, of the laughter with which he had loaded the pickup, but now, as he curled deep in his father's sheepskin jacket, collar turned up against the cold waiting in the whiskey-soaked night, he didn't feel any shame. At least not about that.

When he woke the next morning, he sat up stiffly to confront a group of tourists who had gathered after their overpriced breakfast in the West Glacier Cafe to stare at his wind-combed hair, the month's beard, the old frost-covered shearling jacket, homemade, with a stiff, black bend sinister of blood across the back. They stared, cameras and toothpicks ready, sunburns flaming, considering him as they might a garbage bear waiting by a park road for a handout. Farting loudly, he vaulted out of the pickup bed, laughing like a ghost, sounding like his father screaming as that old sow tickled his innards with long teeth.

"All the oldtime mountain men are long dead, but for a dollar you can take my picture and pass it off for the real thing back in New Fucking Jersey," he shouted, laughing again, watching the tourists flush.

After an overpriced breakfast, he called home again, without asking himself why, but Barbara's mother answered, said that the plane had left earlier.

"I'm sorry, Burke," the old woman said, something akin to sorrow in her voice.

"Yes, well, I didn't call to stop her. Just to apologize for mistakes made long ago. Are the girls awake? I'd like to say hello."

Their voices were shy, guarded at first, then tearful, but they brightened as he told them about the doe that visited each morning, the chipmunk and mountain jay that argued over his breakfast toast, the snowshoe rabbits along the dark road, their eyes burning like rubies. He lied when they asked about the bears, unable to tell them that those shaggy, overweight, diabetic beasts begging candy and white bread in the ditches were bears.

When Barbara's mother came back on the line, she said, "You know, don't you, that she's taking full custody?"

"Yes," he answered, waiting for the rest that her voice implied.

"And you're to have no visitation rights. None at all."

"No. No. I didn't know that."

"In fact, she told me pointedly not to let you talk to them, but I think she's wrong. Not just about this, but about the whole thing. She always did have a head of her own . . ."

"Thank you, Mother MacLane. Kiss the girls for me, good-bye, and thank you."

As he hung up, he thought of the ten years he had refused to call her Mother MacLane, and now he was sorry. Only one of many misjudgements and mistakes. When he took off the heavy jacket, too warm now as the mountain sun pierced the shade around the outdoor telephone booths, he noticed his frozen breath on the collar, melting, droplets skipping down the hard, greasy fluff, and he decided he wouldn't have that morning drink, decided he would fish his way back to the cabin. Getting drunk seemed inappropriate somehow.

There wasn't much action on the North Fork, but he didn't much care. Except for one bad moment, just standing in the river's cool rush as the sun inched overhead, casting bright flakes among the riffles, and working his fly rod awkwardly after all the years away, was quite enough. The bad moment came in the brightness of noon as he thought he saw a bloated body flash by his thigh—a logger from Columbia Falls had gone under a logjam with a rubber raft a week earlier and had not yet been found—but it was only the sunlight and a large piece of plastic sheeting, which he carried to the bank, amazed at the tricks light and water could play. The few trout he landed he released despite his firm conviction that men who put fish through the terror of being hooked and released for sport, who spoke glibly about the nobility of the struggle without the decency to eat what they caught, were fools trying desperately to give meaning where none was ever intended. And so he fished out the heart of the day, occasionally resting on a rocky spit or on a huge fir uprooted by the spring runoff and laid out, still fresh and green, as the waters receded. When the sun approached the mountains in the west and long dark shadows crept across the river, he kept the last four trout, cleaned them for supper, then splashed slowly through the shallows and up the bank to the pickup.

Just before dark, as the western sky flooded red with the sun's last fires and the snowshoe rabbits moved out on the dirt road to catch his headlights in their odd red eyes, while he thought of his daughters' sleeping faces and bedtime breaths warm with toothpaste and youth, one rabbit vaulted the berm, darted in front of the pickup, stopped for a moment's indecision, then dashed back to the left, the direction of Burke's swerve. He felt the slight thump as the left rear tire rolled over the small body.

He would never know if he stopped so quickly out of mercy or sheer fatigue, for the sudden weight of his life settled in his guts and stole the strength from his thighs. There might be something he could do. As he walked back in the dusk, he saw the mountains, rounded heaps, black against the flaming sky, saw the first stars in the east pierce the blue that would soon be blackness, saw the spires of an old burned-over forest, charcoaled snags jutting high above the thick, solid new growth of pine, and he saw the rabbit, crawling in a frenzied circle about his crushed hind legs, front paws scratching the hardpan, and crying in a small, painful wheeze.

The soft furry body, warm in his hand when he picked it up, turned hard, fought as if it possessed talon, sharp teeth and claw, struggled as if it intended to live. There must be something he could do. But the sure knowledge, the vision of the wounded dying, swept over him, and he chose a large rock embedded in the berm, intending to do all he could.

He grasped the rabbit above the hips, his hand hard, squeezing soft belly, and he raised his arm, stretched it up into the red sky, thinking, *Everything wants to live*, and the tired weight in his guts rushed up through his choked throat, flooded his arm, and he swung the rabbit's head down against the rock, hard and fast, thinking, *Everything must die*.

After the last kick and quiver, he threw the body up and over the nearest trees, not wanting to see it rotting on the road day after day. The body spun in a slow circle, ears back and legs flung out, and hesitated at the top of the arc, framed between two snags, dark, the red eye black against the fiery sky. Before it could fall, he turned and walked quickly back toward his pickup and the single burning tail light, the legs of his cold, wet pants wringing against his shins.

1971

The Philanderer

Duane Douglas had this thing about touching women. None of your furtive grasping at the softness shrouded in cloth and no quick feels copped in a crowded bar, not at all. He needed the real thing, and for him that thing was his slim hand cupped over the uncluttered smoothness of a female crotch, gently pressed there for a long still moment, then his long middle finger dividing hair and flesh like a scalpel, his finger into that open wound, warm and grainy and wet and by god sometimes so much like an opening into the viscera that he could feel the very blood of a woman ticking around his finger. That was real, that was touching. All the curious and careless business of seduction was directed at that moment: all the rest was fluff and nonsense, unimportant in the glory and wonder of that moment. My god a woman had allowed his nicely manicured but quite ordinary finger into her body. What an act of absolute faith! And in a way that the following act never did—not even when it resulted in conception—his finger in that pulsing secret place affirmed his belief in life in all its wonder.

But his two brief marriages had taught him that living with a woman complicated the touching. At first he had thought it wonderful, his own private woman to love and touch whenever he pleased. But it didn't work that way. His wives didn't take to being touched while they were washing dishes or trying to sweep, or if they took to it, they misunderstood, and would both say, in identical voices, "Oh Duane—not now honey." So he gave up marriage in his early twenties, took up his quest, to dangle after women, a pickpocket, cutpurse knave. At first he was wildly successful because almost any woman would do—old, young, fat, slim, pretty, foul—and could do, but then he began to seek out those who could appreciate the touch, stolen perhaps as they drove or danced or passed in crowded hallways. Sometimes he even feigned drunkenness, then resigned impotence, releasing his finger to rape and pillage until the woman screamed for mercy. Then he would smile and begin again.

He knew of course that he was limited in his response to women and he accepted it as his burden. He knew too that he was a pervert, but a gleeful and harmless pervert who never confessed his secret. He wasn't ashamed, he never hurt anybody, really. In fact he was reputed among the bored housewives and lazy secretaries and tired barmaids around town as a kind and generous lover, always willing to give of himself. So he thought of himself as happy, his perversion as harmless as private nose-picking or secret toilet paper examinations. And his job was perfect for his work: he sold real estate, residential, and was privy to separations, divorces, and new women entering his domain. At least once a week he returned to his apartment, the fragrant remains of a conquest blessing his finger, and he would sniff in the privacy of his own solitary bed his consecrated finger, thinking, My god, who could ask for anything more? Then he would fall asleep, the deep dreamless sleep of the innocent redeemed.

Then in the summer of his thirty-fifth year he fell in love, hopelessly, recklessly in love with a married woman, a prim and religious woman who would no more let him touch her there than she would a snake.

Her name, like her face and her body and her husband and her life and her taste in furniture, was uncommonly dull: Mary Brown. But he thought her perhaps the horniest woman he had ever met, so horny she must squeak quietly as she walked, must hum when standing still. To be near her was like holding an acetylene torch close to his face, a hissing blue-white flame, fierce in its absolute control; and he thought that to touch her there would send her flying out of bed like a sky rocket sweeping into the heavens, trailing sparks and laughter behind. She carried the burden of her unsatisfied, perhaps unthought, certainly unthinkable, desires with an iron will, a wild faith that she would never succumb to temptation. But beneath the flesh so rigidly held, her very cells swarmed in despair like ants before a summer shower.

When they came into his office, Duane could see even across his office in the blinding summer sunshine that the husband was weak. A gentle man perhaps, but weak. His red hair was pink, his handshake flimsy, his pale cheeks so obviously vulnerable that he should have hidden them behind a beard. And Mary Brown looked as ordinary as her husband did weak. My god who would have thought. . . . Her handshake was brief, firm and dry, but Duane jerked inside as if he had been touched by a hot wire. His knees nearly buckled beneath him, forcing him to kneel before her. Who would have thought just looking. . . . She had a square stubby face with full lips that she kept pursed and large dark eyes, which were usually downcast, but which seemed to pierce Duane's very being with their hunger during the spare moment she allowed him to look into them. Her body might have been voluptuous except for the hold she kept upon it. All in all, a quite ordinary woman, but Duane stepped back from her in awe and confusion. When he went to the back of the office for soft drinks, he sniffed his damp palm, smelled her upon him, dry and hot like a desert wind, and he knew that this was the woman, that when he touched her he would ejaculate with religious joy, know love and hungers he had only dreamt of before.

After they had made an appointment to meet, Duane tried to shake hands with Mary Brown again, but she ignored his hand, and when they were gone, he checked her chair to see if it had been scorched by her passing, and it was all he could do to keep from kneeling and pressing his lips to the still-dimpled vinyl seat. Faint with passion he whispered her name softly, endlessly as the afternoon sun fogged his office in glorious light.

So he gave them half of July and all of August, seeking the perfect house for them, then sold them the house he knew they would buy from the beginning. After the closing he took them to dinner; they ordered the cheapest steaks and refused his celebratory drinks—he for medical reasons, she for religious—but he did manage to press a small glass of wine on Mary, which she touched occasionally with her taut lips. During the dinner Duane found new details with which to be obsessed: her lower lip, plump for a second with the stain of wine, tantalizingly sensuous, and her tiny translucent teeth, and her breasts that must be as firm as apples. He gloried in the newness of these things; this time he would, could, must love the whole woman. But still he thought mainly of the first secret touch.

Mary and her husband ate quickly, as if food were unimportant, then left, walking directly out of the chic restaurant as if they had looked over the menu and found it much too expensive. Mary sliced through the crowded tables without a glance in any direction, single-mindedly on her way out, her purse clasped before her, her husband bobbing adrift in her sturdy wake. That night Duane really got drunk, something he seldom did, and when he got to the apartment of the middle-aged divorcee he had picked up, he didn't have to feign impotence: his disinterest ran deep and final.

So he forced himself on Mary's husband, forced himself to like the fellow, to interest him in golf, which he played like a sick child, and in fishing trips into the nearby mountains, which the husband seemed to barely endure except for those moments when a blind or dim-witted trout would stumble into his fly. Duane shopped where Mary shopped on the off chance that he might meet her, and when he did, she seldom chatted longer than hello and good-bye. He even began to attend church with them, twice, sometimes three times a week, but nothing came of it. Not once during all this time did Mary in even the slightest way suggest that she knew about either of their insane desires, not once did he see the Browns touch in any way that might even begin to suggest that they were any more intimate than two stones resting on the same hillside, and not once did Duane try to force the necessary and accidental touching. Of course there were accidents, their shoulders brushing in hallways, his hand once cupping her hard elbow as he helped her into the car, once their fingers meeting behind a hymnal for all too brief seconds. And each time they touched, Duane tried to make something out of it, goading himself, picking at the fresh scab of this strange and frightening love that engaged his whole body, his whole life, but Mary seemed to remain ignorant of his love, so unaware of him that he felt as if he should reintroduce himself each time they met. Soon, he thought he might die, or do something foolish like rape her then kill himself, something, anything, my god anything.

His life fell into disorder: he sold houses halfheartedly, pursued women without ardor, felt his fingers grow stale with disuse. At night he would wake, his sheets damp and twisted as if he had been dreaming of tortures, some sexual inquisition, wake with his lungs stretched and aching, his penis as taut with desire, as hard as Mary's will to resist. Twice he had wet dreams about Mary, and when he woke from them, he tried to recapture the dreams, but they remained vague, distant, like clouds blanched with lightning locked on the far side of the mountains, lightning whose thunder did not reach his ears. And he would lie awake all night among his destroyed bedclothes, plotting: kill the husband, kidnap Mary and hide her in his ski cabin; or confess his love and need while she kissed away his hot tears, then fell into his hands like an apple after the first hard frost; or he would marry her, fulfill her unspoken desires forever. That was it, he would confess his love and ask her to marry him. He would ask for everything and take whatever he could get.

So in early autumn he drove them into the mountains to see the aspen, to confess.

After the first hard frost he took them up into a narrow mountain valley where a small creek murmured down from a tiny lake, a creek he knew had just been stocked for the last time that year. As usual Mary sat in the backseat with a magazine, silent as a stone, and her husband sat beside Duane trying to make polite conversation but failing to make even as much noise as the car's slipstream, so Duane carried it all, talking lightly of beauty and natural peace. At the creek he convinced the husband to fish for just a bit, to wet a line, nothing more, as they stood under the vaulted blue sky that rose from the mountain pillars, a clear and precise blue as transparent as water. And when her husband caught three small trout in five minutes, Duane got his fly rod out of the trunk, told him to head downstream and he would head up, and Mary could wait in the car while they fished for a short hour. Mary glanced up, nodded silently, the tip of her tongue parting for a moment those prim lips, her eyes in the shadow of the backseat as dark as eternal night.

Duane walked upstream without looking back, went fifty yards or so, and hid in a willow clump for fifteen minutes, panting like a wounded animal, then he snapped the tip off his best bamboo rod, making that sacrifice, then hustled back toward the car and Mary. Whatever happened, she would know of his love this day.

As he walked he dreamed: she would be waiting, standing in the clear cold water, her dress bundled to her waist, her thighs stone hard as they parted the rushing waters, her taut breasts bared to the mountain sun, fallen aspen leaves swirling about her like a golden offering, and she would smile at him, sleepily like a woman fresh from her morning bed, walk to him out of the water, her eyes soft now and dreaming, and he would finally kneel before her, lick the water from her legs, the silver drops from her black bushy hair, he would love her until her tortured flesh stopped screaming, and afterward in their peace she would lie naked on the stones warmed by the sun, her flesh made flesh again, his flesh made whole.

And as he dreamed Duane Douglas finally began to understand his loneliness, to see how he had harmed himself all these years, denied himself life. Whatever that anything more was that he wondered who could need, he knew he wanted it. He paused, listening to the creek patter in the riffles and the deep silence where it pooled, listened to the breeze among the aspen, smelled the pine pitch in the warm fall air, smelled the sunny rocks along the creek, and finally saw how lovely the golden cycle of the aspen, deep gold against the black pine slopes, saw how white and pure brightly cold the early snow packed against the gray mountain peaks, and felt within his own chest this new love for this woman, this life, himself.

But Mary was sitting like a rock in the backseat of his dusty car, the magazine limp in her hands, and when she saw him coming back, she started from the car, stood and faced him, her eyes bright with tears, her arms under her breasts, neither offering nor clutching nor defending them, but holding them in that sensible way women have of being women, and he knew he was lost.

"Mr. Douglas," she said in a voice firm but full of plea.

And his heart fell through that sudden wound in his chest, that bloody gash wherein his hand would seek the tick of his own blood forever. He knew she would say *This is my life and my husband which I have chosen to cleave unto against all temptation so please get away.*

Before she could say anything more than his name, he asked after her husband, then unjointed his broken fly rod and walked off downstream to bring her husband back to her. On the drive out of the mountains back down to the broad and endless plain, Duane spoke lightly of meaningless things, but not his thing about touching women which had fallen from him like a dead leaf. He dropped them at home, then drove aimlessly through the autumn afternoon, whispering her name, remembering the touch of her fingers by god touching his.

1972

Good-bye Cruel World

Standing before the three slim stained-glass panels of Kenneth's door always made Barbara feel vaguely religious, though she hadn't been in a church in years. Even in her anger earlier, she had not been able to slam it behind her, and now she tapped upon it timidly, a sinner begging forgiveness. After the third knock, she waited, her hand poised in the soft cloud of colored light, then tried the door. It opened, swinging back slowly, the translucent glass fading, as dull and leaden as a shadow.

"Kenneth," she said meekly as she wiped off the polished brass doorknob with her brown woolen scarf. "Kenneth?"

But the living room was empty. The fire still crackled happily in the stone fireplace and his reading chair, a large leather rocker, tipped slowly back and forth in a circle of light, as if he had just risen to greet her. She heard the kitten scuffling in the single bedroom and thinking Kenneth there she called his name once more, louder but more hesitantly. When no answer came, she decided he had gone for a late stroll through the dank winter night, and she stepped carefully on into the small room, slipping out of her coat.

If this were a movie, she thought, her square, patient hands resting on the back of the rocker, a cigarette would be burning, its long ash drooping sullenly into the heavy red ashtray on the table beside the chair. But Kenneth, unlike her, never smoked. Or let three martinis loosen his tongue to babble foolishness, as it seemed she had earlier. Barbara had grown up watching her mother pointing out a sign behind her bar to talkative drunks: *Be sure brain is engaged be-*

fore putting mouth in gear. Naturally reticent, she had taken the advice to heart so thoroughly that even Kenneth, who was not disposed to be kind in his anger, had wondered aloud what had come over her.

But what had she really said? Almost nothing until she had devoured three drinks with quick, nervously constant sips. Even then, still almost nothing at all: polite nods, murmured agreements. Until faced with a tall, elegant, middle-aged woman in a long dress, who made Barbara feel especially servile and who turned out to be the hostess and the president of the local symphony society. When she asked if Barbara liked the concert, Barbara felt as if she had been ordered to answer. Too quickly she said:

"Yes. Very, very much. But not as much as the Rachmaninoff last month. Wasn't he thrilling? The Bach was wonderful but so . . . so disjointed, jumpy. YaknowwhatImean?"

The woman had raised her eyebrows, almost as if peering down at Barbara through a lorgnette, answered, "Of course," then politely excused herself. Shortly afterward Kenneth appeared with the brown camel-hair coat he had bought to go with her outfit and they left.

"But that's no reason to call me dumb. Or let that old woman call me 'dear child' as if I were a half-wit," she whispered to the wall of books over his desk, the books whose knowledge seemed as heavy and immovable as the round stones of the fireplace.

But he hadn't called her dumb. She had chosen to take it that way when he had said that the admission of ignorance was the first step to true knowledge and wisdom. She was willing to admit her poor education, her complete lack of knowledge about any world that was not bound by the fly-specked windows of truck stops, where she began hopping tables at fourteen, or inside the soft-lit caverns of cocktail lounges, to which she had moved at twenty-one. But she was not dumb. For ten years she had served the great male public and she had never been fired, had never made a fool of herself over a married man, and had not become hardened by the life. She understood exactly the nature and extent of her accomplishment, understood things Kenneth did not: why he needed her; how and when he would discard her like an old dishrag. Just as long as he did not beat her or try to humiliate her, she was willing to be the rough diamond he had to polish to believe that he, the son of a Des Moines truck driver, had achieved a brilliant luster. She would take what he had to offer; all of it.

A good student, she listened when he said learning comes from a dialogue, and when he repeated his line about ignorance, knowledge and wisdom, she tried to tell him about the years she had listened to men preface their remarks with *Well, I don't know*, then proceed to speak as if they did. When she turned from the fireplace to face him, he sat smugly in his chair, his knees crossed, his hands cradling a pottery mug, a slight smile touching his mouth.

"You don't have to be defensive with me," he had said.

If he hadn't been the only man in years who had been nice to her, she could have hated him, but as it was she was only hurt and angry, ashamed of the hot tears springing from her eyes.

But where *was* he now?

Briefly wondering if it was already over, if her apology would be insufficient, she started as a log cracked and an orange ember arched across the room. Quickly she moved to nudge it off the red rug with the toe of her beige shoe, then closed the metal curtains of the firescreen. How unlike him to leave the house without closing the screen; how unlike her to hope he had forgotten it because he missed her.

Folding herself into his chair, she rattled in her purse for her cigarettes, which were wrapped in a sheet of paper bound by a rubber band. Kenneth was helping her quit. She rolled the rubber band off the pack and let it pop onto the rug. From the shadow under the desk, the kitten pounced at it, killing it with a quick shake, while Barbara silently cursed him for scaring her. Without noting either the time or place of the cigarette or how much she needed it on a scale of one to ten, she crumpled the paper in her hand—she intended to quit quitting; at least she could kill herself slowly if she wanted to—then tossed the balled paper to the kitten. He ignored it, content with the rubbery squeaks of his chewing.

After lighting the cigarette she tossed the pack on the table, meaning to pick up the paper, not to keep, but to keep his place tidy, then the kitten, bored with his rubber band, leaped upon her lap. She moved to brush him off, as Kenneth had told her to do so the kitten would learn that people weren't meant to climb on; instead, for the same reason she let the paper stay on the floor, she gathered the small gray kitten between her hands, stroking his downy fur. As if he understood their sinful arrangement, the kitten responded by licking the inside of her wrist. The slow, careful stroke of his grainy tongue on her skin soothed her oddly and she stretched, much as the kitten might have, slipping out of her shoes.

Midway into a doze she wished she had stoked the fire before sitting down, wished they had made love before the Bach concert, then reached aimlessly for her cigarettes but picked up the pottery mug beside the ashtray instead. Still warm, she noted without thinking, raising it to her lips. The rich, pungent odor of B&B wafted off the coffee and sat her straight up in the chair. Frightened, the kitten leapt off her lap, his claws leaving tiny dimples in the soft brown wool of her dress, then he raced toward the dark bedroom, disappeared through the door with a flip of his stiff, upraised tail.

She sipped the coffee then shook her head. A drink like that would stone crows flying over it. He never mixed drunks like that.

Never. Maybe he really had been upset. What had he said? Something like: "You just can't believe that I need you, can you? You have such a debased opinion of yourself that you can't believe I really need you . . . " Then he had gone on about how he wanted her to be his equal, intellectually, before he asked her to marry him. As usual she dismissed that with a stubborn shake of her head; so hard that her dark brown hair fell across her face, a strand sticking to the corner of her mouth. Nearly, perhaps if she hadn't been crying, she nearly told him to stop feeling guilty for using her—my god, she had been used badly before and could stand his use—to grow up and stop talking about marriage; but when she turned, he wore his superior smile and cocked his head like a very bright child; so she mocked his smile, then headed for the door.

But he had said something more as she was closing it. If she had only slammed it, she would not have heard.

"Barbara, don't leave me. I can't live without you. I just can't."

Perhaps she only imagined that his voice broke, but it sounded as if he might be crying.

Can't live without you.

So much foolishness. She had not driven all the way back across town from the parking lot of the lounge where she tended bar just to hunt the cold, wet night for him on the slight chance that he might do something foolish. Not about to. She hadn't even thought about it until now. Quietly she rose, picked up the wet rubber band and the paper, smoothed the crumpled sheet, dutifully recorded the cigarette—11:15 P.M.; Ken's house; an eight, scratched out, replaced by a nine—then folded and bound it tightly around the pack. Then she poked the gray logs of the failing fire and laid two applewood chunks atop them, waiting until the first hypnotic flames curled around them, releasing waves of tart fragrance. She washed his cup, made a fresh pot of coffee for his return, feeling very safe and domestic in his narrow, well-ordered kitchen, much as she did behind her bar among the stacks of shining glasses when the bar was quiet. Thinking she might undress and steal into his bed to warm it, she dried her hands, flipped her long, dark hair over her left shoulder, then reached behind her for the hook-and-eye at her neck. But he might think that . . . think it *pretentious?* No, *presumptuous.* So she let her fingers drift through the sweep of soft hair down across her chest, curling slightly at the curve of her breast. As she touched herself, she nearly started to look for something to read in bed, but no. Besides, he always made her read at the desk, as if she were a naughty schoolgirl kept in after class, saying that she would not concentrate in bed. The truth was, she could not concentrate at the desk; one of her feet always went to sleep.

So she went back to settle into his chair with hot coffee and a *Time* magazine, which he suggested she read each week for ". . . a slightly conservative but faintly reasonable facsimile of the real world." But it never seemed particularly real to her. There was an article about the economy, but she had only a vague idea what an economy might be if it wasn't a twelve-dollar blouse on sale for six. Then the war, which also seemed far away and vague, perhaps because she didn't watch television news. A girlfriend of hers back in Ohio had done some hysterical mourning over a boyfriend who drowned while on leave; one of the cocktail waitresses had lost a husband there, but she didn't seem grieved at all; and occasionally there would be an argument at the bar over the war, and when it got too loud, she enjoyed 86-ing the participants. Certainly she didn't care if Jackie Kennedy wore a bra or if there were cars with pistons that went around instead of up and down. Like the concerts, she tried to make herself interested, with the same lack of success.

And why the hell should she care? Didn't Kenneth always tell her that the trouble with ignorance was that it bred dishonesty? Well, she vowed to be more honest, especially with him, so she put the magazine aside, then turned on the small television he kept on his desk for news and sports and good movies. She found a Western, which he might approve of because it was Italian—she knew because the actors' mouths seemed to be chasing their words—then curled into the chair, her feet beneath her, and worked at her nails with an emery board in long, steady strokes.

Shortly the actors' mouths caught up with their lines and the movie ended, so she ignored the late news, then the announcer announced a classic Czechoslovakian comedy and she remembered that, since they came home from the party early, Kenneth had said they were going to watch it.

But where was he? He never lost track of time and always knew when movies started on television. Once again she rose, shifting aimlessly through the living room, her hands busy at things already neat and orderly. In his typewriter, open on the desk, a sheet of white paper had been rolled halfway in, but she carefully avoided looking at it. He did not like her looking at his work. But it was only three words in the center of the page, so she looked.

Good-bye cruel world, it said.

She didn't have to think where she had last seen that line. In her mother's place, a rickety joint outside St. Clairsville, on a postcard taped to the dusty, flaked mirror behind the bar. Her father had sent the card from California after he had knocked up a Wheeling carhop and run out on both families. On the card was a line drawing of a long, unhappy face sticking out of a toilet bowl, a skinny hand reaching for the handle. "Hope the turd did it," her mother said occasionally. And Kenneth knew about the postcard.

Suddenly frantic that her single chance in this life might be lost, she raced into the neat, tidy kitchen where she had felt so peaceful only minutes before, her breath metered with sobs, her tears flung from her face as she turned and turned. Then into the tiny bathroom where a face much older than she had remembered stared back at her from the mirror with large, frightened eyes, then on through the house . . .

She found him in the bedroom closet, a paisley tie looped over the pipe and under his neck, the kitten curled asleep at his slippered feet. His tongue hung out and his eyes were crossed in a comic facsimile of suicide.

"Whatever took you so long," he said calmly as she began to shake, her arms gathered to her pounding chest. "I thought you'd never see the note, thought you'd never come. I've been standing here so long my feet are killing me." He unwrapped the tie, placing it neatly over a rack.

"Take it easy now," he said, grasping her trembling shoulders. "Take it easy. Everything will be all right."

"Why, why, why . . . " she stammered through teeth tightly clenched against chattering.

"Part of your education," he whispered softly, pulling her toward him, nudging the kitten out of their way. "So you'd understand how much I love you." His voice, so tender it made her shudder, like a moth brushing her face in the darkness, then his mouth, soft against her eyelids, his cheek held closely against her—with these gentle things, he made her momentarily weak, so that she nearly fell against him, but firm and gentle, ever so gently, his hands on her shoulders held her.

Waiting for him to finish rather than resisting, she let the coldness harden inside her.

"I think I've graduated," she said pleasantly when he finally finished comforting her.

Quickly she went back to the living room before he could put his hands or his mouth on her again, slipped into her shoes and coat, picked up her purse and scarf, and stood at the door as he strolled out of the bedroom, the kitten dodging and circling his feet.

"Where are you going now?"

My god, she thought, he's surprised. It wasn't her voice that answered, but it was a voice she recognized that said, "Out."

"It's a hard, cruel world out there, Barbara, and there's so much you need to know," he said around a small, superior smile. "Hard and cold."

Making herself laugh, she opened the door, saying, "Ain't it the truth, Jack. Ain't it the living truth." Then she made herself go out the door, made herself close it ever so gently as the bright cloud of colored light flooded the darkness behind her.

Back at the lounge the night bartender would buy her a drink and listen professionally to her troubles and in her glass the soft lights would twirl and twinkle, icy and distant against the blackness of the night.

1972

Whores

On long summer afternoons when our idle time lay as heavily upon our minds as the torpid South Texas air, often my friend and colleague, Lacy Harris, and I would happen to glance across our narrow office into each other's eyes. Usually we simply stared at each other, like two strangers who have wandered into an empty room at a party, ashamed of solitude amidst mirth, then we turned back to the disorderly stacks of freshman themes, heaped uncorrected upon our desks. Occasionally, though, the stares held; one would shrug, the other suggest a beer, and in silence we would rise and go out, seeking a dark and calm beer joint.

Sometimes French's, a nigger place south of town, where a cool high-yellow bartender, Raoul, let us bask in the breeze of his chatter, as ceaseless and pleasant as the damp draft roaring from the old-fashioned water-cooled window fan. Sometimes the Tropicana to joust with an obtuse pinball machine called the Merry Widow, while off-shift roughnecks slept drunk at the various tables scattered among the fake tropical greenery. Easy afternoons, more pleasant and possible than hiding in the air-conditioned cage of our office, where the silences had no meaning. Dusty air, dark bars. Outside, the sun, white-hot upon the caliche or shell parking lots, reminding us how pleasant the idle afternoon was. Dim bars, cold beers, our mutual silence for company. Harmless.

Or so they'd seem until I'd catch Lacy's hooded blue eyes slipping toward the heated doorway. His wife, Marsha, was already prowling the town like a lost tourist, looking for him in the bars. Almost always she found us. One moment the doorway would be empty, the next a slim shade stood quietly just inside, perhaps a glint of afternoon sunlight off her long blond hair, her dark brown eyes like holes in her face. Somehow I always saw her first. When I said "Lacy," he never moved, so I would walk to Marsha, welcome her with the frightened ebullience of a guilty drunk. She seldom spoke; when she did, in a hushed murmur, too quiet for words. She moved around me to Lacy's side, slipped her hand into the sweaty bend of his elbow, led him away. At the doorway, framed in heated light, his face would turn back to me, an apologetically arched eyebrow raised.

On those rare occasions when she didn't find us, we drank until midnight, but without frenzy or drunkenness, as if the evening were merely the shank of the afternoon. Then I drove Lacy home, let him out in the bright yellow glare of his porch light. As he sauntered up the front walk, his hands cocked in his pockets, his head tilted gently back, his tall frame seemed relaxed, easy. A tuneless whistle, like the repeated fragment of a bird song, warbled around his head as he approached that yellow light. At the steps he'd stop, wave once as if to signal his safe arrival, then go inside the screened porch. Sometimes, glancing over my shoulder as I drove away, I'd see him sitting on the flowered pillows of the porch swing, head down, hands clasped before him, waiting.

On the mornings after, he never spoke of the evenings before, no hangover jokes shared, never hinted of those moments before sleep alone with Marsha in their marriage bed. And on the odd chance that I saw Marsha later, no matter how carefully I searched that lovely, composed face, no matter how hard I peered beneath her careful makeup, I caught no glimpse of anger. Unlike most of my married friends, the Harris' kept their marriage closed from view, as if secrecy were a vow. Aside from her sudden intrusions into our afternoons, his too casual saunter toward the bug light, as casual as a man mounting a gallows, and a single generality he let slip one night—"Never marry a woman you love"—I knew nothing about their marriage.

On rare and infrequent summer afternoons, when the immense boredom that rules my life stroked me like a cat and the heavy stir of desire rose like a sleepy beast within me, when our eyes met, I would say *Mexico*, as if it were a charmed word, and Lacy would grin instead of greeting me with a wry smile, a boy's grin, and I could see his boy's face, damp and red after a basketball game, expectant. On those afternoons, we'd fill a thermos with gin and tonics, climb into my restored 1949 Cadillac, and head for the border, border-town whorehouses, the afternoon promenade of Nuevo Laredo whores coming to work at the Rumba Casino or the Miramar or the Malibu, the Diamond Azul or Papagayo's.

Perhaps it was the gin, or the memory of his single trip to Nuevo Laredo after a state basketball tournament, whatever, he maintained that grin, as he did his silences, all the way across the dry brush country of South Texas, my old Caddy as smooth as a barge cresting the swales. Or perhaps it was the thought of Marsha driving from bar to bar, circling Knight until full dark, then going home without him. He never went intending to partake of the pleasures, just for the parade.

Sometimes it seemed the saddest part, sometimes the most pathetic, sometimes the most exciting: the dreadful normalcy of the giggling girls. Dressed in jeans and men's shirts knotted above their brown dimpled bellies, they carried their working clothes, ruffled froth or slimy satin, draped over their young and tender shoulders. Although they chattered in Spanish, they had the voices of Texas high school girls, the concerns of high school girls. Dreadfully normal, god love them, untouched by their work, innocent until dark.

Occasionally, because I knew the girls more intimately than Lacy—unlike him, I'd never married either the loved or the unloved—I could convince one or two to sit with us a moment before they changed clothes. But not too often. They seemed shy, unprotected out of their whore dresses, like virgins caught naked. If the mood seemed right, the shyness touching instead of posed, I'd have one then, slaking my studied boredom on an afternoon whore as the sun slanted into the empty room. Afterwards, Lacy often said, "I'll have to try that again. Someday." I always answered, as if wives were the antithesis of whores, "You've no need. You've a lovely wife at home." To which he replied, "Yes, that's true. But someday, some summer afternoon, I'll join you . . ." His soft East Texas accent would quaver like a mournful birdcall, and a longing so immense that even I felt it would move over him. Even then I knew he'd want more than money could buy.

Most whores in Nuevo Laredo are carefully cloistered in a section of the city called, appropriately, Boy's Town, a shabby place with raucous bars spaced among the sidewalk cribs, but the better-class whores worked in the clubs we frequented, outside the Boy's Town. By *better-class* I don't mean more practiced, for Mexican whores don't go in for the precision of the Japanese or the studied depravity of the Germans. I mean more expensive, less sullied by the hard life. More often than not, they're just good old working girls, pleasant and unhurried in bed, not greedy, and sometimes willing to have fun, to talk seriously. Many were sold into the business as young girls, many are married, making the most of a bad life. And then there are the rare ones, girls a man can fall in love with, though I never did, never will. Whores help me avoid the complexities of love, for which I am justly grateful. But even I have been tempted by the rare ones. Tempted.

One afternoon in Papagayo's in the blessed stillness after the parade—the waterfall silent, the jukebox dead—Lacy and I sipped our Tecates. A moist heat had beaten the old air conditioners. Behind the bar one bartender sliced limes so slowly that he seemed hardly to move; the other slept at the end of the bar, his head propped on his upright arm. Lacy's whistle seemed to hover about us like a swarm of gnats. All of us composed, it seemed, for a tropical still life, or the opening act of a Tennessee Williams play. Absolute stasis. And when Elena came in, moving so slowly that she seemed not even to stir the hot air with her passing, she seemed to hold that moment with her lush body. As I turned my head, like some ancient sleepy turtle, she too turned her's toward me. A slack indifferent beauty, eyes always on the verge of sleep, the sort of soft full body over which frenzy would never leap. Otiosity sublime. Surely for a man to come in her would be to come already asleep.

I clicked my Tecate can lightly on the tile bar as she eased past us. The sleeping bartender, knowing my habits, looked up. I nodded, he asked her if she would join us for a drink. Halting like a tanker coming into dock, she nodded too, her eyes closing as she lowered her head. A life of indolence is really a search, I thought, a quest for that perfect place to place one's head, to sleep, to dream . . . but behind me, Lacy whispered, "This one, Walter." So I let her go. Walter

Savage, perfect languor. Habits can be restrained; passions should not.

After the preliminaries, an overpriced weak brandy, an unbargained price—local airmen had ruined the tradition—Lacy left with his prize ship, walking away as casually as he wandered into the force of that yellow porch light, hands pocketed, loafers shuffling, head back, his aimless whistle. But as he held the door for Elena with one hand, the other cradled itself against her ample waist. I meant to warn him, but in the languorous moment all I could think was, "You've a lovely wife at home," and that seemed silly, the effort too much.

They were gone quite a time, longer than his money had purchased, so I knew it had to be an amazing passion, impotence or death. Afternoon slipped into evening, the waterfall began flushing. Two students from the college came timidly in, then left when they recognized me. The girls returned in bright plumage. I took the gaudiest one, ruffled her as best I could, but when I came back, Lacy hadn't returned. The bartender cast me a slimy smile. I drank.

When Lacy finally came back, Papagayo's hummed with all the efficiency of a well-tuned engine, and I would have stayed to watch the dance, but Lacy said, "Let's go."

"Why?" Though I could guess.

Hesitating, unable to meet my eyes, he shook himself as if with anger, a flush troubling his pale face. Then he answered, "I don't want to see her working."

Not just impotence, but love, I thought, wanting to laugh.

More silent than usual on the trip back, he drank beer after beer, staring at the gray asphalt unwinding before us. Outside of Falfurrias, I ventured, "Impotent?" To which he answered, with hesitation, "Yes."

"It happens," I said. "Guilt before the deed. With whores and wives and random pieces . . ."

"Don't," he said, almost pleading.

"Hey, it doesn't matter."

"Yes," he whispered, "I know."

When I dropped him at his house, he said good night, then walked into that yellow haze quickly, as if he had unfinished business.

During the twenty years or so I've been beating love with border-town whoring, I've had it happen to me—drink or boredom or simple grief—and I knew most of the techniques with which whores handled the problem. Those who took simple pride in their work, those honest tradeswomen of the flesh, usually gave the customer his best chance, along with motherly comfort and no advice except to relax. Then they would try to laugh it off. Others, working just for the money and those few natively cruel, would pointedly ignore or even scoff at the flaccid gringo member. Or, as happened to me once, they would act terribly frightened, whimpering as if caged with a snake or a scorpion instead of a useless man, occasionally peeking out of the corners of their sly brown eyes to see if you'd left yet. Whatever the act was meant to do, it did. Perhaps because of my youth, when it happened to me, it kept me away from the whores for months, nearly caused me the grief of marriage with a rather chubby woman who taught Shakespeare very badly.

But Elena did none of those things. She was after all only a child, in spite of that woman's body, so she just started talking aimlessly, in her child's voice, winding her black hair with her fingers. What she did was, of course, more cruel: she talked to him, told him about her life. The dusty adobe on the Sonoran desert, the clutch of too many children, both alive and dead, the vast empty spaces of desert and poverty. When their time was up, he asked if he might pay for more, to which she shrugged, lifted a shoulder, cocked an eye at his member. And she answered, why not, she covered her breasts with a dingy sheet and smiled at him. God knows what she had in mind. When I told her, months later, of his death, she also shrugged at me, slipping into her dress.

Although Lacy and I were both in our thirties and both knew that, except for a miracle, we were going to ease out the rest of our academic careers at South Texas State trying to make them as painless as possible, I accepted my failure more gracefully than he. I'd been born in Knight, still lived in a converted garage behind my parents' house, and I taught because it was a respectable way to waste one's life. Unlike my mother's attachment to morphine and my father's to the American Conservative Party, teaching is respectable. The salary may be insulting, the intellectual rewards negligible, but when I tried doing nothing at all, the boredom drove me to drink. So I teach, my U.T. Ph.D. a ticket to a peaceful life. Eventually, because of the awful laws of attrition, I'll be chairman here, perhaps even a dean, but my ambition is for an untroubled life. And don't suppose that my whoring will ever be considered remiss. No one will ever mention it; it would kill my mother, drive my father insane. Or vice versa, depending on the moment.

But Lacy, like so many bright, energetic young men, once had a future. Articles published in proper journals, one short story in a prestigious quarterly, an eastern degree, that sort of thing. And he came to South Texas State for the money, just for the money. When he came, he thought that, like a boulder tumbling down a hillside, he had only lodged for a moment, a winter's rest perhaps, and when spring came with heavy rains, he would be on his way once again. By the time he realized that no more showers were going to fall, he had been captured by the stillness, the heavy subtropical heat, the endless unchanging days of sun and dust. He hadn't accepted his defeat, but it didn't matter. By the time of this last summer, he had stopped writing letters of inquiry, had ditched his current Blake article, replacing somehow his fiery vision with Elena.

II

They say the second acts of all boring plays take place at parties, where truth looms out of the drunkenness with all the relentless force of a tidal wave. But in Knight the parties were dull, deadly dull, and whatever shouted insults rose above the crowd like clenched fists, whatever wives were hotly fondled by whomever in dark closets or under the fluorescent glare of kitchen lights, were beside the point. The truth lay in the burnished dullness, not in the desperate cries of hands clutching at strangely familiar bodies. The last party at the Harris' seemed no different, perhaps was no different, despite the death of our chairman.

Even Lacy had risen from his torpor long enough to become a bore. Each time he found me near enough to Marsha for her to overhear him, he would remind me loudly of our golf game the next day, suggesting earlier and earlier tee offs. But he had El Papagayo's in mind, not golf. We had been back three or four times in less than a month, more often than was my habit, and his love remained unconsummated. He had passed through acceptance to sorrow to rage, and on quiet midnights in my apartment I had begun to think of Lacy and Marsha abed, he cursing his errant virility, she pliant upon their bed. His untoward passion had begun also to disturb the tranquility of my life, and when he reminded me about our golf game the fifth or sixth time, I answered queruously, "I don't think I'll play tomorrow, I think I'll go to Mexico and get fucked." Then I left him, his stricken face like a painted balloon above the crowd.

It was then I noticed our chairman, a pleasant old gentlemanly widower who asked no more of life than I did, leaving the party. He wore a tweed jacket, as if fall in South Texas were autumn in Ithaca, that smelled slightly of pipe smoke, paper and burning leaves. We chatted a moment, the usual graceful nothing, then bid each other good night. He suffered a coronary thrombosis just off the porch and crawled under the oleander bush at the corner of the Harris' house; slipped away to die, I like to think, without disturbing anyone. The party continued, somewhat relieved by his absence, until those wee dumb hours of the morning. Shortly before noon the next day, Marsha found him as she worked in the flower beds. On his side, his head cradled upon his clenched hands, his knees lifted toward his chest, the rictus of a smile delicate across his stubbled face, the faint stink of decomposition already ripe among the dusty oleander leaves. She brushed bits of grass and dirt from his face as she knelt beside him; she began crying and did not stop.

In an ideal, orderly world, on this day Lacy would have performed his necessary act, a final act of passion before we went home to his mad wife, but the world is neither ideal nor orderly, as the life we forge from the chaos must be. Elena, who was I can attest a very dull girl despite her interesting beauty, decided that day to become interested in Lacy's failure. She no longer babbled about her past but promised to cure his problem, if not with her antics, then surely with a *curanderas* potion. Of course, neither worked, and Lacy's life was complicated for the next month with an infernal dose of diarrhea. Even now, even in my grief, I know he deserved better.

When he returned that night, we both noticed the absence of the porch light. He took it as a favorable omen, I thought it an oversight. Even as I unlocked my apartment door—unlike most folk in Knight, I lock my door; I have a small fortune in medieval tapestries and Chinese porcelain, two original Orozco's—the telephone's shrill cry shattered the night. Lacy.

After the bodies had been disposed of, our chairman's beside his wife, Marsha into a Galveston hospital, instead of driving Lacy back to Knight, I made him stop with me in Houston, not so much to cheer him up as to hold him away from the scene of disaster for a few days. We stayed at the Warwick, drank at the nicest private clubs, where my father's money and name bought us privacy. Finally, on our third night, as we were sipping Scotch at the Coronado Club, our nerves uneasy in their sheaths from seventy-two hours of waking and sleeping drunk, Lacy began to talk, to fill in the gaps, as if by breaking his silence he could restore his shattered life.

His mother, as she often said, had made only one mistake in her life; she'd fallen in love with a Texas man and followed him out of Georgia and into exile in East Texas. In exile her native gentility grew aggressive, proud. No girls in Tyler met her standards, none quite good enough for Lacy, so except for one wild trip after a basketball tournament his senior year, a single fling to the border, Lacy knew nothing of girls. Where he found the courage to remove his clothes before a strange dark woman in a dank cubicle behind the 1-2-3 Club, and how he overcame his disgust long enough to place

his anointed body upon hers, I'll never know. What guilt he suffered, those days he carried himself carefully around Tyler as if a
sudden knock would unman him, he never said. I like to think of
that first time, Lacy's body, lean and as glossily hard as a basketball
court, yet tender, vulnerable with innocence, a tee shirt as white as
his buttocks, flapping as he humped, his wool athletic socks crumpled about his ankles, his soul focused on the dark, puffy belly of a
middle-aged whore with an old-fashioned appendix scar like a gully
up the center of her stomach.

In college, his career as young-man-about-campus kept him so
busy that girls were just another necessary accessory, like his
diamond-chip K.A. pin, his scuffed bucks and chinos with a belt in
the back, and it wasn't until he began graduate school at Duke,
where all the other teaching assistants seemed to have thin, reposed
women at their elbows, that he discovered the absence of women in
his life. He looked over a freshman composition class and mistook
that dark quietness in Marsha Long's wide eyes for intelligence, mistook her silence for repose.

The brief courtship could only be described as whirlwind, the
wind of his stifled passion whirling around her pliant young body.
Surprised that she wasn't virgin, he forgave her nonetheless, then
confessed his single transgression in Mexico. Marsha nodded wisely,
just as she did when he suggested marriage, expecting her to hold
out for magnolia blossoms and fourteen bridesmaids. But she didn't.
They were married by a crossroads justice of the peace on the way
to South Carolina to tell her parents.

They lived on the old family plantation on the Black River in a
columned house right off a postcard, and as he drove up the circular
way, Lacy thought how pleased his mother would be. But inside the
house he found an old woman, perfumed and painted like a crino-
lined doll, who called him by any name but his own and confused

Marsha with her long-dead sister. In Marsha's father's regal face he saw her beauty, larded with bourbon fat. Everywhere he turned, each face—black, white, or white trash—every face on the place had the same long straight nose, the broad mouth, the wide dark eyes. Only the blacks still carried enough viable intelligence in their genes to maintain some semblance of order. Marsha cried ten solid hours their first night, only shaking her head when he inquired as to why. By dawn he expected a black mammy to waddle in from the wings and comfort the both of them, but none came. At breakfast, Marsha had redrawn her face, and stare as he might through his own haggard eyes, he could see neither hint nor sign of whatever endless grief lay beneath her silence.

They left later that morning, since nobody seemed to mind. Mr. Long ran wildly out of the house, spilling whiskey, and Lacy, fearing now for both sanity and life, just drove on. But he heard the shouted, "Congratulations, son." He looked at this mad child, now his wife, seeing her now, dumb, painted, pliant. Perverse marriage vows followed; he made her silence his, vowed to love her.

They were so old, old enough to be her grandparents, they didn't have her until they were in their forties. God knows what her childhood must have been like, locked on a movie set with those mad people, and every face she saw for ten miles in any direction, every club-foot, humpback, gross-eyed genetic disaster, was her face. She thought she was ugly. You know that, ugly. In all the years we were married, I saw her without makeup just twice. Once, when she had the flu so bad that she couldn't even crawl to the mirror. I found her like that, on her goddamned hands and knees, mewling and crying and holding back the vomit with clenched teeth. When I tried to carry her back to bed, she fought me like a madwo . . . fought like a wildcat, hiding her face from me as if she'd die if I saw her. . . . Listen, I shouldn't be here, I should be back in that room, room, shit, cage with her. She needs me, she needed me and I wasn't there . . . And all those niggers in that house, so goddamned servile, so smug butter wouldn't melt in their assholes. Listen, drive me back to Galveston, will you? This isn't helping."

I led him out of the club, holding his elbow as if he were an elderly uncle. And it had helped. In the car he slept, quiet, not mumbling or twisting or springing awake. Slept really for the first time in days. I checked us out of the Warwick, drove us back to Knight on benzedrine—border-town whorehouses are filled with more vices than those of the flesh. When I woke him in front of his house, dawn flushed the unclouded sky as birds chittered in the mimosa trees of his yard. He mumbled a simple thanks, grabbed his grip, and went into this empty house, his toneless whistle faint among bird song. I thought he'd be all right.

III

He seemed all right for the next few months, more silent perhaps, uninterested in afternoons at French's or jousting with the Merry Widow, but accepting his life on its own terms. I hadn't the heart to suggest a trip to Nuevo Laredo, and Lacy didn't invite me to accompany him on the frequent weekends he spent in Galveston. So we began to see less of each other. He had his grief, I had a spurt of ambition and energy that threatened to destroy my wasted life. I handled it, as usual, by spending a great deal of my father's ill-gotten money. Christmas in Puerto Vallarta. An antique Edwardian sofa. Two Yung Cheng saucers in *famille rose* that made my father take notice of me and suggest that I was worse than worthless, expensively worthless. I even gave a party, a Sunday morning champagne breakfast, fresh strawberries, caviar, an excellent brie, and although Lacy didn't come, those good folk who did, didn't make church services that morning, not even that night. For reasons beyond me, I made the mistake of resuming my affair with my chubby Shakespearean cunt, an affair it took me until spring to resign.

Spring in South Texas lacks the verdant burst of those parts of the world that experience winter, lacks even the blatant flowering of the desert, but it has its moments. A gentle mist of yellow falls upon the thorned *huisache*; tiny blossoms, smaller than the hooked thorns of the cat-claws, appear briefly; and the ripe flowers of the prickly pear, like bloody wounds, begin to emerge. And the bluebonnets, sown by a grim and greedy highway department, fill the flat roadside ditches.

On a Sunday when he hadn't gone to visit Marsha, I took Lacy out into the brush country north and east of Alice to show him the small clues of our slight season. But it only works for those who take pride in the narrowness of their vision, who stubbornly resist boredom, whatever the cost. By one o'clock we were drunk in the poolhall in Conception; by three, drinking margaritas at Dutch's across the border in Reynosa; at seven, stumbling into the waterfall hush of Papagayo's in Nuevo Laredo, giggling like schoolboys.

Lacy, standing straight, asked loudly for Elena, but she wasn't working that night, so he collapsed into his chair, morose and silent for the first time that day. I, ever-present nurse and shade, bought him the two most expensive girls in the place, sent him with them to find Elena's room. *Dos mujeres de la noche. Caro.* Where love had failed, some grand perversion might work.

And of course it did. When we met at the dry fountain in the courtyard afterwards, Lacy had a bottle of Carta Blanca in each hand, a whore under each arm, his shirt open to the waist, and a wild grin smack on his face.

"Hey, you old son of a bitch, you set this whole fuckin' thing up, didn't you?"

I smiled in return, trying to look sly, but failing. My eyes wouldn't focus. "I'm responsible," I said. "How was it?"

"Ohhh, shit, wonderful," he said, stumbling sideways, his two ladies holding him up with a patient grace that my father's money hadn't purchased. "Listen," he said to them, "I want you to meet my best friend in the whole damned world, he's a good old boy." He lifted his arm from the right one's red-satin shoulders, gathered me into his fierce grasp. "Stood by me, held me up, laid me down, introduced me to the woman I love . . ."

"We've met," I said, putting my arm around the abandoned whore. Her skin, warm and sweaty from the bed, smelled like all those things that men seek from whores: almonds and limes, dusty nights, cheap gin, anonymous love. I buried my face in her neck, had a moment's vision in which I bought both girls and fled south across the desert toward some other pleasantly idle life, a Yucatan beach, a mountain village, Egypt. But even as it came, it passed like a night wind. Lacy began to shout and shuffle our circle around.

"Ohhhh, what a great fucking night." The girls slipped out of the circle, whores again, leaving the two of us. Lacy hugged me until my breath faltered, repeating, as if it were a litany, "Ol' buddy, ol' buddy, little ol' buddy."

It had been years since I'd been frightened by a man's embrace, or ashamed, or I must add in all honesty, aroused, but Lacy held me with such a fierce love, so much drunken power and love, that I clutched him, hugged him back, and for a few seconds we whirled, stumbling about the dark courtyard. Then—perhaps he thought it a disgusting revelation, perhaps he responded, I'll never know—he flung me from him as if I were a sack of dirty laundry. My knees hit the fountain wall, my head the fountain. As I fell into darkness, I tasted blood in my mouth, dust, and the lovely stink of a whore.

IV

The next morning I woke in the back seat of my car, not a great deal worse for the night. A bit stiff and sore, but no more. Because I am terribly responsible about the way I exhaust my life, I cleaned up, made a thermos of Bloody Marys and went to my office. Lacy was already there.

"Listen," he said as I sat down, "I'm sorry."

"Hey, it doesn't matter."

"I know, I know."

He smiled once, nearly grinned, then raised his hand and left the office, walking with a bounce and energy that I'd never seen, striding as he must have onto the hardwood courts of his youth. I never saw him again.

Elena says he was drunk, but I doubt it. She thinks he was drunk because of the wad of bills he offered her to flee across the border with him, because of the wonderful grin on his face. When I asked her answer, she shrugged, slipping into a yellow frothy dress that gave her skin a touch of jaundice, "*Cansada.*" She held up her ring, not as if it were a trophy, but as if she had been born with it on her finger.

"Did he make it?" I asked.

She shrugged again, not knowing what I meant until I showed her. Then her whore's face brightened, like a cheerleader's welcoming home a winner. "*Bueno*," she said, "*Muy bueno.*"

I tried to excuse her, telling myself that the craft of whoredom is lying; I tried to excuse myself, blaming my grief. But it didn't work. I paid her for another time, and as she slipped out of her yellow dress, she shrugged once again, as if to say *who knows about these gringo men*. Inside her, I slapped her dull face until she cried, until I came.

I don't go back to Nuevo Laredo anymore: I satisfy my needs up or down the border. Of late my needs are fewer. I visit Marsha occasionally. We sit in her room, I talk, she nods over the doll they've given her. Her parents would rather have her back than pay for her keep, so I pay; that is, my father pays. Even in her gray hospital robe, without a trace of makeup left on her face, she is still lovely, so lovely I know why men speak of the face of an angel. She neither ages nor speaks; she rocks, she nods, she clutches her painted doll. I believe she's happy. When I told her about Lacy, just about the accident, not the cause, she smiled, as if she knew he were happy too. I didn't tell her that it took a cutting torch to remove his body from the car.

As they say, the living must live. I don't know. From my parents' house I can hear them living; my mother's television tuned to an afternoon soap opera, the volume all the way up to penetrate her morphine haze; in the kitchen my father is shouting at a congressman over the telephone. I don't know.

I'll marry my chubby Shakespearean, or somebody so much like her that the slight differences won't matter. I'll still go border-town whoring, and it will never occur to her to complain. And we'll avoid children like the plague.

1974

The Things She Cannot Write About, the Reasons Why

*H*ouses. She has a gift for houses, sees what they might be, and beneath her tanned and capable hands, they become what they might be, their possibilities realized. When she house-hunts, which she has done too often to suit her, she stalks the right house, want ads circled, realtors in tow like native bearers, and she follows the scent through dumb houses so badly planned that no matter how large they are they are always crowded and lonely as train stations; through sad houses where small empty rooms have crushed marriages, lives, and joy; through pretentious houses, lovely but sterile, where families had lived as if in a museum display. The excitement of the chase is so intense that her large bowel, usually her most reluctantly functioning organ, pleads to be emptied into the toilets of each new house.

But in the right house, her brain begins to flow. Her eye slices walls away, she thinks colors and drapes, and dark cluttered rooms become light and airy, breathing, laughing, living space. Possibilities shimmer before her like distant mountain vistas. Kitchens organize themselves around her; pots fly to her hands, stoves become submissive. Bathrooms become as gay as nurseries. In the right house, she feels it can be hers and hers alone, a work of love and craft and devotion, a work of living art. So she sets to work, makes that house that might be become, always by herself, alone. Neither of her husbands had helped—the first busy shifting from job to job, the sec-

ond bored with anything except his own painting—and she pre-
ferred her own mistakes to those of over-paid carpenters, lazy
plumbers, and electricians who shocked themselves with their own
incompetence. So she worked at the houses, pausing to bear two
children by each husband, going at birth as she did at her houses,
with honest labor and quiet pride. She could saw a straight line,
build a cabinet with square corners and doors that fit so snugly a
shipbuilder might have made them, and she gave birth quietly, too;
naturally proud, competent. And when two of the four died, leaving
her with a son by each husband, she knew it was not her fault. And
each time the disjointed lives of her husbands forced her to other
towns, other states, other houses, she tried to follow without looking
back, believing in her gift for houses.

As a younger woman, this talent had pleased her, made her confident, but too many times she had settled a house about her, fluffed
her nest, then raised her hands to write, only to find that she was
about to be tugged away from her house as her husbands pursued
their dreams. Too many moves, too many houses, scattered behind
her like lost children. Five or six in Southern California with the
first husband; a lovely brick one in St. Louis where she had met her
second husband; two in Colorado, two in Idaho, one in Oregon, two
in Montana as he drifted west, seeking a clearer light and found ob-
jects with only natural history, seeking the next bend of the river. As
a younger woman, her way with houses had seemed a gift, but now
as she pauses on the bare wooden stairway of this, her last house,
pauses with a cup of coffee in her hand on her way up to write, she
wonders if this gift might be an obsession.

Coffee splashes from her cup onto the sleek varnish of the stairway. Even through the dark stain, the aged yellow of the oak glows
dully. This must be her last house, if only because she has brought
this one the farthest, had rescued it from condemnation, if only be-

cause she will never marry again; she will tenant there young lovers
with soft hands and long hair, but she refuses to marry again. This
will be her last house, alone, in a way the others were not.

But when she thinks of the others, as she bends and wipes up the
coffee with the tail of her shirt, she feels a vague resentment, not
directed at the men who moved her, but toward the people living
there like animals crept in from the cold. She tries not to think of
the houses, but she sees people happy there, laughing, always laughing, children giggling in nurseries, two lovers chuckling with spent
passion, their bodies rosy in the warm light she had arranged for
herself, and in the kitchen meals bursting forth like bouquets of
spring flowers laid for a jolly feast. When she hears the laughter, she
tries not to think of the abandoned houses, but she does, and the
laughter seems that of winter vandals wrecking a summer home.
Her life lies in wreckage behind her, barbarians and vermin inhabit
the ruins, but still she must climb those bare wooden steps, her bare
feet cool against the sleek varnish, but still she is not happy, cannot
write, not even about the houses.

*P*oetry. Poems about poetry bore her to tears.

*L*overs. Although her first husband had her before they were married, had her in the backseats of cars, on living room couches, on the
beach at Newport, when they had their honeymoon night in the hotel room on Catalina Island, she understood that not just passion
made her body shudder when he touched her: she could not stand
his grimy hands upon her flesh, could not bear his skinny flanks, his

blotched buttocks retreating from her as he walked toward the bathroom to wash himself. With some pride, she understood the depth
and nature of her sexual desires because she could sleep with him
for eight long years. No. She slept with him just that once after they
were married; after that she closed her eyes, and whoever entered
her wore the face and hands and body of whomever her romantic
notions had last focused upon. It was best when the man above her
was vague, still unformed in her mind, a cloudy figure, an incor-
poreal shape out of which that distant man she loved could become.
In the vagueness, her longing saw possibilities. And when that was
not enough, she waited until he slept, then she crept into the gay
bathroom to masturbate; she learned to manipulate herself with
competence, without guilt, not thinking the act infidelity, but
necessity.

Only once during either marriage had she been unfaithful, driven
not by desire but pity to allow a pathetic insurance salesman to have
her behind some shrubbery during a party. She let him because he
wept when she laughed at him; she laughed because she was drunk,
and his face clenched itself around his pain, tears leaked from the
cracks. And her only shame was her lack of involvement. She
opened her eyes widely, primed her senses, prepared for passion, but
nothing came. Small things only, details, the clatter of the dry leaves,
the flakes of the brick wall needling her back, her only really good
dress bunched at her waist. Even his tears, hot on her face, were cool
on her bare shoulders. She wanted to slap him for not even baring
her breasts, but he came so quickly, staggering away as if struck,
hobbled by the baggy slacks around his feet, that she could not hit
him. She felt nothing, not even used. Beyond the reach of the lawn
sprinklers, she felt an arid landscape, the desert night, nothing.

Later, despite the force of her memory, she made more of the
moment, sometimes thinking of it as she masturbated. It was not

much, she admitted, but for many years it was all she had. She had other chances, she had a face that men made much of, but she never took them when she was younger. Her second husband, who used her to flush away his frustrations, taught her to keep her eyes open, once had slapped her when she closed them, so she learned to hide behind her open eyes, to imagine him a more gentle lover, imagine no laughter.

After he left, she slept with whoever pleased her and discovered with some pride that she could come with any man who was neither too rough nor stank, and and sometimes even with those, with her eyes open or shut as she pleased. Often, even now as she raises her face toward the second story of her last house, toward the yellow room where she will write, she suspects her passion as she suspects her gift, fears them both forced and mechanical, meaningless, but she consoles herself with the thought that it always feels good, she likes the way she sleeps afterward, and she seldom judges herself. She needs it, she gives and takes it pleasantly. Because she had never tried to write about it, she assumes it not nearly as important as men make out. And it does not make her sad.

*S*leep. Usually she sleeps quickly, easily, and well. But sometimes when she closes her eyes, she feels his hand slap her face, hears his laughter, and she wakes shaking. Her first husband ceased to exist when she left him, but the second ranges through her mind like a wolf, his grinning face outside the dark windows of her house.

*D*reams. She does but seldom remembers.

*S*hit. She tries.

*C*hildren. Bearing children ruined her breasts, left them as empty as an old woman's dugs. The two dead ones left her with bad dreams she cannot remember, the two alive confuse and frighten her. As she climbs the bare wooden steps toward the yellow room where she will write, the smell of their bedrooms greets her. No, not smell or odor or stink, but stench, a stench that only she can smell, the faint odor of a carnivore's lair. As it strikes her in the face, warm and damp perhaps with raw flesh, she wonders why she placed her room upstairs with their bedrooms. She and her current lover sleep downstairs, so there are no extra rooms, no other place. The kitchen commands cooking and eating; the living room, an easy grace so pervasive that when friends visit, they fall among the large pillows and low couches as if never to rise again. So she writes upstairs, among the stench of her sons.

Of late she has been able to accept the fact that she sometimes hates them as she hates their fathers sometimes, for forcing her life, for binding energy and time better spent. And she has gathered courage to admit this much, to love beyond that, and she has carefully explained to both boys how she sometimes feels and why, quietly explained the rules of life in this her last house. She needs time and will take it; they must learn to live with themselves. She admits this truth even to casual friends, but has told no one beyond herself about the stench, the other truth.

The older boy is as sullen and spoiled as his father, as finally lazy, and within his artfully constructed, very hip and aware teenaged pose, he covers his fears with a love of violence that terrifies her.

When first he let his hair grow longer, she was pleased because it fit so neatly into her redecorated life, but then one night she saw him.

Even as a child he had been quiet—intelligence, she thought—and stubborn and violent. Once he set his mind against her, only physical force could move him, and even then he preserved some kernel of stubborn meanness with himself. When struck, he refused to cry, even as a child; when struck, he fought back however he could. But she always thought the best of him, pitied his torn and fatherless life, until she saw him one night after a high school dance when she had driven to pick him up, saw him leaning against a street lamp, alone, away from the boys edging the gaggle of teen-aged girls laughing and flushed after the dance. A cigarette hung from his tight lips, and the smoke furled about his face, pinched and white as a convict's, up through the stiff wings of his straight black hair. He stood alone, one foot propped against the post, his bloody defiance electric about him. As the crowd broke up, one group strolled past him. His foot snaked out, a smaller boy tripped, sprawled upon the gray sidewalk. Her son flipped his hair out of his face, set his feet, and laughed. She thought: a stupid hoodlum, a punk. How? She lay her forehead on her cool wrist.

When he was in the VW bus with her, she tried to be pleasant, asked him if he had had a good time. *Buncha shit.* From, by god, the side of his mouth, where he quickly placed a cigarette, lit it. She did not look at his face in the match's flash. When she touched his shoulder for an instant, she felt the thick muscles like stone: he was already the man he meant to be, he had no other possibilities. She prepared herself to love beyond the hurt, but the glare of headlights, the blue metallic glow of mercury-vapor streetlights, pinched her eyes as she drove home to her last house. When he was a child and tossed off her motherly caress, she assumed a little boy's normal embarrassment, but now she would no more hug him than she would a wounded grizzly bear.

The younger boy demands her touch, her love, too often and too much. When it is not there exactly when he wants it, he runs to his room to sulk, to lick his wounds, and when he sulks the air in her house grows hot and gray like fresh ashes, desert dust. And he looks so much like his father, that despite herself she keeps his curly hair shorn. She cannot remember spoiling him either, but he wills his way right through her with persistence and anger, an intelligence like a knife. She can do nothing with him. When she loves him, his arrogant acceptance dismays her; when she disciplines him, he agrees loudly, then does as he pleases; when she strikes him, he either screams with such horror that she quits, or stands up to her and says, as his damned father has taught, *Oh, the old battered child syndrome, huh?* Then she wants to kill him, and her guilt gives him his way. A tyrant, a petty tyrant as sly as an animal, standing on his father's bowed legs among his Lincoln Logs and clay. And when he is happy, he sings at the top of his voice until she could strangle him.

From her place on the stairs, she can see across the oak floor of the landing into the disorder of his room. He has more Lincoln Logs and Tinker Toys than she ever imagined existed, and with them has constructed his own world, and to get to his bed he travels a mazelike burrow. Down the hall the older boy's spartan room sits like a cell, bare and devoid of decoration. She tacks up posters, pictures of bands or actors he has mentioned in her hearing, or day-glo prints, but they cannot cover the bare spaces of his walls. She touches her hard flat stomach muscles, still slightly sore from her morning exercises, but it seems that there has never been life there. She lifts her foot, moves one step up the stairs.

Sometimes she thinks she loves them only because she had borne them so gracefully, loving the child within that would become her child without, thinking good thoughts as she carried them, bearing them undrugged and awake and happy. They had not been wrenched from her body, but had flowed. And now they were worse than strangers, and both the little bastards loved their absent fathers more than her.

Once on a bright morning, the sun rich in her yellow room, pleased with her new life and forgiving of her old, pleased that both boys seemed willing when she explained the new rules, she tried to write about their births, which she, like her houses, had suffered alone. The doctors and the nurses had been so damned pleased with her, proud of her, and the boys, unlike the two who died, had been so red and healthy, and she had been so brave. A glorious moment earned, and she would write about it, yes, but when she tried, the poem that came was about the death of the aunt who had raised her. A sweet gentle woman so mortified by cancer that she became even uglier than she could bear. Her hair fell out, her flesh retreated before the knives, and when her family came in the hospital room, she yipped like a puppy hit by a car. On that bright morning in the sun, she wrote about the death of her aunt, the stinking room, the wailing, rubber tubes writhing like snakes, and it seemed a good poem, perhaps her best, but for days afterward the sadness cloaked her, a sorrow as hot and dry as desert air.

And then she wrote a poem about birth, titled it *I am the mother of death*; a bad poem that not even her friends would publish.

*H*er body. As she mounts the stairs, the hard new muscle of her legs seems as sturdy and solid as the old brick and wood of this new house, but her breasts are still meager, fleshless sacks hanging off the tough bones of her chest. She must live with that, and the blood flowing from her womb, must live with these wounds as she lives with her past. This will be her last body.

*H*er lover. A man so kind and gentle that she suspects him, sometimes, of deceit and craft, a man younger than she, who must surely turn to a younger woman someday. She will not marry, but fears she may lose him, even though he seems perfectly content to tenant her house for as long as she cares. Only of late has she begun to suspect that he is not very smart, to suspect that he is wiser than she. Her second husband once told her that he had no time for smart wives, but she thought it a lie, thought it her he had no time for, thought . . . So she tries not to think of smart or wise, tries to appreciate everything that can be. She suspects this new man loves her, which she fears, and fears that he does not. When her sons obey him, she trembles, as she does when they do not. He is a tall, graceful man, too much wiser than her, with soft hands, and he smiles kindly when her sons trouble her, smiles and gathers her more closely to his strong chest. A tall, graceful man, but sometimes tenderly awkward with his strength. Sometimes when she is with him, she wonders if her second husband would like him, or want to kill him, and sometimes she hears old laughter baying about the house. He is a lovely young man, and she suspects she loves him, fears she does not. She cannot write about ambiguity, so she does not.

*H*er husbands. She forgets the first, she remembers eight years of cheap houses as cheerfully bright as a maniac's smile, houses that seemed to scream to be allowed to descend back into the ruin from which she had restored them. As she slips into her yellow room, the sun scrambles among the branches of the blue spruce outside her window. A pad of lined yellow paper, cocked at an angle only she knows, awaits her. She closes the door against the present, seals herself within her past. She sits at the desk, sets down her empty cup; her new house breathes softly around her, a bunch of strawflowers rattles. She forgets the first, but the second stays with her.

She had loved him and confessed the need to evacuate her large bowel in new houses, and he laughed at her, each time they went house-hunting, he laughed at her. Once he carried a roll of toilet paper with him, offering it to her at the door of each house. And he hated houses, he used them, defiled them, filled them with his disorderly laughter, then left them. He lurched through her life like a drunk down an alley, dragging her along from house to house, and when he had finally destroyed her last resistance, thoroughly bewildered her, he walked out. The sigh she released filled that house, and even before he had driven away she clutched a pen and a week-old newspaper, began looking for a house in a town she knew she would not live in. But he stuck his head in the front door, shouted *I'll be back*, laughing. She had collapsed into a chair, waited for his return for days, crying until the newspaper in her hands had become wet pulp.

As the sun climbs through the spruce, she still waits. Sunlight fills the yellow room, around her this last house lows like a slow wind, inside her the ache labors to be a poem, her large bowel feels like a hard knotted stick, a spear. She writes one word, *shit*, then presses her cheeks against the smooth page. He is still out there. He will come back.

She could find him, tracking through ruined houses, littered like a den with his debris: whiskey bottles and beer cans, a lumpy mattress on a bare floor, bits of shattered charcoal, paint droppings, splatters, feathery clumps of dust, shards of canvas as dry as dead skin, and perhaps in a corner his furry scat. She could find him, follow his spoor: rage and laughter, the wet smoky smell of burned houses. But if she could write about him, it would be with love.

*D*eath. It tempts her, she suspects it.

. . . so she climbs each day to her yellow room in this her last house, she sits, feels its breath, watches the sun scattered by the spruce. Poems rise in her like gas bubbles; she catches some before they burst, the others drift away to mix with the animal stench of the upstairs, to lurk with the laughter. Divorced from her husbands, from marriage itself, divided from her sons, left only with abandoned houses behind her where vandals creep, she is not sure how many more times she can lie in ruins but she intends to live until she cannot. Her chair creaks, her house breathes as regularly as a sleeping child, the sudden sound of her pen on paper is so much like a child's first cry that she shudders. Among the dark spruce needles the sun is divided, outside her house wild animals pace. To be safe she will give up her new lover. Her large bowel clenches like a fist.

Given a choice, she would climb upon her desk, mount it as if it were a step, curl up there and sleep, but she looks at the smooth sheet of lined yellow paper, as cold as a sheet of ice, and she sees its possibilities. Touches it once with her cheek, writes.

1974

The Real Story

Interview

by Bryan Di Salvatore and Deirdre McNamer
Missoula, Montana, 1985

James Crumley was born in 1939 in Three Rivers, Texas, and grew up in Mathis, thirty-five miles outside Corpus Christi. He attended Georgia Tech for a year on an ROTC scholarship, spent two years in the army (which provided the material for his first novel, an initiation story with no detectives entitled One to Count Cadence, *published in 1969), graduated from Texas A & I and later, the Writers' Workshop in Iowa City. He has taught writing and literature at the University of Montana, University of Arkansas, Colorado State, Reed College, Carnegie-Mellon University in Pittsburgh and at the University of Texas at El Paso.*

Crumley moved to Missoula, Montana, after he finished the writing program at Iowa in 1966 and has tended to return between teaching jobs elsewhere. He lives there now, in the lower Rattlesnake Valley. His eight-by-ten office is attached to his garage and equipped with a good-sized space heater and a porta-potty. His cluttered desk faces south. On it are an IBM Selectric II and typed pages, a two-volume Oxford English Dictionary, *a wooden file basket, a Spanish/English dictionary, an Austin, Texas, city directory for 1975 and a field guide to the birds of Texas.*

The north wall is floor-to-ceiling bookshelves. Among the hundreds of books are The Alexandria Quartet, *a Louis L'Amour,* Fat City, Dog Soldiers *and* Under the Volcano. Women in Love *is next to* Don Quixote *and not far from* The Memoirs of Pancho Villa. *There are also some translations of Crumley's own books:* L'Ultimo Vero Bacio *and* Kerle, Kanonen und Kokain.

From one shelf hangs a plaque from the Private Eye Writers of America, announcing Crumley's nomination for a Shamus Award. The metal shield of the plaque is ripped outward where a .30-30 shell (from Crumley's father's rifle) tore through it. The tiny office holds, in addition, a baseball cap bearing the legend "Space Shuttle Team Member," a can of Iron City World Champion Pirates memorial beer and a framed photo of Crumley with Linda Ronstadt at a publication party for Dancing Bear *at the Pettler and Lieberman bookstore in Los Angeles. Also in the office is a Ruger Mini-14, which Crumley calls "the survivalist rifle of choice," a 6mm Remington rifle and a framed flat of a recent* News-week *cover story which included Crumley and his "surreal version of Montana" in a select crop of the best detective fiction going.*

Crumley is wearing khaki Patagonia shorts and a tee shirt reading "Texas Institute of Letters." He is five-ten and 215 pounds, with a massive chest and a stance left over from his high school and army football days.

It is one of those infinite lavender evenings that Montanans don't like to tell other people about. We pull up chairs around a metal table outside Crumley's office. An ice chest packed with Sol beer is handy by Crumley's right hand.

He smokes Benson and Hedges 100s and speaks in a husky, Texas-accented voice, occasionally breaking into gleeful, high-pitched, almost helpless laughter. A tattoo of a large spider hides near his right underarm. On his left calf is another tattoo, this one newer and brighter. It's a road-runner and its middle finger is raised high.

What about that tattoo, Jim?

The roadrunner? I've had it since some recent times in El Paso. I got a spider under my arm because a friend of mine had a fly under his arm. The guy who did the fly, Little Johnny, got too far into whiskey and amphetamines. Finally he couldn't hold a needle anymore so they recommended this one-legged ex-biker over by Fort Bliss. We became friends. He did the roadrunner because I felt unbalanced with just the spider. Later he goes to jail for arson. You have to edit everything about my mother and drugs.

Right. Where was your mother when you were born?

Three Rivers, Texas. It's west of Corpus Christi where you get out of the black-land plain and into what they call the brush country. The three rivers are the Nueces, the Frio and the Atascosa, and they make the Nueces River. Which is a river that means "nuts." They say it means "pecan," but I know it means "nuts."

My father was an aircraft-maintenance mechanic. Later, he went back to work for the same oil company he worked for before the war and we moved to Mathis. We lived in the servants' quarters behind the big house for six or eight months in a shack while they were building the company house. We lived in that company house until I graduated from high school.

For a time during the war, my father and mother ran a photography studio, taking pictures of World War II guys in uniforms holding me on their laps. There's hundreds of pictures of me in the arms of some drunken sailor—practice pictures to get the guys to relax.

Were you poor, growing up?

I don't think we were really in dire dangerous shit. Especially because, after my father moved to Mathis and got a job, my mother's younger sisters and their husbands came down. And some cousins. So the clan sort of moved parts of itself from central Texas to form this terrible matriarchal clan.

And so there was always family around to take care of you. A very strong sense of family. But it was also very easy to be ostracized from the family. You know, like two or three divorces and you're out.

So are you out?

No. And mostly because of my father. He was what they wanted everybody to be. He didn't drink; he didn't chase women; he never got divorced two or three times. And even though I've done those things, I remind them of him.

What kind of student were you, what kind of kid?

I got straight "A's" in high school, had a 3.5 average as an undergraduate and only two "B's" in graduate school. But in high school I just wanted to be accepted, so I did everything. I was a juvenile delinquent and I was in the bookworm club. I was on the annual staff. We'd hunt lizards at lunch. Throw rocks at 'em, or sewing needles. When I was a kid Mathis was an onion-packing center, so there were a lot of sewing needles you could steal, and onions. Balloon fights were something that Yankees did. We had onion fights.

Mathis was one of those tiny little towns. When I was a kid there were 5,000 people and 3,000 of them were Chicano, but they were called Mexicans then, and a small core of white minority Baptists and Methodists, and a sort of sea of poor people. It was a very suspicious kind of society. You know, once you were accepted it was really friendly and open in a funny kind of way, but that first acceptance was really hard to get.

Were you a reader as a kid?

Yeah. I taught myself to read before I started school. And I grew up with the Hardy Boys, Collier's Encyclopedia, the *Book of Knowledge*. You know . . . whatever. My parents both said I was gonna be smart and so they better start giving me some books, because smart gets you into another kind of world.

And detective books?

Yes. My aunt turned me on to Mickey Spillane. There were all those books and all that fucking adolescent sexuality and all that wonderful violence and moral breadth—a set of moral precepts that seemed flexible—and so I loved him.

I started a novel when I was twelve. It was a Mickey Spillane. It was called *The Brown Case*, as a matter of fact.

And when did you discover serious literature, the classics?

It wasn't until I was in the army that I started turning on to so-called serious novels. I was in an odd kind of outfit and most of the guys had more college than I did. One guy had a B.A. in English from Harvard. There were a whole lot of people who read books and who'd been to decent colleges and so it was OK. There was no stigma attached to getting drunk and talking about novels. I started reading novels and I just went berserk. Read everything wrong for a long time. Read the second-level guys like James Jones and John O'Hara. Years later, I show up in graduate school in Iowa and I've never read any Faulkner or Fitzgerald or anybody. In graduate school there was another attack of berserk when I discovered the first string. The Russians. *Anna Karenina*, *War and Peace*, *The Brothers Karamazov*. My first year in graduate school, in 1964, I was jumping up and down in the snow in the park in Iowa City in my shorts screaming "Hooray for Karamazov!" I discovered that there were novels that were fun, and I discovered there were novels that were magical. . . .

What did you study at Texas A & I, and how did you get from there to graduate school in writing?

I majored in geology and petroleum engineering, physics, education, pre-law, English and then I finally got a degree in history because it's just what I had the most courses in.

It must have been when I was getting out of physics into something else when I met this strange and wonderful friend across the street from me, a guy named MacDuffy. He was an insane redneck from East Texas who'd done essentially the same thing I had in the service, except he'd actually gotten an education, you know. He had really read.

He told me there's this writer coming to campus. I'd written some drunken poetry and I remember going up to this writer, Bill Harrison (who wrote *Rollerball*, the novel and the screenplay) and telling him I had these poems I wanted him to read.

He read those poems and suggested I should read some poems before I tried writing more, so I went home immediately and read the collected Frost and the collected Pound and the collected Dylan Thomas and two awful anthologies of American poetry and wrote some more poems. And he read those and said, "Perhaps you should try fiction." So then I did.

I wrote a story called "Labor Pains," which eventually became *One to Count Cadence*. I wrote another story called "An Ideal Son for the Jenkins Family." It was about a son who comes home from the army and is going back. His mother doesn't want him to and his father ends up hitting him in the head with a sledgehammer, giving him brain damage to keep him home. But it's all accident.

Anyway, Harrison told me I had to become an intellectual. He also showed me that writers didn't have two heads and that they were guys you could have beers with and guys with their own successes in life and their own failures.

Right down the line—the books, their sales and critical response. First, One to Count Cadence.

Cadence got all kinds of strange reviews but not really enough to make it do anything. They printed 17,500 and sold about 10,000. I got a good review in the *New York Times*, then others suggesting that the book should be submitted for psychological analysis and I should be incarcerated. That kind of shit.

It got good play for a first novel. I didn't read it for ten years after it came out.

Then came The Wrong Case.

It got almost no critical response. Very few reviews. A couple of good mentions here and there but "Newgate Calendar" in the *New York Times Book Review* went to a great deal of effort to pan it. Really snotty remarks. "Same old shit," something like that. Which is funny because I always thought of it as an anti-genre novel. It's so goofy and strange. They printed 5,000 and remaindered 2,000.

The Last Good Kiss?

It got a pretty good critical response, including the *Kirkus Reviews*. They were really high on it. For some reason, rock 'n' roll critics like me. I got a good review in *Heavy Metal*, plus a telephone interview.

They printed 9,000 or 10,000 and sold about 5,000 copies.

Dancing Bear?

It got a good response for a genre book. It had two printings, 6,000 and 3,000. It will probably almost sell out. And it went into a Vintage Contemporary Classic and sold 10,000.

You've also been working for years, on and off, on a big non-detective novel set in Texas. Do you think of it as a different kind of effort than your detective books?

Well, the Texas novel has a lot more characters and covers a lot more time, but I don't think it does anything really different. I think what might be wrong with the Texas novel is it's meant to be somewhat political and I don't seem to have much politics left. . . . I don't think it will have a big strong plot line. There are a lot of set pieces that I want to do, and shit, all kinds of goofy things I just want to do.

At one point, I had 800 pages. Now there are about twenty-six pages I put together for a grant I didn't get. But you know, I remember all that stuff; it's all still here.

Sughrue is a character from the Texas book. When I finished *The Last Good Kiss* I had that Sughrue voice rolling and I thought I could step right into the Texas novel with that voice and burn right through it. It turned out not to be true.

I need at least two years to write it. That's a 600–800 page novel. I suspect that I'll need to make enough for two years or so where I don't have to teach or do any screen work unless I want to. Then maybe I'll finish it.

What do you think has held you up?

One of the things is that I think I lost a lot of confidence after *One to Count Cadence*. I had some kind of serious shock in there; I don't know what it was.

I rewrote the first hundred pages of the Texas book so many times it squeaked when you read it. Jesus, was it tight! But I couldn't stand to read it that much. I suspect, looking back, that I was doing right things. But there were a lot of things I needed to know before I wrote this big novel, and I just didn't know them yet.

Meanwhile, you've written detective novels.

Well, with *The Last Good Kiss*, I was getting a lot of attention and I mean I'm getting reviews in the *Atlantic*, shit like that. And so that's when I decided that I'd be happy to do detective novels. Somehow that seems more honest than to do serious novels. Gives you something to say in bars besides that you used to work for the phone company.

And so I had a little of that, and then I decided that oh, Jesus, I can't write another fucking question-and-answer session. Never. And then I wrote *Dancing Bear* under the influence of dire need. Like it was either write that book or go roughneck. That's why it only took a year and a half.

But at the same time, I feel those detective books have done a lot for me. They taught me a lot about writing and I think they stand up fairly well as literature. I think I can say that without having to sound too arrogant.

Here's the big one: What is the difference between "serious" literature and detective literature in general?

Well, okay. Serious fiction is sometimes serious. Detective fiction is sometimes serious, but ofttimes not. Serious fiction, on the other hand, sometimes when it's serious is ludicrous. And detective fiction is never ludicrous when it's trying to be serious.

Okay.

No, that's not right.

It was rolling.

Yeah. Well, when I read a book I can tell if there's somebody back there who has control of the craft and who's serious in intent, even if he's trying to be funny. Then that seems like a writer to me. When there's a guy back there whose craft you can see working all the time, but who's sort of missing something, that's a good hack. And then there are hacks, you know.

Do you get to say what you want to say when you write within the bounds of the genre, or do you feel frustrated?

Well, the only things that I've ever been trouble with my editors about are, uh, the occasional bodily function. But I've never been, you know, stifled. The trouble I have, most of all, is they want me to explain more than I'm willing to. And, you know, I don't want to have everybody in the drawing room at the end.

The only conventions of a detective novel I refuse to fall into are the detective that gets captured and gets away by sheer destiny or nerve or wit; or the detective who fucks the bad girl and she becomes the good girl. You know, I have some semi-respect for the genre; I think I can play against it.

What's the difference between Sughrue and Milo?

Well, Sughrue seems to love what he's doing most of the time but he's kind of mean about it. Sughrue is easier to write but Milo's a nicer guy.

Dancing Bear started off as a Sughrue novel because *The Last Good Kiss* had done so well for me eventually in terms of making a cult following, or whatever it is they call it. But I got halfway into it and it wasn't right, and so I went back and it was really nice to be back in that Milo voice. They're not the same at all. As I hope to prove someday by writing a novel using both voices. They like each other; they know each other.

How has Milo changed during the years between The Wrong Case *and* Dancing Bear?

Well, he's getting older and he's despairing more. It's all catching up with him. I tried using him on the book I'm working on now, and because he's trying to be sober he's a little bit sad. And I don't like that sad turn at the beginning, so I expect I'll give up and use Sughrue. But until I work on it awhile, I won't know.

What about booze? It's important in your books.

It's important in life. It wasn't invented by accident. I've always been a hard drinker. All of my friends seem to be hard drinkers, for the most part. They're all writers and writers seem to drink hard. Sometimes I can write when I've been drinking a bit, but usually after the third beer is when I quit, unless I'm really cooking and if I'm cooking the adrenaline burns up the alcohol just as quick as you put it in. So that's about the extent of drinking and working.

So you're working on a detective novel.

Yeah. It's set in El Paso and it's either called *Soledad City* or *The Mexican Tree Duck*.

Any other projects in the works?

Warner Brothers has an option on *Dancing Bear* and Tim Hunter and I are doing a screenplay.

How do you work? Do you work out plots beforehand?

I know what happens next by writing what happens before. A lot of the early rewriting is not just working on the chapter itself but also finding out what happens next. I sort of write by the seat of my pants. I don't think about what I do much; I think about the characters. The characters are always in my head so it's not like they go into a book and stay there and then pop into another book, changed. They're the same. For me there's a continuum because they're there all the time. There's not a day goes by that I don't think about Milo in some form or another.

You write at night, and have been known to write standing up at the typewriter?

I've never slept well. Not since the Spanish-American War. Sometimes I feel like Alice Roosevelt, who said that nothing important ever happens before two in the afternoon.

Generally, I write at night. Though I have written in the early evening a couple of times. I wrote the middle of *Cadence* in Guadalajara in the summer of '67. I was living with two other couples and a friend of mine in a house. I worked in the early evening in the living room at the mantel over the fireplace while lots of things were going on around me. Polysyllabic poetry and friendly fights and coupling—that sort of thing. I got a lot of work done.

I don't write standing up as much as I used to. It's hard to find something the right height.

Why do you keep coming back to Missoula?

As a general rule, people in Missoula are about as nice as people get. You know, just the general populace. I'm constantly amazed at how nice people are in this town, even though they can't drive worth a shit.

Plus, I like to go out and sit in the country sometimes. Plus, there are more working writers in this town than anyplace in the world, per capita. And working writers are about the only people I can talk to. They're the only people that understand how serious having fun is and how much fun being serious is. David Reisman said that in *The Lonely Crowd*, I think.

I don't know why this town has so many writers. It's at the bottom of an ancient lake bed and writers just like dead, stinky places.

I've had my troubles here but this is where I intend to live as long as I can. Remember that matriarchal crazed clan I used to belong to? It's not that they had a bad idea; it's just that they were crazy people. We in Missoula have a good idea; we're not too crazy and it's a large circle. Just keeps growing and people belong to it that don't even live here anymore. It's like coming home to your family.

Watch much T.V.?

I keep T.V. on all the time. Almost no network T.V. except reruns and the CBS late movie. Sometimes I try to catch "Miami Vice." I watch T.V. when I'm reading. I mostly watch old movies, Australian Rules football, "Golf Tips," "Northwest Logger."

If you were going to reread three books—three favorites—what would they be?

Durrell. *Under the Volcano* and *The Brothers Karamazov*. I read at least 100 books a year, maybe 200. In a week's time, when I'm not writing, I'll go through maybe four or five novels, mostly trash, but not all.

Do you read detective novels?

More than I used to. I wasn't staying away from them deliberately; it's just that so many of them are not very good and so many of them are awful. But there's a lot of good new guys right now: Michael Z. Lewin, K. C. Constantine, Stephen Greenleaf. I also reread Chandler a lot, much more so than Hammett. And although I don't do it much anymore, I've probably been through the Ross MacDonald novels half a dozen times, at least.

Who is your favorite working detective writer?

Me.

Besides you.

Son of a bitch. K. C. Constantine. He does a wonderful job. Anybody who can write books and come up with a title *The Man Who Liked Slow Tomatoes*—there's got to be a book there. He seems to have a sense of decency and justice, without being sober-sided at all. He's got a great wealth of ethnic characters and he does unusual kinds of crimes. He's an original.

He didn't make the Newsweek *detective-writer story, did he?*

No. He should have, but one of the reasons is that he doesn't do interviews and nobody knows who he is but his editor.

What do you like best about what you've written?

I don't know. Some of the stuff about Milo's father, maybe. A guy going around buying the fucking clothes off drunks' backs and shit like that. I can't be a truly bad person if I've actually invented something like that. And in the Sughrue book I mention when his father ties him to the back of the motorcycle and takes him up to see the snow at Estes Park—I kind of like that.

Whatever happened to that long-ago detective novel, The Brown Case? *The one you started when you were twelve?*

I don't know what happened to it. I still remember the first line though. It was something like, "I came back into the office and there was my secretary—naked. And there was a note pinned to her breast and it said: 'Get off the Brown case!' 'What Brown case?' I said."

I think my literary career is summed up in those lines.

Novel Beginnings

The Muddy Fork

If you must go back, go back in November on the windy blue wings of a norther. . . .

Or so Galen Moody always said. Sometimes as if it were a plea and November the safest month in South Texas, sometimes with a curse—*go back, goddamnit, go back*—and once when we were coming down off acid and hunting rattlesnakes in eastern Colorado, he said it with tears rolling down his large face and his giant hands waving before him. *If you must*, he said, *if you must . . . go back*, then wept into his hands.

Trouble was, though, Galen had not spent a November at home since our senior year in high school. He summered there all those years, sucking at the sugar tit of his Daddy's money, but come September, he was gone. Come June, he was broke and back. Unlike Pancho, who never left; unlike me, who stayed away nearly twenty years; unlike Maudie, who came back when it suited her, Galen kept returning like a docile boomerang, kept taking the money, kept paying. But, in spite of what he said, never in November.

Well, this is not November now, but March, and here I am back for the second time in less than a year, and everybody else is gone. The Big House stands alone and empty, except for me, tops the shallow rise south of the Muddy Fork of the Nueces like a forgotten war memorial. At least there was a norther this morning, my first morning back. Maybe Galen would have liked that.

Just after midnight, the Gulf breeze died, wet and warm, in my face, and then the air filled and quivered with mist as the cold front packed the damp before it. The widow's walk and the old canvas chair where I waited were touched with a mighty dew, wet unto dripping. Just before sunrise but after first light, the first chill gusts whispered with a slithering of scaly, lizard-tail leaves through the salt-cedar windbreak, and the single bantam rooster left, one wing drooping from an encounter with a coyote or a fox, lifted his crow toward the murky sky, then had it snatched from his beak as the wind became serious. The abandoned windmill squealed around to face the wind, the ungreased gears screaming as the blades began to spin, the broken rod pumping air. In the Spanish arches across the front porch, untrimmed vines in hanging pots swayed and rustled like dancers in a ghostly promenade. A volley of cold raindrops splattered against the flaking plaster walls, leaving stains like tears on the pages of an old book, then stopped. In the green, scummy water of the half-empty pool, the wind had cornered a batch of floating beer cans, and they tinkled and nodded like a coven of gossips talking about you. The thorns in the prickly pear fence screening two sides of the pool chattered like teeth, and across the concrete pool deck chinaberries, yellow and withered, shot into the pool with soft, puckering splats. A greedy field mouse, who should have been curled warm at home, found himself lifted and blown into the pool. I watched as he swam around and around, his tiny nose tracing a delicate border on the sides of the pool. I watched and wished I had a longer arm, wished I had a gun, wished I had not come.

As the rain began to fall in earnest, somewhere out over the Gulf, the sun cleared the horizon for a moment before the rolling clouds slammed it shut, but in that brief burst of light the earthen scar gleamed among the mesquite down the river where the Army Corps of Engineers meant to dam the Muddy Fork for good, then it too disappeared beyond the cold, slanted rain.

That was enough for me. I retreated into the wild emptiness of the old house, back to Mr. Vernon Moody's rolltop desk, back to capture our pasts before the waters finally rose over the Moody Ranch, and bass fishermen and water-skiers came to frolic over the years.

This is, of course, the end—no, beyond the end, this is the beginning of the reconstruction. I must admit that I do not know where the story begins; this is the first day, and I am back until the story ends no matter where it began.

Begin with the land: South Texas is easy to find. If you have a map, you can see it dangling like a withered dug off the heart of America, a tattered remnant left over from the Mexican War and the grand notion of Manifest Destiny. Without a map, just head for the heartland and wait for a north wind; ride it south until you can smell the warm romance and poverty of Mexico. Before the Chihuahuan desert scrubs crept north into South Texas, carried in the bellies of Spanish stock, aided and abetted by the withering feet of the cyclical droughts, it was a land belly deep in grass; now, except where the brush—the mesquite, *granjeño*, prickly pear, cat's claw, *et al.*—is beat back with root plows and crops, everything wears a thorn. South Texas is hot and damp, like a tidal flat or the bottom of a shallow sea. It is not America at all.

Or begin with the beginning of the ranch: In 1871 the Moody, Delany, and MacSwayne Land and Cattle Company hauled enough pine plank from East Texas to put one hundred sixty thousand acres under fence; it took twenty *vaqueros* thirty-four days to kill all the mustangs on the ranch, the grass meant by God for the mouths of cattle not horses.

Or begin with a list of the names: Judge Smith Moody, Mr. Vernon Moody, Senior and Junior, Mrs. Edna Moody, Mrs. Maribeth (the second Mrs. Vernon Junior) Moody, Galen Moody, and Maudie Mae Moody Theriault Crawford Kinder MacSwayne; Teal and Tike and Booger MacSwayne, Dummy and Hannah MacSwayne, and Pancho MacSwayne; and me, Sonny Sughrue.

Or, better yet, begin at the end: July 4, 197—.

Another time, another place, it might have been a lover's moon, a silver coin in a star-studded reticule, but this is South Texas, summer, a hunter's moon, and the small beasts of the night tread with care. In the low sand hills on the western verge of the Moody Ranch, a coyote howls at the moon as he waits for his mate to push the jackrabbit back through the long circle, and down along the bottoms of the Muddy Fork, an owl, banked on sibilant wings, hoots once, then cocks an eye toward the ground. Not even the snakes sleep in this hot night, and only the feral durocs, who have no enemy but Pancho MacSwayne, root peacefully under the dying live oaks.

In the distance, the growl of a high-powered engine warms the night as Pancho's black Ranchero roars down the county road toward home. A mile or so before the bridge, it stops, idles, the three-quarter-grind cam making the engine chortle like a contented beast. Pancho steps out, but before he can slam his door, a scrap of a Bach fugue escapes across a cotton field. From the toolbox in the bed of the Ranchero, Pancho lifts a grubbing hoe, with which he quickly digs another pothole, his third of the night, in the thin, patched asphalt of the county road. If truth be known, Pancho thinks he owns the road, knows he would blow the bridge over the Muddy Fork if he thought the county would not build a better one to replace it, as the county had done when Mrs. Edna Moody took the old bridge out. He digs the pothole a little deeper, a bit wider, then presses on toward home, driving by moonlight alone down the narrow, flat road.

When the Ranchero drops off the shallow rise and hits the one-lane bridge over the Muddy Fork, gravel scatters, planks rattle, the iron girders squeal. Someday, he thinks, if he hits it fast enough, the bridge will simply give up and fall into the murky waters while he rides on air and momentum to the other side. But tonight the bridge holds one more time, and he has to punch the brakes so hard that the Ranchero fishtails into the turnoff, where he stops, where he always stops.

This time he kills the engine, pops out the tape, opens a fresh longneck Lone Star with his teeth, then steps easily out to stare at the gate. Two stone pillars flank the cattle guard, and between them rises a double arch of two-and-one-half-inch water pipe, the aluminum paint silvery in the moonlight. Between the arches, written in a script of welded chain, it says: MOODY. And from the center of the lower arch, dangling from a chain, hangs an old, worn out rotary bit. When he squints, through his sandy lashes, it could be the head of a deposed king, still crowned, too heavy to blow in the gentle Gulf breeze.

He stretches then walks to the nearest pillar, where he pees, marks his spot like a dog. Then he laughs—what the hell, it is his birthday. Up the rise, the white plaster walls of the Big House glisten like bone. The fire pit is dug, the mesquite sawn, the steer dressed and resting in a trough of sauce—like his father, Dummy, before him, today Pancho will barbecue for the Company picnic. Everything is ready, waiting, but still he does not hurry.

As he shakes the last few drops off his pecker, his fingers feel the dried crust of the woman. He lifts them, sniffs, then grins. He could not pass the oatmeal test tonight, should Maudie take a mind to give it. Then he laughs at the idea of Maudie rushing to the kitchen for a handful of dried oatmeal, then throwing it on his dick to see if any sticks. He thinks again of the woman, then of his wife asleep in her father's house.

When he walks back to lean against the Ranchero, he listens, thinks he can hear the muffled snouts of the pigs rooting. Any other night but tonight, he would strip, butt naked but for a jock, barefoot, carrying nothing but a sharpened persimmon spear, then smear himself with mud from a wallow, and crouch beside a trail, waiting. Sometimes he thinks he is crazy to hunt the pigs, but other times it seems the only fun he has in life. He tosses the empty bottle in the ditch, climbs back into the pickup, opens another, and searches through the tapes until he finds the Brandenburgs. He props his feet in the notch of the open door, gives in to the music.

After three days out on the rig outside of Palacios, waiting while the crews fished for a ballpeen hammer a roughneck worker had accidently kicked in the hole, Pancho was tired. So he stopped at a truck stop in Victoria on the way home.

The waitress was not much to look at—mostly bone and lank hair, scuffed flats and a sickly pink nylon uniform—but neither was Pancho. He was short, five-six, with bowed, runty legs trying to carry the chest and shoulders of a much larger man, and except for a close-cropped fringe of bright red hair from ear to ear, he was bald. His nose did not seem to point the same way as his face and his worn teeth were stained with Copenhagen, but he was the head hog, the number one honcho of Moody Drilling and Production Company. Charlie Dunn up in Austin made his boots, at three hundred dollars a crack, and a Mexican tailor named Galindez down in

Corpus made his western shirts, and he never left the house with less than a thousand cash in his Levi's pocket. So when he looked at the waitress—Mona, her name tag said—she looked back.

Something about the way she worked caught his eye, the calm motion of her hips as she carried four plates of chicken-fried steaks to a table of truckers, the smooth strength of her hand as she poured a steady, glittering stream of sugar from a bent can into a bowl. She carried herself like a much prettier woman, as if she knew her own secret value. And when he asked her what time she got off, she answered "ten" and looked him in the eye. He waited for her.

In the motel room, though, immersed in the seagreen streetlight seeping through the drapes, she seemed all knee and elbow, smelled stale and sour, and even her bush felt like steel wool. He could not get it up no matter how hard he tried.

"Guess you're gonna have to go down on it, lady, just to get it up," he said, and realized that these were the first words spoken in the room.

"Honey," she said, "I don't know you from Adam's off ox."

"Right," he answered as she climbed out of bed to dress. "Sorry."

After they were dressed, he kissed her by way of apology, tender and easy, and her mouth opened under his, and he was enveloped in the flood of her breath, and the smell of worn tile floors and old grease, of bad teeth and long hours afoot, his hands clutched the tired stringy muscles of her arms, worked at the knots in her back. Then he lay her back down on the bed, took off her shoes, and softly rubbed her feet, her aching calves, the backs of her knees, her skinny thighs, and when he kissed her crotch, the hair was soft and wet, like burying his face in warm, dewy Bermuda grass. They made love like old friends, then talked until they went again.

Ah, he thought, resting in her arms, cuddled against her meagre breasts, too often like this. He went looking for a piece of strange and found some kind of love he could not name. To hell with it, he thought, blessed are those nighttime seekers in foreign beds, those ricochet lovers. Poor Herman, the husband horned while he worked morning tower on a drilling rig out by Mission Valley, poor Maudie sleeping home alone. Pancho pressed his lips into the stubble of her armpit, then his tongue. She giggled. They shared a spit-warm beer as they dressed in the dim grotto of the room.

Outside the air-conditioned room, the night struck them hot and damp, and they had to walk across a carpet of suicidal crickets to get to his pickup. They held hands like teenagers as Pancho drove her home to a clapboard house with peeling paint hidden behind a forest of oleanders.

"Is it really your birthday?" she asked, one hand on the door handle.

"Damn straight."

"I don't believe you," she said calmly. "Show me your driver's license."

While she peered at it in the dash lights, Pancho lifted a hundred dollar bill out of his billfold, and when she handed his license back, he tried to slip her the folded bill.

"What's this?" she asked, confused, half-angry.

"Lemme give you a birthday present," he answered lamely, knowing he had already ruined the moment.

"No thanks."

"Please."

She glanced at his face, her eyes damp and hurt.

"Why?"

"A hundred bucks don't mean shit to me," he said, "and I know you can use it." Then he added, "Please. As a favor to me."

"You any kin to that MacSwayne who used to be married to Mary

Helen Heard up here?" she asked, the money still held out in her hand.

"Some," he chuckled.

"You?"

"Me."

"I'll be damned," she said, curling her fingers partially around the money. "Me'n Mary Helen were in the same grade all the way through school. How come you got divorced?"

"She couldn't fuck for shit," Pancho said, and Mona laughed as she closed the bill in her fist.

"See you around," she said, smiling, then she slipped out of the pickup and skipped through the oleander hedge, her pink uniform glowing warmly against the night.

Pancho felt so good on the way home that he was five miles out of Vado on the county road before he remembered to stop to dig a pothole. When he did, the hole was as big around as a truck tire and six inches deep, a real axle breaker. That'll teach the bastards to use my road, he thought as he grinned across the wide, flat fields of milo and cotton toward the brushy smudge that marked the Muddy Fork.

Instead of parking in the driveway, Pancho eased the Ranchero around the rock fence and the curving line of salt cedars to the fire pit behind the Big House. In the bright moonlight, he saw Mr. Vernon Moody—junior, though nobody had called him that in nearly sixty years—sleeping in a lawn chair beneath the huge old live oak, a tree so large that it took three men to reach around the trunk. An uncorked bottle of Jack Daniels, three-quarters empty, rested between the old man's legs.

"Off the wagon, huh," Pancho muttered to himself as he stepped quietly out of the pickup.

Washed in the moonlight, the old man looked dead, but Pancho

did not even bother to check. He was convinced that the old bastard
would live to be a hundred. A hundred, hell, a thousand. The old
man was a tall, rawboned piece of work, dressed as always in the
summer in cavalry-twill khaki pants, a white cotton long-sleeved
shirt with a silk tie hanging loose at the neck, a Panama-styled hat
like a banker's Stetson, and the only pair of lace-up cowboy boots
Pancho had ever seen.

He glanced at the old man once more, then took off his shirt, and
went to work at the pile of mesquite logs, dropping them into the
pit with the same smooth, easy rhythm he had learned by watching
his father, had had to learn watching because his father was deaf and
dumb.

When he finished stacking the pit, Pancho paused to brush the
drops of sweat off his hairy shoulders. As if to compensate for his
bald pate, Pancho's chest, shoulders, and back were covered with a
red furry pelt. It had been a long time since he had been ashamed
of his hairy body, but he still remembered the shame occasionally,
and before he opened another beer, he put his shirt back on. Then
he dumped a gallon of gasoline on the hard wood, stepped back,
popped a kitchen match with his thumbnail, and flipped it toward
the pit.

The gasoline went off with a great, roaring whoosh, flames leap-
ing twenty feet into the air, and it brought Mr. Vernon Moody right
out of his slumbering chair. He caught the open bottle, though, before it hit the ground, and Pancho heard the gurgle and plop as the
old man took a long hit of bourbon.

"Gonna kill yourself, old man," Pancho said.

"Lay off, weevil," the old man answered, then hit the bottle again.
"I'm celebrating."

"Thanks. I didn't know you cared."

"What?"

"Cared enough to celebrate my birthday."

"To hell with your birthday, boy," the old man, growled, "Galen's coming home, my boy's coming home."

"Shit, he's been home for a month—where the hell have you been?"

"No—he's home to stay."

Pancho took a long pause to think about that while he dipped a new pinch of snuff into his lower lip, then he spit a sizzling splat of juice into the fire.

"We don't need no goddamn hippies 'round here," he said finally.

"He's my son," the old man said, "he don't need no reason to be around here. This is his home, boy."

"He ain't no more blood kin than I am, you old bastard."

Mr. Moody tilted the brim of his hat back from his eyes and stared across the fire at Pancho, shook his head, then said, "Someday, boy, you're going to remind me of that one time too many, and I'm going to run your ass off this place."

"You best bring a sack lunch, old man, and a dozen friends, 'cause you'll be at it for a piece of time," Pancho said, then added, "No, I guess since you ain't got no friends, or if you do the old farts are either dead and buried or sitting on a bedpan, you best hire some help."

Mr. Moody sputtered, sipped at the whiskey, then grinned slyly. "Where the hell you been, boy? Maudie Mae cooked up a real big feed for you, boy, and you didn't show up. She is, to say the least, somewhat pissed."

"Don't make a gnat's-ass difference to me," Pancho said, "Besides, she just fixed Mexican food to impress Galen and all his goddamned hippie friends—I didn't want me no hair in my birthday taco . . ."

"Hippie, hippie, hippie," the old man chortled. "Get off my ass. I saw you out by the pool smoking that marijuana cigarette with that big-titted little girl—what the hell is her name anyway?"

"Her name is Purple."

"What?"

"You heard right, old man—Purple—and just 'cause I smoke a little dope with big-titted little girls don't make me a hippie. You're just jealous, that's all."

Mr. Moody shifted in the lawn chair, his bulk making the dowel joints creak, then tilted his hat brim back over his eyes. Pancho tossed the empty bottle into the pit, waited until it popped softly, then went to the cooler for another bottle.

"Mind if I have one of your beers, boy, this expensive whiskey is about to give me the acid indigestion," the old man said quietly. Pancho got two beers, and when he opened them with his teeth, Mr. Moody complained, "Goddammit, boy, you're going to break off a tooth someday doing that."

"Well, don't matter. We got that new company dental insurance, so I'll be covered."

"You know, I'm not convinced we ought to be spending all that money we do on these insurance plans," the old man said, calm now, doing business. "The next time I'm down at the office, I'm going to look at the books on this."

"You ain't been to the office in three, maybe four months, you old bastard, and besides, all this insurance stuff works. Shit, we got a better plan than Mobil or Exxon, and when we get a good hand, we can sometimes keep him even though we have to pay shit for wages." Mr. Moody grumbled a bit, but finally stopped. Then Pancho said, "And speaking of hands—I had to fire that Hartsell boy you made Boomer hire."

"You what?"

"I run the kid off the location."

"Where the hell do you get off firing somebody I hired?"

"Anytime you wanna run this junk-house s.o.b., old man, you just let me know."

"You ought not fired him without asking me, boy, his Daddy and I go way back."

"Listen, I been three days fightin' mosquitos up at Palacios while we were fishin' for a goddamned ballpeen hammer that kid kicked in the hole," Pancho said. "It was supposed to be one day while we ran a sidewall core, not three days fishin' for a goddamned hammer."

"Running whores in Nuevo sounds more like the truth," the old man grunted.

"I figure that hammer only cost us about thirty thousand dollars, give or take a thousand, so I run the kid off."

"Ought to run you off," Mr. Moody said, then shook his head and raised his face into the firelight with a broad grin. "I called the tool pusher on the mobile phone, boy, and he said you left the location about eight o'clock. I've never known it to take you five hours from Palacios to the house, not the way you drive. Shit, you keep that one lawyer working full-time on your speeding tickets."

"Well, I did stop there in Victoria at the truck stop to talk to that waitress . . ."

"The one with that high, hard nigger ass?"

"Other one."

"The skinny one. How was it?" the old man asked, leaning forward in his chair so far that the whiskey flirted with the neck of the bottle.

"We just talked—that's all."

"Talked, my ass . . ." Then Mr. Moody jerked himself erect in the chair as if he had just remembered something very important.

"Goddammit, boy, you are married to my only daughter. Seems to me that you could either keep your pecker in your pants or your mouth shut. I don't know why Maudie Mae puts up with you—shit I don't know why I do."

"Me'n Maudie been married less'n three years, old man, and you and me been runnin' whores since I was a nubbin, and I done seen how you behaved both times you had wives around the house, and hell I seen you sneakin' 'cross the river to shack up with Sonny's Momma way back when, so don't you give me no lectures, you old bastard . . ."

"You think Sonny knows about that," Mr. Moody interrupted seriously. "It sure makes me nervous having him around. What the hell's he doing down here anyway?"

"Well, sure he knows. Hell, he knew at the time," Pancho said, "we used to talk about it all the time—and I don't have no idea what he's doin' down here, except I know that Galen's payin' him a thousand dollars a week just to be here . . ."

(Excuse me a moment, dear reader, indulge me for a bit. Of course, Pancho thought he knew why Galen had hired me. I thought I knew, but that was not the case at all, and I was only getting eight hundred a week to protect Mr. Vernon Moody, even though I still hated the old bastard for fucking my mother way back when. Mud under the bridge, as we used to say as kids, mud under the bridge.)

"Well, I wouldn't miss him if he was gone," Mr. Moody huffed, then settled back into his chair and fell promptly asleep.

"Old farts need naps," Pancho muttered.

In other more exotic places—the south of France, Egypt, southern California—they have names for those hot, irksome, steady winds, those winds that drive men mad, that cause wives, to paraphrase Chandler, to thumb their bread knives and gaze longingly at their husbands' throats. They call them Mistral, Khamsin, or Santa Ana—words that ring off the tongue like a tocsin. But there is no name for the wind in South Texas, the wind that rises off the Gulf each afternoon from February until October, that rises off the sea-foam scum, picks up sand off Padre Island and salt specks off the tidal flats of the Laguna Madre, and blows, a constant, endless abrasion, grinding and scrubbing your skin until your nerves hang from your flesh like withered vines, until your very soul flaps from your body like a sheet hung out to dry. Sometimes they call it the Gulf breeze, this goddamned nameless wind.

Just outside the washhouse, where the dressed steer lies in a trough constructed of two lengthwise halves of an oil drum, Pancho MacSwayne struggles in the false dawn with a portable engine-block hoist. The steer is already spitted on a piece of pipe, and the chain and hook already shoved through a split beside the backbone, but Pancho is drunk, and the hard rubber tires of the hoist seem to turn and lock no matter which way he tries to push across the sidewalk, like a petulant child with a grocery cart. Even when the wheels flip sideways, he shoves harder. Finally, his shirt soaked, he steps back, then walks away. There is still no hurry. He goes back to his pickup for another beer, but instead his hand snakes into the glove box for the vial of crystal. He has managed to leave it alone for nearly a month in spite of the long hours he works, the pressures that strain every summer when Galen comes home, but now he thinks he will not make the day unless he has a line. Very carefully on the small mirror, he chops a healthy line, pausing often to glance at the old man. When he snorts it, the almost pure methamphetamine crystal fills his sinus cavities with fire, as if his face had been cut off with a sword then cauterized with a piece of white-hot angle iron, but he dips a palmful of ice water from the beer cooler and snorts that too. Not that it puts the fire out, but the water banks it for a bit, and after the pain comes the lovely clarity.

He gets another beer, stuffs it in his back pocket without opening it, then goes about his business. He does not fight the hard rubber tires but guides them to his will, hooks the steer to the hoist, then runs the endless chain until the dripping meat lifts clear of the trough. Even with the weight, he glides across the lawn toward the pit, slowly but surely, then positions the spit above the forked poles, and lowers it into place. The electric motor and the long chain are already waiting beside the pit, but after he unhooks the hoist, Pancho takes the spit handle in both hands, and turns and turns, like his father did, watching the sauce and the fat fall sizzling into the fire, little puffs of flame lifting off the coals. He turns and turns and watches the fire, remembering a time before he could remember, feeling his father's hands in the iron handle, softly turning and turning the meat against the fire.

It has been said that on the day he was born, Pancho's father kept turning the spit until the steer was ready to carve before he went down to the board-and-batten shack, down the hill from the Big House where Hannah had just given birth to a boy-child she had already named Francis Troy MacSwayne, after the romantic sergeant in Hardy's *Far from the Madding Crowd*; when Dummy went down, his job on the hill was done.

The birth had been hard, the labor long, and the veterinarian attending had long since shook his head and given both mother and child up for dead. But Hannah was tougher than that and with her own hands she positioned the child and forced it out. The left elbow, though, or the arm—something was dislocated or broken, and the screams of the child could be heard all the way up to the long tables where the employees of the Company sat over pitchers of warm beer waiting for the beef—heard, that is, by all except the father.

When Dummy went down, he only knew the child was crying by the screaming "O" of the mouth, the crooked arm, and those rough, horny hands that coaxed tomatoes the size of oranges and watermelons the size of pigs out of the Moody garden plot, those hands straightened the arm, gently as one might lure a bean vine around a string, and the child stopped crying. They said a hush fell over the tables, that lanky men with white circles from new haircuts above their ears and pale wives, embarrassed under homemade marcels, all fell silent with the knowledge that the child had died, and even the happy booming of Dummy's fists against the shack walls seemed to them the cadence of grief.

When Dummy came back up the hill a few minutes later, his son cradled in his large, rough hands, it was told that all the folks stood and cheered. Everybody except Mr. Vernon Moody and his wife, Edna, victim of four miscarriages already. Mr. Moody sat heavily in his chair, Mrs. Edna Moody took herself to her room, and two weeks later Mr. Vernon Moody went up to the Baptist Orphanage in Waco and brought back a son, whom they called Galen, named after Mrs. Moody's father up in El Dorado, Arkansas. For years it was rumored that Galen was a bastard issue of Mr. Moody's, and like rumors, it never completely died. And, as often happens after an adoption, shortly after Mrs. Edna Moody carried a baby to term, and eighteen months after Pancho and Galen, here came Maudie Mae.

As Pancho turns the smoking steer, he understands, remembers, misunderstands, thinks this is the beginning of the story.

After a bit, he nails the electric motor's base to the ground, hooks up the drive chain to the gear welding on the spit, re-greases the forks, checks everything twice, even the old man sleeping in the chair, then heads toward the Big House. For reasons he refuses to understand, he needs to hug his wife, to fall to his knees and beg her once again for a child. Perhaps he will confess the crystal and the Mexican girlfriend, Rachel, in Vado, who supplies him the speed, perhaps he will finally confess to Maudie that he loves her more than he loves the ranch, perhaps—no, he will not confess the waitress in Victoria, whatever her name was.

The norther has blown itself out quickly. This afternoon when I went out to sit on the roots of the old live oak by the fire pit, the sky was as clear at the whites of a baby's eyes, and light blue, not the blue of the mountain sky in Montana where I call home now, but blue like a pastel wash in the hands of an artist. I watched the sun fall through the spare limbs of the mesquite beyond the pasture and leaned against the old tree. Live oaks lose their hard, glassy leaves in February, and the Bermuda grass under the tree was still littered with the tiny golden fragments. Most of the live oaks in Moody County have died, given way to some alien fungus, but this one lives on.

A hundred years or so ago, somebody, a MacSwayne or a Moody or a random vaquero lodged a board, something like a modern two-by-four, in the crotch of the tree, stuck it there and augered through one end. A place to clean deer, I suppose. Now the tree has grown around the board, and the end with the hole juts out from the rough trunk a full eighteen inches below the crotch. It is as if the live oak has this giant splinter locked in its heart, but the old tree has grown on around it, and when I reach up, hook my fingers about the board, and swing my weight against it, the board does not give, and I lift my feet higher and higher until my arms give out.

1981

from *The Mexican Tree Duck,*
a novel in progress

There was a time. It didn't start with the Vietnam War, and it didn't quit just because we did. Maybe it started with Elvis mumbling jive to Ed Sullivan, and maybe it ended with the Arabs squeezing our nuts at the gas pumps. But somewhere in there, I swear, there was a time when we were free. Our choices were our own, and they seemed important. Black was beautiful, fat was funny, and hairy legs mingled when love was free.

But that was then and this is now. The insidious forces of oppression have taken a form we never would have guessed. In the name of good health, good behavior, and good taste, once again Americans are being taught to behave, to be good little boys and girls. (Even the poor Arabs are discovering that desert sands and oil reserves do not freedom make.) Drugs, sex, rock 'n' roll is no longer the cry of freedom, but just another corporate slogan.

No matter how they tell it, this country was not founded or freed by the well-behaved.

"So fuck that," I shouted at the end of my tirade to my old buddy Solomon Rainbolt as he played out the two-hundred-foot extension cord behind me as I dollied the jukebox out of the back door of the Hole-in-the-Mall Bar through the snow toward the railroad tracks.

"You understand?" I shouted. "You remember?"

"You're just mad," he said as he plugged in the jukebox and I eased the dolly from under it, "for no good reason."

"The world's fucked," I screamed as the jukebox glowed like a spaceship in the softly drifting snow, "and the bastards took Hank Snow off the machine and replaced him with a butch drag queen. You call that no reason?"

"Yes," he answered calmly, then huddled in the lee of the machine. He dumped a pile of crystal into his hand.

"It's gonna blow away," I said.

"I've got plenty," he said, then handed me a glass straw with a fluted end. Never argue with a speed-freak drug lawyer. They have all the answers and most of the drugs.

After we had destroyed a major portion of our mucous membranes and cooled the fire with jolts of Glenmorangie Scotch, Solly gave me a long, thoughtful look.

"You have any idea what the fuck you're doing, Sughrue?" he asked.

"That's not my job," I answered.

Solly and I went way back. All the way to the late sixties with the 1st Cav in the Central Highlands. He'd been a captain then, on his second tour, and I was one of his platoon sergeants on my first. We owed each other.

"You're not a PI anymore, Sughrue. What is your job?"

Solly just sighed and shook his head so slowly that he didn't even disturb the halo of light snow on his bald head. Out in East Meriwether the 3:12 through-freight touched its horn at the crossing. I stood up, counting off the seconds while Solly fingered jazz-piano riffs on his knees. As I thumbed a quarter into the jukebox, Solly rose, his stiff left knee creaking in the cold. He raised his eyebrows.

"Last chance to back down, C.W.," he offered.

"Hey, I didn't get where I am by backing down."

"No shit," he said.

When the giant sparkling light on the engine rolled around the last turn before the straight shot through Meriwether, I punched P-17 on the machine, then followed Solly, limping heavily on his cane, back to the middle of the parking lot to wait.

In my weaker moments, in my cups lamenting lost loves and missed chances, I could stand behind the bar of the Hole long after closing, since I lived in the basement, and listen to Hank Snow sing, "It don't hurt anymore." I could raise my glass to Hank's rasping voice and answer, "It don't hurt any less either." And sometimes the laughter, alone in the bar, was enough. It had been eight years since I had gone looking for anybody, professionally, and I didn't miss it. It wasn't that I quit, but that other people stopped running away, or people stopped looking for them. I never found out which.

At first I worked for Wilbur the Weasel part-time to raise rent money, but by the time he had sold the Hell Roaring Saloon to a group of local developers, who put up a small mall with what passed for a fern bar, Wilbur and I had become partners. And we'd done all right. I didn't have to live in the basement. It was cozy, convenient, close to the job. I didn't even have to tend bar very often. Just when I felt like it. Not a great life but a damn sight better than working as a security guard or a repo man.

So eight years slipped by sort of easy. Then in the late summer before Solly showed up in the fall with five pounds of pure crystal methamphetamine supposedly stolen from a biker gang down in Texas, it all went to hell in just one week.

First thing, The Weasel, whose eyes had for years only brightened at the ringing song of the cash register, fell madly in love with the dumbest and meanest of our cocktail waitresses, Betty Boobs. She looked a lot like The Weasel's wife, Betty Books, except she had tits and claimed to give the best cross-country head in America. Goddamned Wilbur climbed into his Caddy, telling Betty Books that he was on his way to the Betty Ford Rehab Center in Palm Springs to take the cure. When she asked him why he didn't fly, he claimed he was afraid he would show up drunk.

When she finally caught on, Betty Books didn't say a word to anybody. She didn't make a deposit or pay a bill for two weeks, then she cleaned out the account, stuffed the cash into her purse and caught the first flight out of Meriwether heading west. The ticket agent, Mr. Polish Joke, said he heard her muttering something about revenge fucking in the Third World. But Leon was a regular in the Hole, and sometimes regulars made up stories just to have something to talk about. I almost believed him because he seemed hurt that she hadn't asked him along.

"Fucking Polacks," he told me over brandy-rocks. "If we ain't the Third World, I don't know who the fuck is." Then he looked at me as if I knew. "I believe I'll have one of them B-52's," he said, "see if I can get bombed."

"You tell me how to make it, Leon, and I'll tell you how much it costs."

After he told me how to make it, I gave him the first one free. He paid for the next five or six, but I paid for his taxi home and cleaned up the rest room. Chuckling to myself as I mopped, I admit.

Isn't it odd how often the beginning of the end seems comic at first. The next day the bank called me to let me know that all the salary checks were going to bounce. I thought about having a B-52, and when Big Linda, my cocktail waitress for the shift, hit the front door with her check in her hand, I offered to make her one. She told me to piss up a rope after I made her check good out of my pocket, and spent the rest of the afternoon glaring at me.

About three-thirty a woman's fast-pitch softball team from Billings stopped in for a quick beer to celebrate a tournament win. Fifteen pitchers and a quart of tequila later, the third baseman, a stocky girl herself, said something to Big Linda about getting in shape. Big Linda hit her hard enough to make her house plants dizzy.

"You don't pay me enough to put up with this shit!" she screamed at me, then picked up a half-full pitcher off the table, chugged it, and drew back like an outfielder making that long throw to home plate.

"Take it easy," I said. "I talked to Weasel a couple of hours ago, and the check's in the mail."

"And I won't come in your mouth."

"That's not completely true, Linda," I made the mistake of saying.

"This used to be a nice bar," the woman's softball coach said, almost sadly, as she tried to revive her third baseman.

Big Linda sighed, stepped over to the single remaining fern, the only one to survive four long, hard, drunk Montana winters. She jerked the wan fern and its pot out of the macrame berth, then dashed it to the floor. It went off like a grenade.

"Not anymore," she said quietly, then picked up her purse and sailed out of the bar. In the draft of Big Linda's exit, the third baseman muttered softly, wondering what the score was.

Rumor has it that Big Linda was seen that very same evening packing her three children from two marriages into a Falcon station wagon beside two broken television sets, and before good dark she was heading south. Word has it she's either laying bricks or installing cable television in Tucson. I hope somebody's paying her enough to take their shit.

It took an hour, three free rounds of Joe Crow Gold for the softball team, and a long pleading call to Little Linda, the only cocktail wait-

ress I could reach, to make the Hole back into a bar again. Thirty
minutes would have been enough, but Little Linda insisted that I
step over to the boutique next door and pay cash for a really radical
jacket in the window. Radical is right, buckles and straps resplendent on a field of camouflage. A relic from a war we haven't fought
yet. She spent most of her shift turning down the thermostat, ad-
miring herself in the back-bar mirror, and eating animal
tranquilizers.

When Dotty called in drunk, deep in sorrow because her husband's step-grandmother on his step-mother's side had died, I fired
her over the telephone. Then I fired Little Linda when she forgot a
drink order after the third trip back to the table.

"And leave the fucking jacket," I shouted as she flew out the door.

"It's too young for you, Sughrue," she smirked over her shoulder.

The next day, still bombed, Little Linda joined the Air Force,
they say, and became a national-security problem instead of mine.

Rather than run the bar by myself, I thought about closing it, but
cracked a bottle of single-malt Scotch instead, and bought the house
a round, too.

Before sundown, the last flat rays of golden light flooding the bar,
things had gotten out of hand. A gypo-logger with a broken arm
kept trying to get a lady insurance agent with a broken leg into the
men's john. She maintained that the only comfortable way was leaning over the pool table. Everybody was so drunk off the free rounds
that nobody might have noticed, but I felt some obligation to civilized behavior.

"At least wait till it's dark, Doris," I suggested.

It seemed to make some sense to her, so she jerked the logger up
by his bad arm and dragged him into the men's can. The lovers
slipped my mind for a bit, then I saw them sneaking out the back
door. When I checked the men's, I found the remains of the toilet,

a heap of porcelain shards, sitting in a fountain of water. In the parking lot, I found the crippled lovers giggling in the front seat of Doris' Buick.

"I'm outa cash, C.W.," she giggled, then handed me a quarter-ounce bundle of cocaine, "but will that cover the damage?"

Before I could answer, Doris dropped the Buick into reverse and kicked it out of the lot. The last anybody saw of them for several weeks was me. As they hit the interstate ramp just beyond the rail-road underpass, bits and pieces of their casts tumbled out of both front windows.

"True love," I said as I dropped the coke into my shirt pocket.

But back in the bar, I discovered a love even truer.

The Original Linda, who had been a rock-steady hand behind the bar for seven long years—never missed a shift, never got too drunk to work, never forgot a joke or left a dirty bar—was standing at the end of the bar with her ex-con husband, both of them drunker than pigs in sour mash.

"I take it you're not working tomorrow," I said as I popped two beers and sat them in front of the lovers.

"I'm not working ever again," Linda said, then fell on her ex-husband, Bill, with a drunken, sloppy kiss, "ever again." Then she fluffed her short blond hair and flounced toward the john.

"How you doing, asshole?" Bill inquired, giving me his hardest stare. Some dudes come out of the slam at Deer Lodge with eyes as hard and flat as nickels mashed by a train, and some come out with eyes that are just mashed. Bill glanced at his feet, then softly added, "She means it, man. We're done with the bar life. Tomorrow we start the AA meetings, the next month, we get married."

"Best of luck."

"You'll understand, man, if we don't invite you to the wedding, right?"

"Right," I said. Linda and I had done a brief number while Bill was in the slam. She had shit-canned me for a minor dalliance with Betty Boobs. Or maybe for my excuse: sometimes a dumb, mean woman can be more fun than a bright, pretty one. "That was a long time ago."

"Not for me," he said, then took a tiny sip of beer, "asshole."

"Get the fuck out of here, Billy," I said, "while you still can."

"Right," Linda said, stepping up to the bar. She took her paycheck out of her shirt pocket, tore it into tiny pieces, then tossed them on the bar. "Let's get out of this shithole, honey, while we still can."

So they went, and I wished them the best, bought the house another round, then slipped into the cooler in the liquor store for a quick lift of artificial fun. When I finished, I picked up the Help Wanted sign, taped it on the wide glass front door.

Occasionally, when the light was just right, I imagined I could see where I had scraped the painted letters off the door. HELL ROARING, it once said, but that night I couldn't even hear the creek a block west as it tumbled, roaring down to the Meriwether River.

By closing time, though, numb and glad to be alone in the silence of the bar, I thought things might work out. I played Hank Snow a couple of times, had a last drink, turned out the lights and turned on the alarms, then drifted down to my hole in the Mall.

About the only good thing that happened when they tore the Hell Roaring down—except for the fact that we kept the same customers, stayed a neighborhood bar and never became a cocktail lounge, and our neighborhood was hell—was that the front door kept the same south-southwest angle, so that when the autumn sun drifted toward the southern horizon, the same flood of golden light filled the afternoon easiness of the bar.

On that October day when the Original Linda and Bill re-plighted their troth in a dry, wilderness setting, I sat in the empty bar, considering the rush of fall light. It had been October, nearly twenty years before, when I came into the Hell Roaring for the first time. This poor schmuck from Redwood City had tried to change his life, faked a robbery at this pharmacy, then fled with the money, the drugs, and a hippie chick for the mountains of Montana. By the time I caught up with him, he was glad to go home. As we sat at the bar while I explained the easy ways and the hard ones back to California, he wept like a child, then laughed crazily, a man leaking everywhere. He had a junkie's sniffles, oozing tracks inside his elbows, and a dose of the clap that modern medicine couldn't cure. But it hadn't all leaked out. When I told him his wife still loved him—she'd hired me, hadn't she?—he muttered something about a fat bitch and a weak bladder.

Maybe if I hadn't been looking at the light that afternoon, I would have understood what the muffled thump from the john meant. Five minutes later, when I went to check—even the most painful of leaks shouldn't take that long—I found the leaking man hanging by his belt from the toilet door. Everything had finally leaked out.

When I thought of him, as I did every Montana fall, I had a drink for the Leaking Man and me. And on this October afternoon I poured a good unblended Scotch, a double with a splash of water, then raised my glass to the Leaking Man, who knew how to stop the flow. With the drink halfway to my lips, though, a shadow fell across the door, a slim hand removed the Help Wanted sign and the directions to the wedding. Then she opened the door, stepped through, glancing at the empty bar quickly.

"Who do I have to fuck to get a job around here," she said, "and how long do I have to work to get a nickname?"

I don't know how long I held the whiskey in the air. Long enough to watch the sunlight blaze through her gauze blouse, leaving her deep, full breasts in heavy shadow; to watch the sun sparkle red through the dark Indian hair that fell to the rounded love of her butt, lovingly stuffed into tight jeans; to see the smooth skin of the half-moon scar beside her left eye reflect the light off her dark skin. As if she didn't already have my attention, she slammed one of her high-heeled strapless pumps against the tile floor. Somehow I drank my whiskey without choking.

"Want one?" I asked, holding up the bottle.

"You got shit for tequila," she answered, swaying slowly toward the bar, "but the Glenmorangie will do."

We gunned the two shots I poured, then she looked around. "Well?" was all she said, then took my hand, led me around the bar and into the liquor store. Straight to the cooler, as if she knew exactly where to go.

Inside, she leaned against a stack of Coors cases, lifted a crystal vial of coke from between her breasts, unscrewed the solid-gold top, then gave both of us brief hits off her long red fingernail. Then she pulled my face to her chest, warm with the furious fall light, and held my head there for a long time before she made room between us to open our jeans, shove them to the floor.

"Fake cowboys," she murmured, raising her mouth to mine, lifting her legs just enough for me to enter, "and brass buckles."

Connected, it was only the work of a few endless moments, then we came together as we always had. It was like coming into the dark Mexican sun, blinding and timeless.

She caught her breath first, her easy laughter filling the cooler like silk flowers. "Ah, Sonny," she sighed, "we always had that . . ."

"Goddamnit, Gloria," I whispered between her breasts, "out of

all the fucking gin joints in the world, you had to walk into mine."
She laughed, her lovely neck tight against my lips. "Goddamnit,
Gloria, I still love you."

"You haven't seen me in nearly twenty years, Sonny," she said, sitting up and pushing me softly away, "what the hell do you know?"

"You haven't changed."

"You've got less hair and more belly."

"Less time, but more money."

"Speaking of money," she said, tugging up her jeans, "do I get the
job?"

"Shit, you can have the bar, love."

"Still the same Sonny—giving away more than you have, more
than was asked," she said.

"It's half my bar," I said.

"Proves my point," she said, smiling.

"You got the job. You got anything you want."

"Call me Connie Rodriquez, okay, and let me work off the
books?" she asked as she buckled her belt and I tugged my jeans
back.

"Need a place to stay?"

She nodded, running her fingers through the long, thick hair.

"With me?"

"If you don't mind . . ."

"Anything you want."

"I'll hold you to that, Sonny." She looked at me seriously, then
smiled and led me out of the cooler. Back at the bar, another Scotch
in hand, she asked for a price list. After a moment's scan, she flipped
it back.

"You're still quick," I said.

"I can still do the bones of the body, Sonny," she said, then
paused. "Probably nobody calls you 'Sonny' anymore."

I shrugged.

"C.W.?"

"Whatever."

"*Mi corazón.*"

But before we could talk, wedding guests began to drift in from the dry reception, and Gloria went to work as if she had always been there, as if her name were Connie Rodriquez instead of Gloria Remojadas.

When I closed the bar, we sipped Scotch a while, talking of the old days in Colorado, danced twice to Hank Snow, then retreated to my cave, entwined in the darkness as if we'd never been apart.

She stayed six weeks, then disappeared just as she had twice before in my life. At Colorado, where she, Solly, and I were all members of the Vietnam Veterans Against the War—the two of them honestly; myself working for the Defense Intelligence Agency—she was eighteen months into her premed program, her time as an Army nurse in Vietnam convincing her that she had to be a doctor, and had been living with me for six months, when she decided that she had to go back to Nam. She didn't talk about it, she just did it.

There were times when I thought it my fault, her leaving. Solly knew I worked for the DIA to keep out of Leavenworth—hell, we got stoned and made up my reports every week—but when Gloria discovered that I was a spy, that the extent of my moral qualms about the war only extended to keeping my ass out of a ten-year jolt in a military prison, she seemed disappointed in me. Justifiably, I thought. But that was only a small part of it. The real part was her love and concern for the kids, dead and dying and maimed, the kids without student deferments who were now fighting the war. I loved her heart, and that made her loss even sharper.

For Solly and I, well, we'd bought into the Army—I had done

two earlier hitches playing football, and Solly was meant to be a soldier: when he took three AK-47 rounds on a hot LZ, he was calling in an air strike while I pinched a thumping bleeder in his thigh— but none of those drafted kids had any business there. Gloria was right to go back. Or so I told myself that hard winter in Boulder.

Four years later, flush with money made from lost parents of runaways, I tracked Gloria down to her mother's house in El Paso. We flew to Mazatlán for a week, then she sent me back to San Francisco, promising to call.

When she showed up in Meriwether, I could almost forgive her for not calling, I could almost resist not copying down the Colorado license-plate number on her old VW Beetle. But she insisted on no questions, while I waited for the other shoe to drop.

I have to give it to Gloria for style, too. When she dropped it, we had been eating mushrooms and driving around Flathead Lake on a brilliant November day, and had stopped at the Outlaw Inn in Kalispell for sparkling martinis and shrimp cocktails. I don't know how long I had been holding a serious conversation with my martini before I noticed her absence.

"What happened to that woman?" I asked the bartender.

"Who's that?" he answered, as if he hadn't been bug-eyed since our arrival.

"The one sitting next to me, idiot."

"Maybe she went to the john . . ."

He didn't even try to keep me out of the woman's can. But he followed me in, so he saw the note on the mirror when I did. "See you around, soldier," it said.

"Goddamnit," was all I could say.

A woman in Levis and a cowboy shirt stepped out of the nearest stall. "You boys fuck up your eye shadow?" she asked as she pushed through the door.

Even though I knew it was a waste of time, I went out to the parking lot to look for my little Jap truck, but I'd taught her how to steal cars myself. The bartender had followed me outside, too.

"Gone, huh?"

"Third time's the charm," I said, "this time I'm not even going to chase her."

"By God, I would, son."

"You wouldn't cash a check for me, would you?"

"Damn straight."

But it didn't help. When I got back to the bar about midnight, my truck was parked behind it, and Gloria was gone like the last warm, golden day of fall.

Ten lousy days later, my old buddy, Solomon Rainbolt, arrived in an orange Dodge pickup truck with Texas plates, which looked as if it had been driven on dirt roads the whole way. And Solly looked like a man who had been chased all the way. He was wearing a brace on his short leg, something he seldom did, and his right elbow had finally fused in spite of three operations. Even before he said "Hi," he tugged me out to his truck, showed me the five pounds of crystal, and asked, "Can you lay it off for me, Sonny? Quick?"

"Gloria was here for a while," I said, as drunk as Solly was cranked.

"What? What the fuck? Gloria? Who? Can you do it?"

"What?"

"Lay it off, man? I lifted it from these bikers, right, down in Albuquerque. If you can't sell it, can you at least find someplace safe to cache it, man, I gotta get away from it for a while. Okay?"

It didn't seem to matter. Not after Gloria. Which is how I came to have Solly living in my hole, his crank tucked away in my safe, which was behind the bar's safe in the basement. One combination opened the bar's safe; another allowed the safe to be lifted out of the concrete floor, exposing my safe. The sigh of relief Solly released when I locked the crystal away sounded like a death rattle.

When the engine pulling the 3:12 fast-freight hit the jukebox two weeks later, the collision filled the snowy night with an explosive rainbow shower of plastic and pot metal that covered the parking lot like some postapocalyptic snowfall. With the juke's volume cranked to the max, the butch transvestite let out a terrific squeal, then died under the thundering freight train.

"Well, I hope to hell you're happy, Sughrue," Solly shouted over the noisy passage of the train, which hadn't seemed to notice the collision.

"I am happy," I said, lifting the Scotch into the night. "I am happy, and I'm damned certain that Hank Snow is ecstatic."

"Oh, I'm sure," Solly commented in his best drug-lawyer's voice.

"Now let's go back to the after-hours party," I suggested, "and establish my alibi. Give the people enough crank so they forget what time it is."

"I can't tell you how glad I am that I'm not your lawyer," Solly said.

"Me too," I said, and tossed the extension cord and dolly into the back of my truck before we climbed in, bound for the confusion of darkness.

1989

James Crumley is the author of *Dancing Bear*, *The Wrong Case*, *The Last Good Kiss* and *One to Count Cadence*. He lives in Missoula, Montana.

Interior illustration and cover painting,
The Muddy Fork, by Russell Chatham.
Cover design by Anne Garner and Russell Chatham.
Book design by Jamie Potenberg and Stacy Feldmann.
Composed in Granjon and Bembo
by Wilsted & Taylor, Oakland.
Printed and bound by Malloy Lithographing Inc., Ann Arbor.